New York born Mario Martinez studied at NYU and the American Academy of Dramatic Arts. After military service several years followed in films from which he switched to work for the Catholic Church in the US, UK, Ireland and beyond.

No longer active in fundraising he now lives in England. 'Ghost of a Guttersnipe' - historical fiction - is his fourth book. Life experiences give Mario much to draw in his writing. To mention just a few, he's been followed by the KGB, acted with Robert Redford, socialized with Salvador Dali, been taken for 'Carlos the Jackal' in Kenya, produced a film for UNICEF in Sudan, worked for Cardinals, lived and worked with Jesuits in Ireland and was behind the Iron Curtain at the height of the Cold War...

Ghost of a Guttersnipe

Mario Martinez

Ghost of a Guttersnipe

Olympia Publishers
London

www.olympiapublishers.com
OLYMPIA PAPERBACK EDITION

A CIP catalogue record for this title is
available from the British Library.

ISBN: 978-1-84897-764-8

This is a work of fiction.
Names, characters, places and incidents originate from the writer's
imagination. Any resemblance to actual persons, living or dead, is
purely coincidental.

First Published in 2017

Olympia Publishers
60 Cannon Street
London
EC4N 6NP

Printed in Great Britain

In memory of my mother Cecilia Martinez, 1909-2010 and Marion M. Parry, 1923-2012.

May they rest in peace.

My thanks to Johanna Schneider and
Erika Green for providing the appropriate German words
in this book.

Are we not Spirits, which are shaped into a body, into an Appearance that fade away again into air and Invisibility?

Oh Heaven, it is mysterious; it is awful to consider that we not only carry a future Ghost within us; but are, in very deed Ghosts!

Thomas Carlyle
Sartor Resartus: Natural Supernaturalism

During The Second World War Winston Churchill called Adolf Hitler a 'Bloodthirsty guttersnipe'.
Webster's dictionary defines guttersnipe as a contemptuous term – a common snipe, a neglected child of the street

FORWARD

Although Adolf Hitler has been dead for many years his passive ghost lives on, he's as conspicuous in death as he was in life. Despite the scale of deaths and misery that he caused, perhaps his pull is the talent to capture one's attention and in a way hypnotise.

In life his charisma spoke for itself, his speeches certainly transfixed. Although the words from his lips were a drip, drip, drip that corroded and poisoned people's minds, Germans and others fell under his spell. In 1938 when his takeover of Europe was underway, when his extinction of Jews was gathering pace and when his practice of eugenics was poised to begin, Time Magazine named him 'Man of the Year'.

His magnetic character and the speed in which he elevated Germany to a world power seduced the American magazine. Rather than condemning him for the ruthless tyrant that he was they were lost in admiration.

But that was then. Today, seven decades after he killed himself Hitler's passive ghost continues to transfix. New generations view him more as a figure of fascination than the killer that he was. His attraction is ever gripping and whether we like it or not Hitler has once again defied the reality of his life and is now not the 'Man of the Year' but the almost ever present 'Man of the Moment': A man where words at rallies provided the clothing for ugly, naked thoughts.

When it comes to Hitler and commercial profit all seems to have been forgiven or put aside by those who retell World War Two. For book publishers, documentary filmmakers and others, the subject of Hitler and Nazism is gold dust. Its commercial value is immense. Tours to Nazi sites in Germany and beyond are common as is an even darker tourism dealing with the

Holocaust. Huge sums of money also change hands for Nazi memorabilia.

The failed artist who once lived among Vienna's destitute under the Hapsburg Empire prior to WWI and who, with his Storm Troopers rose to power from the streets of Munich will never suffer from too much grief disturbing the dead. There is no chance of that, his passive ghost lives on. But that's not the end of it.

Hitler in death has another dimension beyond the mere passive, a wheel within a wheel in a world of supernatural spirits.

Although this tale is historical fiction it's really a 'Dead Poet's Biography' with layers of truths. Readers of this book may find its stitch so tight that it's hard to tell where the yarn ends and the facts begins much like the Holy Trinity.

Even though this book is historical fiction, readers of this work should be in no doubt that the subject of Hitler and the many relevant characters of WWII have been deeply researched.

ONE

Great Britain's surrounding islands have for centuries been subject to paranormal activity. The Isle of Wight for example is known as Ghost Island. One of the strangest paranormal events in recent years took place on the Isle of Man, a thirty mile-long island of 80,000 souls situated in the Irish Sea between Ireland and England.

In the morning hours of Tuesday April 30th 1991, a black bottle washed ashore at Point Ayer on the island's north coast near a keeperless lighthouse. It was not lying flat on the pebbled beach; it stood upright as if seeking attention. Some twelve inches long with square sides, it had a chunky neck and on each of its four sides black swastikas stood out against circular red backgrounds. A red cap, meant to unscrew, sealed the bottle's mouth.

In the course of the day a Golden Labrador named Neptune found the bottle and holding it in his mouth by the neck he trotted home to his owners Peter and Heather Moore. As he made his way home a few of his local friends observed him and wondered why the smart dog was carrying what looked like a wine bottle. He was well known for bringing home all manner of items from the beach but never a bottle.

Acquired by the Moores as a gift, The Labrador had been given his name due to an event that took place on the same day and year of his birth – the 20th of April 1989 – the same day that Nasa's Voyager 2 spacecraft passed near planet Neptune's north pole on its tour of the Solar System. Neptune was found to be a planet of astonishing surprises and similar to earth despite being in the outer reaches of the solar system. Perhaps by chance, perhaps not, the 20th of April also marked 100 years since the birth of Adolf Hitler.

Clever Neptune was no ordinary Labrador, his eyes, his human instincts, his psychic nature and even his name suggested qualities that were out of this world He was a big, happy fellow whose face always said hello and though everything about him spoke of pure Labrador breed, his deep blue eyes posed a mystery. A top vet on the island could not get over the anomaly. "It's down-right supernatural", he said.

Peter and Heather Moore lived in coastal Port Cranstal not far from the beach where the bottle had washed ashore. Only recently retired, the couple's home was a lovely yellow bungalow named 'Avoca' which sat near a winding lane with neatly cut hedges.

On the afternoon of Neptune's find Heather was not at home. She had driven to Peel on the west coast of the island for kippers which Peter had a yen for. He was home in the living room up a ladder spacing a two panelled curtain along a wide window rail when Neptune scrambled in with the bottle in his mouth and a swiftly wagging tail. Having announced his arrival he lowered the bottle to the floor perfectly upright. With his back to the Labrador and while spacing the curtains the tall Peter asked.

"What have you there, Neptune?"

The Labrador's response was a crisp bark and two steps back. *Look what I found* said his eyes and tilt of the head. Peter knew that whatever it was came from the beach near the lighthouse, which was Neptune's home away from home and around which he was often seen at high tide or when the local school let out.

Still up the ladder Peter turned and glances down at the bottle. When his eyes fixed on the swastikas an intake of breath followed, and then the memory of the sounds returned that on a night in 1942 caused his ears to bleed - General Montgomery's preamble to The Battle at El Alamein, the ground-shaking thunder of 900 heavy field-guns firing in the desert of North Africa. For a spell time stood still but Peter soon snapped out of it.

He descended the ladder, sank into his armchair and stared at the bottle on the floor. With his tail wagging at a rapid clip Neptune sniffed around the bottle. Peter wondered if its content was wine or God knows what, there was something spooky about it. He leaned forward in his chair for a closer look fearful of touching the bottle until apprehension gave way to curiosity. He was about to reach for it when there was a knock on the front door. Neptune barked but when Peter answered no one was there. Then there was a knock on a window. Neptune barked but no one was there. Then there was a knock on the kitchen door. Neptune barked again but no one was there. Peter scratched his head, shrugged his shoulders and returned to what he was doing before the knocks. Neptune remained in the kitchen, his blue eyes riveted on the kitchen door.

Peter lifted the bottle from the floor and thought, *What on earth have we here?* There was no sound of liquid when he shook the bottle only clinking against glass. Except for the swastikas there were no other markings on the bottle's surface. Peter stopped... Then he thought, *better not go any further... better wait for Heather.*

When his wife returned and was shown the bottle she froze where she stood almost lost for words.

"What on earth..."

"Neptune brought it home," said Peter. Heather's mind raced...

"Did it come from the beach?"

"Without a doubt," Peter replied. Time stood still again.

The sight of the swastikas had reached into the couple's memory box of the war, of Hitler, of Churchill, of bombs and destruction, of their sisters and of the war's terrifying madness when they were young. No words were spoken, only thoughts and questions about the bottle. The Moores drew breath and pulled themselves together.

"Shall I open it?"

Heather hesitated – she was thinking – then she said, "Go on, but be careful." Peter began to unscrew the bottle's cap It was resisting.

It was afternoon, a bright day in April, none of the bungalow's lights were on. Enter the uninvited again. For no apparent reason every light bulb in Avoca started flickering one after the other until the last one stopped. Then they did it again. Neptune barked and his ears shot up. But Peter and Heather were strangely unperturbed, they think it's a brief power blip but such was not the case and Neptune knew it. He was out of sight behind the sofa, ears up, eyes darting, chin on the floor, body ached, tail rigid.

With her eyes fixed, Heather looked on as Peter applied more strength to the bottle's cap. When it finally yielded a pungent odour escaped from the bottle. The Moores fanned the air in front of their faces with their hands and Neptune barked. And when the smell had eased and Peter turned the bottle upside down a voice from the past slid out of a dead man's presence – fate or afterlife destiny had delivered the supernatural ghost of Adolf Hitler to the Isle of Man fifty one years after he had sent the bottle on its voyage along with his spiritual self.

No sooner had the bottle been opened than a chill ran through Neptune who reacted by disappearing from behind the sofa and into the kitchen. Peter and Heather never noticed, their eyes and Peter's hands were on the bottle's content, a rolled up hand-written letter in German dated July 4th 1940 whose body had been held inside a silver finger ring along whose outer edge the word Zenitram was engraved.

The letter was in pristine condition as if written yesterday. So too was the bottle like new. Neptune was nowhere to be seen.

The letter's script and signature was that of Adolf Hitler's. And now, forty-six years after his suicide he was back and talking but Peter and Heather had no clue what he was saying; or that his spirit was at liberty in Avoca. Or that Neptune could sense him. The Moores would never know the bottle's story.

Rewind to 1940; the bottle had been thrown into American waters by Wilfred Schulhart, the commander of U-Boat 29 on the night of Monday, July 1st. He had flung it in the ocean at high tide four miles from the east coast of a lighthouse at Montauk Point in Long Island, New York.

That night little did Tom Buckridge, the Montauk Point lighthouse keeper know that a U-Boat was lurking near the coast of Long Island poised to deliver a letter to America from Adolf Hitler.

It had been sent to America and thrown into its waters at high tide believing that it would drift to the Long Island coast and wash ashore on or before America's Day of Independence on July 4th. And that it would be found and that its letter would make headlines and convince an already sceptical US public that it should not again meddle in a war to help Britain and France as they had in World War I.

Ruled by the madness of self-belief, Hitler was certain that Irish Americans had no wish to help Britain, a nation that for centuries had bullied Ireland. And that German-Americans were not eager for war with their ethnic kin. And that the isolationists in congress would not stand for it. And that most Americans had no desire to aid the pompous, two-faced French who had so easily caved in to his army despite their military strength.

But Hitler was not totally a fool or insane, his letter aimed to reinforce the opposition of millions who had no appetite for taking part in another war in Europe thousands of miles away to save the Imperialist British and the snotty, cowardly French. Of all this Hitler was sure.

In fact Hitler's letter was the notion of a fantasist, a man certain that he was destined to lead Germany to greatness. Nevertheless, by June 1940 he had conquered or had under his control any nation he chose in Western Europe with little opposition. All his military ventures had met with success.

Believing that Britain and France were preparing to occupy the Scandivanan counties, in April his Army had struck first and only met resistance from Denmark. By May he had conquered the Netherlands, Belgium and Luxemburg. By June Norway and France had surrendered. And with Norway and Denmark already occupied, Sweden and Finland was his by default. The countries of yesteryears prowling Vikings had been no match for his army or had the stomach for a fight with their Teutonic aggressors of old.

President Roosevelt, whose hands were tied by a Neutrality Act as well as a mostly isolationist congress, knew he must join the war in Europe sooner rather than later. Hitler hoped Japan would not give him an excuse. But he was worried. Unlike Italy, his other ally Japan were motivated, they had cunning and grit, but he was well aware that behind their smiles and bows lay the knife that might stab him in the back. They had done it to Russia in the past and they might do it to him when least expected.

Now that Hitler's supernatural ghost had surfaced it was able to reflect. Unlike his passive ghost he was free of bitterness, free of frustrated ambitions, free from his journey of fifty one years through time and watery space. Unlike his passive ghost he was now at ease. His life had been a nightmare of his own making from which he was finally awake. In death no god to reprimand him had appeared.

TWO

In the mix of lectures to his generals Hitler often professed to be a Catholic. He would quote the bible and speak of God and His Will while at the same time denouncing Christianity. In a 1938 speech he said:

Hence, today I believe that I am acting in accordance with the will of The Almighty Creator. By defending myself against the Jew, for which there is no earthly reason, I am fighting for the word of the Lord.

Hitler had studied the works of Blaise Pascal, one of the most brilliant minds of the Age of Reason who when asked by Louis X1V for proof of the supranational had answered simply; *The Jews, my lord, the Jews.*

In 1941 Hitler said to one of his ministers: *I am now as before a Catholic and will always remain so.* In fact Hitler and Mussolini hated the Catholic Church and its sway over people, seeing it as a challenge to Nazism and Fascism. The sex-mad Benito stayed close to the church to maintain the illusion that he was a god-fearing Catholic. In 1928 Ernest Hemmingway interviewed him in Paris and labelled him the 'great pretender'.

Hitler once said of the Church: "While always talking about love and humanity, the clerics are interested in only one thing, power over men's souls and lives. The Catholic Church is like a scheming woman who at first gives her husband the impression that she is helpless, only to take over power, finally holding it so tight that the man has to dance to any tune she plays."

Hitler would subject his plans to the scrutiny of his Swiss astronomer Karl Ernst Krafft, a man who had never actually met Hitler. The readings would be done by Krafft then passed on to Hitler through an aid. Many were certain that Hitler had no faith in astronomical forecasts. In fact throughout most of his years of power astronomy one of his core beliefs, the first of which was the faith he had in himself and the certainty that he was destined to lead Germany to greatness. Churchill also had an astrologer, the cigar-smoking, self-promoting German fake Louis de Wohl.

Krafft had assured Hitler that given the Fuehrer's hour, day and year of birth – six thirty p.m., April 20, 1889 – that the positions of his planets Neptune and Pluto conjoined in Gemini were favourable for any venture he undertook in early July. Hitler was certain that he would be reaching a receptive US audience if news of his letter and method of arrival had reached their media and public.

It was no secret that Roosevelt was already helping Britain and that citizens of America, Canada and other nations were sending aid as well. In any event, what have I got to lose was Hitler's view in 1940. "My letter might tip the balance and keep the US out of the war."

What Hitler did not know was that with the help of Churchill's Special Operation Executive, the SOE, America and Canada had begun building Camp X, a secret facility in Canada for spies who would be sent to occupied territories to gather information and help the local resistance to damage the enemy's infrastructure. The SOE was already active in France with Churchill's mandate 'to set Europe aflame'. The construction of Camp X started in 1940 when America was neutral, which is why its location was in a remote area of Canada. As a member of the British commonwealth Canada was already at war with Germany.

Hitler's letter was a silly pipe dream, but what man with power had not hatched odd ideas and succeeded. Was his plan less likely to succeed than landing men on the moon less than thirty years later?

"I have no wish to awaken America," Hitler told his always questioning General Ludwig Beck: they helped defeat Germany in the first war and have not forgotten the cost. My aim is to unbalance them, but Roosevelt 'The Jew' is dangerous. I aim to infiltrate the minds of the American populace and hope the Japanese do nothing to stir them. They can deal with China at some point, and when the time is right they can strike Russia from the east while I attack from the west. I need nothing more from Japan.

Hitler was euphoric when his troops marched into Paris in June 1940. Three days later, on his first and only trip to the city he paid a visit to the tomb of Napoleon. Wearing a white raincoat, his cap removed in deference and flanked by generals, he stood gazing down at the tomb of the man who, like Frederick The Great, he adored. Surrounded by his staff Hitler said this was one of the proudest moments of his life. Conscious that the hero he was honouring was known only by the name Napoleon, Hitler said that he too would not need a title on his gravestone. He ordered that sandbags be placed around the tomb to guard against damage.

For years it has been said that Hitler lost a testicle in the first war. Not so, but had it been the case he would have felt in good company because when Napoleon died it was found that he only had one testicle. As in the case of Hitler, many have considered Napoleon to be the embodiment of the antichrist. A close contemporary of Hitler also had one testicle: General Franco of Spain, though as in the case of Napoleon no one knows if they were born with the condition of Monarchism, or were victims of a mischief in life.

Until recently the French would bristle over any comparisons between Napoleon and Hitler, but new revelations show that France's greatest hero presided over atrocities, which in ways compared with Hitler and certainly influenced him.

During his reign as Emperor concentration camps were common and gas was used to kill people. There were hit squads in France, mass deportations and Jews were persecuted. Napoleon, who like Hitler rose from the rank of corporal, hated democracy, for him the state was supreme. All this had taken place 140 years before the Holocaust, so nearly a century and one half before Hitler's rise, his hero had set an example of 'brutality', a word Hitler used often. And if he learned only one lesson from Napoleon, it was that to achieve victory callousness was required, not only in a leader, but in those around him. Hitler learned the lesson very well and chose his henchmen accordingly, Heinrich Himmler and Reinhard Heydrich were but two of his followers who killed Jew on a scale so unprecedented that even Winston Churchill was lost for words when he descried the killings as a crime without a name.

Now that Paris was his, Hitler was bursting with pride. His troops had crushed the French Army. Some had been killed, many taken prisoners, the rest had escaped to England from Dunkirk along with thousands of British soldiers. Others had been routed, killed or captured. But more than three hundred thousand had escaped due to his own vacillation.

France had fallen and more victories were sure to come, his troops had swept through the Balkans in a lightening manner to secure the Ploesti oil fields in Romania. His eyes were now on the rich oil fields to the east in the Caucuses but he needed Italy's help in the Balkan countries, he needed to free his troops there for the Russian campaign to come. Nothing could stop Hitler now. Who would oppose him? He would soon occupy the undefended Channel Islands near the north coast of France. And there were those in European countries who also hated Jews and Communists and viewed them as Europe's greater threat. Occupied lands like Poland, Denmark, Belgium and Holland were but a few to say nothing of Vichy French collaborators and sympathetic neutrals like Sweden, Spain and Portugal. Hitler's old feelings of Germany's humiliation over the French instigated terms of the Versailles Treaty would now be redressed. The moment was sweet!

His terms of surrender would be sent to the French envoy and signed in the same railway coach in the forest of Compiegne where the German envoys had been humiliated into signing the 1918 armistice. After France had signed, the railway coach would be taken to Germany and in time destroyed. This thought was so delicious that Hitler could taste it. He was a hurry, on a mission to everlasting greatness. But he had to keep America out of the war!

In 1940 his generals had said don't do it, don't move so fast, we are not prepared for war, we don't have enough troops, only two and one half million trained. General Beck and others felt that war would lead Germany to destruction. General Rommel also had his doubts, but Hitler hadn't listened. His astrologer had been telling him what he wanted to hear so he pushed on. The result was victory after victory. Not a peep of opposition now came from his generals, at least not to his face. Now they did what they were told but always with a measure of reluctance. Always, as in the case of some generals from the German upper classes with smirks on their faces and whispers behind his back. Many could not accept that their bombastic leader was a high school dropout who had never risen in the army above the rank of corporal in WWI.

Britain would next come under Hitler's hammer. The Channel Islands would soon be his, the country was sure to crumble from the Blitz on its airfields and cities.

Hitler felt he had the measure of Churchill, he thought him to be a drunken imperialist fool with a mother that not only was American but a Jewess to boot. Even before becoming prime minister there were rumours that the old bulldog had homosexual tendencies despite being married with children because he always had young men around that he would often call dear. And that his motto was KBO: *keep buggering on*. And that he had allegedly slept with the entertainer Ivor Novello and had found the experience to be 'musical'. None of this was true.

How could Churchill with his nasty habits match him, the anti-smoking, vegetarian, apple pie loving Adolf Hitler. He would best the half-American, half-Jewish aristocrat, a failed politician disliked by many in his own party and the working class; a glutton who was easily satisfied providing that his cook Mrs. Landemare served him the best of everything.

What Hitler didn't realize was that if ever an hour waited for a man it waited for Winston Churchill, a sixty six year-old egoist who was besotted by war, who had killed men with his own hands in past wars and that cometh Britain's hour of need, cometh his super-human courage and strength of character.

Hitler was crossing swords with a man who was never happier than when the cannons of war were roaring. This was no boy-loving queer like Ernst Rohm of the Storm Troopers, the only one allowed to call Hitler 'Adolf'. War intoxicated Churchill. He loved its intrigue. To be killed in battle in the name of the British Empire would for him be paradise. When Britain needed a wartime leader no one but Churchill possessed the complexity of personality and oratory skills to galvanize a nation in the defeat of Nazism.

That he had political failures behind him, that he could be rude, impatient, intolerant, fanciful and disliked by some in his wartime cabinet like Stafford Cripps was well known. In ways Churchill and Hitler were similar in their interests and talents, both were artistic and good painters. Hitler was keen on architecture and Churchill with the physical act of laying and cementing bricks in the construction of garden walls. He was a member of the Guild of Bricklayers and cultivated butterflies.

That he had made errors in the past that cost lives and lost many elections spoke for itself, but no man was better equipped to be Prime Minister when the survival of Britain was at stake. Despite his gruffness he could be charming and absorb criticisms. He was indeed the man of the hour. None of these strings to Churchill's bow did Hitler and others recognize. What he and others chose to see was an old fool with a chequered past whose mother was a Jewess, not a man whose beacon to guide by were persistence and the belief that courage is the ability to go from failure to failure without losing heart.

THREE

The Fuehrer was in two minds about little Britain. He admired how it ruled huge India with only an 'elite' of 1200 Britons under whose direction 20,000 Indian civil servants worked. His favourite film was the *Lives of a Bengal Lancer*, the tale of British cavalrymen trying to defend their base at Bengal against rebellious natives. He also admired its schools and architecture but these were only one side of the coin.

At the same time he didn't think much of British people, viewing the upper classes as a snooty bunch without substance, the middle class as social climbers and the working class as those that deserved to be at the bottom of Britain's human heap.

For him former Prime Minister Chamberlain was an example of British manhood, a jellyfish to the core who always seemed carried a silly umbrella. Lord Halifax too was another spineless man in Hitler's view, a tall man born without a left hand and withered arm who could have been Prime Minister but lacked the courage to take up the challenge. He remained Hitler of the Kaiser, Although Kaiser Wilhelm II, another pampered fool and Queen Victoria's grandson also had a useless left arm, his disability had resulted from nerve damage to his neck at birth.

Then there was the monarchy with their jewels and crowns and stagnant German blood springing from the House of Hanover, the House of Saxe-Coburg and their now English sounding House of 'Windsor' sobriquet. No problem from them would come when faced with adversity. At best they were inbred idiots whose backsides were daily kissed by the Peers they created and their humble subjects who were all too eager to pay homage with bows at the waist and bends of the knees.

To his way of thinking George VI was no better than a child. Edward VIII had tossed away his crown to his stuttering sibling not only for Mrs. Simpson, a twice wed American with a

Halloween face - who was seeing a Nazi officer while seeing Edward - but also because he was more drawn to nightclubs and African Safaris than duty.

He had met the couple, the now married Duke and Duchess of Windsor after Edward's abdication and he didn't think much of either one. Edward was fluent in German and pro-Nazi and this Hitler liked but that's where his admiration ended. Recently released files reveal the scale of the couple's pro-Hitler leanings, how they tried to keep Britain out of the war, and how Hitler planned to put Edward back on the thrown and the lengths to which Britain and America had gone to keep the embarrassing couple out of public gaze.

According to Hitler Britain had an unforgivable degeneracy, they were somewhat sympathetic in their leanings towards Jews. Lord Balfour's 1918 Declaration was sure to speed the day when an Israeli State would be created. By 1929 more than 80,000 European Jews had moved to Palestine and now, in 1940, with German and other Jews running for their lives, the number was greater. Yes, Britain posed no problem as far as Hitler's was concerned because despite Balfour's declaration, many in Britain's upper class and beyond disliked Jews and were in awe of him.

In America they included Charles Lindberg, Henry Ford, Joseph P. Kennedy, the film star Errol Flynn and others. In 1937 Hitler had created the German Eagle Order medal for foreign friends of the Reich. It's first and second recipients being Ford and Lindbergh who were very anti-Jew. Ford had built Hitler's Volkswagen assembly plant in Berlin. Hitler's upper-class English fan Unity Mitford as well as Sir Oswald Mosley and John Amory, son of Leo Amery, Secretary of State for India in Churchill's cabinet were also in awe of Hitler. Another keen admirer was Robert Baden-Powell, national hero of the Boer War and founder of the British Boy Scout Movement. They, in Hitler's opinion, were an example of how the British would willingly melt when the Luftwaffe came calling over Britain.

Then there was William Joyce, *aka Lord Haw-Haw*, Hitler's New York born half English, half Irish propaganda mouthpiece whose radio broadcasts from Germany aimed to demoralize the

British public. He had a listening audience in Britain of eighteen million. And there were other Nazi friends in Britain like the anti-Semitic Fascist 'Right Club' headed by Archibald Ramsay, a Scottish blue-blood MP. Another Jew hater was Tyler Kent, a cipher clerk at the US Embassy who, in 1940 was copying messages between Churchill and Roosevelt dealing with Lend Lease ships from America. Kent, a committed isolationist, aimed to pass the secret messages to the Right Club so that Ramsey could expose them in Parliament and show that the American president was breaking the neutrality act passed by congress. MI5's Maxwell Knight recovered the documents from the US turncoat and they remained secret until after the war.

So besotted with Hitler was young Unity Mitford that she fired a bullet into her head the day Britain and France declared war on Germany. Somehow, with Hitler's help, and despite the bullet in her skull, she survived and returned to England. For years rumours abounded that she was pregnant with Hitler's child at the time. Maybe yes, maybe no, who can say for sure. But it's doubtful, Hitler was inclined to fire blanks on the rare occasions that his weapon was primed, his appetite was never equal to the menu's allure. Then there was Winifred Wagner, another admirer, Hitler's alleged lover, the English born wife of Siegfried, son of the composer Richard Wagner.

As for the lustful Mosley and Diana, Unity's Mitford's sister, the couple were in trouble. They were interned in 1940 for belonging to the British Union of Fascists, which, under British law, put then under 'foreign influence and control'.

Once he had smashed Britain Hitler planned to expand Germany's living space by dealing with Russia and their uncouth, web-toed leader with a Jewish mistress who may have been his third wife and whose Jewish fathers of the Bolshevik Revolution he had thieved for to help finance. Was Russia a threat? Not in Hitler's view in 1940. After their military shambles in Finland, he was certain that the Russian Army were useless. Russia was, after all, a weird country occupied by odd people – *in ways a riddle, wrapped in a mystery, and surrounded by an enigma,* Churchill's words - not Hitler's.

Like the actor James Cagney in the film White Heat, in his mind Hitler was calling up to his mother Klara in heaven, " Look mom, top of the world", he was all but clicking his heels that 14th day of June 1940 when Paris fell to his troops. And he had reason for joy, like Rumpelstiltskin, everything he touched turned to gold. Every country that he wanted he took with little opposition – 'smash ruthlessly and grab' was his order on any given day. His strength was 'speed and brutality'; his father's swift, angry whippings had taught him that.

At home his 'Hitler Youth Movement' had struck a rich vein. Flush with pride in their Nazi attire, Germany's youth revelled in the blue eyed, blond haired Aryans that most were and the Jews that they were not. The boys were besotted when Hitler demanded that they be slim and slender, swift as greyhounds, tough as leather and hard as steel. Few Germans failed to notice or care that Hitler and many of his henchmen looked anything but Aryan and that hardly any fit the profile that he asked of youth. Two-ton Hermann Goring did not fit the mould.

FOUR

By 1940 Hitler had Western Europe under his control. The Allied landings in Norway had been swiftly dealt with, scores of men had been killed or captured but two hundred thousand British and one hundred forty thousand French and Polish troops had fled Dunkirk and slipped through Hitler's fingers.

One of his concerns in 1941 was his Italian Ally's poor performance in the Balkans: he already had troops there but he needed them elsewhere to the east. The Balkans were an array of nations friendly with Germany like Bulgaria, Hungary and Romania, the others drifted where the wind took them.

Italy had invaded Albania but failed to use it as a springboard to conquer Crete and Greece so Hitler had to help with troops to finish the job. Nor had the Italian army fared better in Yugoslavia so again Hitler had to send soldiers. These distractions were upsetting Operation Barbarossa, his plans to invade Russia. In the 1920s Hitler looked up to Mussolini but now the lustre was fading. With some reservations from the start of their alliance in 1936 Hitler was optimistic, but in 1941 his suspicions were bearing fruit.

He thought Italian troops to be questionable soldiers. In 1940 he had already sent troops to North Africa in aid of Italian soldiers who were being routed by the British Army.

As far as Italy was concerned, in 1960 US President Lyndon B. Johnson echoed Hitler's sentiments when he said about the opponents in his own democratic party that it was better to have the bastards in his tent pissing out than outside pissing in. In the case of Mussolini, his listless troops were streaming both ways, two hundred fifty thousand were in North Africa and many had already surrender to British forces of much smaller numbers.

Two other unreliable Mediterranean in Hitler's eyes were Franco of Spain and Salazar of Portugal. Having used German arms in his own Civil War, as well as some of the Italians, Franco now refused to back him unless his territorial demands were met. Although fascist on the surface, Salazar was selling sugar, tobacco and tungsten to the Allies and some of his military was helping the British. As far as Hitler was concerned, Franco and Salazar were double-crossers hiding behind neutrality.

Hindsight has 20/20 vision but what, on reflection does Hitler's supernatural ghost have to say now that he's free to speak from the unknown.

What say you Herr Hitler, if only randomly tell us with yesterday's voice the things on your mind today.

Speak! Speak!

"Jawohl, Jch werde sprechen" – "Yes, I will speak!

"My life is a nightmare from which I have escaped…

"I loved my mother…

"I was born with Neptune and Pluto conjoined in Gemini. I hung suspended between Aries and Taurus in the Zodiac. I never knew what this meant except that I had a destiny. Even when I despaired I could feel it…

"I loved my dogs, how lovely that one of their species found me on the beach…

"I loved mineral water, vegetables, apple pie and chocolates but hated meat and especially smoking: a nasty habit that ruins ones health. I would reward associates with a gold watch if they quit…

"Polish and Jewish slave labour were important during the war. I could not have progressed without them…

"I was once Man of the Year. How lovely!…

"Like Salvador Dali I loved money. My wealth was immense. I never paid taxes. If a couple married they would get a copy of Mein Kampf which the state would pay for, I would receive royalties on the sale. And if my image appeared on a stamp I would receive royalties on each stamp sold. How lovely!…

I wonder who has my money now…

"I did not have good Allies, Italy was useless, Japan could not be trusted…

"In 1912 I was destitute in Vienna trying to sell my sketches in beer halls to people like me. They were that type of beer hall. A strange old man who smelled of urine said he liked one of sketches but he was poor, the only thing he had of value was a silver ring on the middle finger of his left hand. It was his birthday, he said he was his father's sixth son, and that his father was a sixth son, and the father before him was also a sixth son. Always six, six and six. I gave him the sketch as a gift. In order to repay me he gave me his silver ring, it had the word Zenitram engraved on the outer rim - he said it would bring me luck. While looking down at the ring I asked what Zenitram meant and said I could not accept it but it was too late. The old man had closed his eyes and died sitting at the table...

"I loved cars but never learned to drive. My friend Henry Ford was surprised...

"I was fond of Diana Mitford. We had nice talks. I would ask her about her cousin Winston. She said he would ask about me. I attended her wedding to Mosley...

"I didn't care for him. He and Wallis Simpson had faces like rats. Their faces were like five miles of bad Austrian road. They were both sexual animals. Diana was known as 'the three way girl' – no orifice was sacred or safe with her...

"The British upper class like the Mitfords were in the palm of my hand; some Greek royals too but not princess Alice, a heavy smoking Jew lover. Her son Philip was like me in my youth, a lost soul without a home...

"My father was a civil servant. I wanted to be an artist. He hated the idea. "You need a job with a pension at the end," he would yell. We argued a lot, he beat me if I talked back, he beat me if I was late, he taught me violence...

"Mother feared for me when the blows came. I didn't love my father, I feared him, I was glad when he died. I felt free...

"When I failed the entrance exam to art school in Vienna I hoped of becoming an architect but having dropped out of high school that dream was also gone. Had my dreams been realized I might been a different person. Instead I became 'Man of the Year' in 1938. How lovely!...

"My mother died of breast cancer when I was seventeen. Her doctor was Jewish. I liked him. I fell at his feet with grief when she died. I felt lost. He was shocked and moved...

"My little sister Paula cried when I left Linz for Vienna after mother died. My half-sister Angela looked after her. When I became known I made Paula change her name from Hitler to Wolff...

"I hated the Austro-Hungarian Empire and the House of Hapsburg. The Austria of my youth was a patchwork of ethnic groups from the Balkans. I hated them too. Ethic Germans like me were second-class citizens in the mix that made up the Empire...

"I had my first real sexual experience in Vienna with a Jewess. I met her in a beer hall, I was twenty-one. Was it a sin? If so my punishment was greatness...

"I knocked around Vienna until 1913 living from a small inheritance and my sketches...

"I loved Vienna's architecture. The city was a contradiction, a smiling face, a rotting heart. There were prostitutes everywhere; thousands of miserable souls lived in sewers with rats and like rats. I lived in rat-infested hostels. In the morning someone would be found dead in his bed, killed by the cold, or hunger or by Lady Vienna. I was young and survived hostel life, that's when I started to go grey...

"I wanted no part of Austria; I hated Germany too, they failed to include German-Austrians in the new unified Germany. I always felt an outsider in Austria...

"As a boy in Linz I liked a Jewish girl named Stephanie but I never approached her. I was a *dummkopf* – invisible to her...

"To avoid serving in the Austrian Army I moved from Vienna to Munich and then to England for a short spell in 1913. I joined my half-brother there Alois Hitler Jr. He lived in Liverpool with his Irish wife Bridget. He worked as a waiter for Jews, he was a terrible gambler, he had a two year-old son who grew up to be loathsome. I stayed with them for six months. I spoke very little no English. They got sick of me so I left. I never got on with Alois. He lent me money to get rid of me, I was broke, had wasted my small inheritance. I was a stupid daydreaming *dummkopf.*

Alois and Bridget were not to be trusted, their rotten son grew up to be a rotten man like that whore of the sewer Lady Vienna...

"When I rose to power Bridget and her son tried to profit from my status and wrote bad things about me. William Patrick, the son, tried to blackmail me...

"I returned to Munich before the first war. I was back living in a hostile, a lost soul with no hope, no money, no purpose, no future. I was like a dog looking for a master – a *dummkopf*...

"I now hated Jews – they were outlaws – people without a country who could live and profit anywhere...

"My salivation began in 1914, The First World War. I was then twenty five-years old...

"Where else would the war be triggered but in the Austro-Hungarian Empire in the Bosnian city of Sarajevo. A Serbian shot dead Archduke Franz Ferdinand and his wife. How lovely! I was thrilled. I hated the House of Hapsburg. They had created the mixed-raced nation that Austria had become. The result was war, beautiful war: Germany and Austria-Hungary against Russia, France and Britain with others thrown in. America took part in 1917...

"I joined the Bavarian unit of the German Army and became a corporal. I was wounded and gassed and lost my sight but I recovered and was decorated. The war ended with Germany's betrayal by German Jews and communists not by the army's defeat. News of Germany's surrender was a shock to me and others. I heard it in hospital while recovering my sight...

"Being gassed taught me a lesson about the weapon. It was cheap. Napoleon had used it, in years to come Heinrich Himmler and Rheinhard Heydrich would use it to kill Jews. I saw it as necessity – they revelled in the job...

"I lost my faith in God and the Holy Trinity when the war ended. Justice had abandoned Germany, Jews and Russian communist and Germany's leaders had conspired to trick her into surrender...

"I hated von Hindenburg and the Versailles Treaty but I found my purpose in life when I was thirty. I found it in the streets of Munich in 1919. It was there that I made speeches to anyone who would listen, that's when I started dying my hair, I was only thirty and completely grey…

"My subject was always the evils of the Jews and communists and their role in Germany's downfall. I would rehearse them over and over and over. They words thrilled me. My audiences grew. How lovely! Only mother ever listened to me..

"I joined the Nazi Party and become more committed to racial hatred than ever. I was soon in charge of party propaganda. I organised public meetings. Within a few years I was party leader. What a thrill, how lovely, at last I was somebody…

"But I made mistakes…

FIVE

"I failed to overthrow the Weimar Republic in 1923 and was jailed but I did not waste my time. I wrote Mien *Kampf* with the help of fellow prisoner Rudolph Hess...

"My mother, my mother, my mother. The thought of her and the way she died haunted me. I wrote a poem called Mother. I had never written one before....

"I was inspired by books on sterilization and racial purity, a view held by many. One book was by the English advocate of family planning Marie Stopes. She would write to me allot...

"After my release from prison the first thing I did was buy a car, then I created the Schutzstaffel - my SS bodyguards. Heinrich Himmler would be its leader under Hermann Goring. Many attempts were made on my life, I survived most through luck. The SS and the Brown Shirts under Ernst Rohm would soon be in competition. This caused problems. So too was Gregor Strasser being difficult, he tried to take over the party leadership while I was jailed...

"If Schindler had a list of Jewish names Bormann and Goebbels had them first; lists of communists, intellectuals and others that needed to be culled. Many were on the run. They included writers, artists, film and theatre people, philosophers, scientists and musicians. Even Charlie Chaplin who was neither Jewish or in Europe was on the list...

"Others too had to be scrubbed from Nazi Germany: gypsies, homosexuals, the mentally ill, the physically disabled. If they were flawed and outside the mould of Aryan appearance, or expressed views contrary to the Party, the Gestapo had them in their sights...

"In 1928 my party held twelve seats in the Reichstag. By 1932, with Germany on her knees, stripped to the bone by the Versailles Treaty and with millions out of work I held 230 seats.

I campaigned for votes flying to many cities and towns in a single day and felt safe flying with my pilot Hanz Bauer. A special train also allowed me to sweep Germany for support...

"By the will of my destiny and bankers I was made chancellor in 1933. I simply made myself head of state in 1934 when von Hindenburg died. A fire in the German Parliament, which I blamed on Communists, helped me. The Brown Shirt were really responsible...

"I had loose ends to deal with...

"Himmler of the SS and Rohm of the Brown Shirts were at odds over who had more power. My generals were fearful of the four and a half million storm troopers Rohm had under his command and their thuggish ways. They also hated that many of their leaders like Rohm were homosexuals. Himmler planted the idea in my mind that Rohm was plotting against me...

"The storm troopers had to be brought under my command and sworn to obey me. I arrested Rohm personally and had him shot. He was in bed with a man when I broke into his hotel room in Munich. I had others done away with too including Gregor Strasser...

"The next year I began rearming in defiance of the Versailles Treaty and the Nuremberg Laws began. German Jews now had no rights. I didn't care what the world thought; there was little they could do about it...

"I later learned that Rohm was not plotting against me, that Himmler made up the story in order to bring the Brown Shirts under his leadership. I felt bad about having Rohm killed, despite his sexual leanings he had always been loyal. We didn't agree on everything but he did not need to be shot. Only he had the guts to tell me that Churchill had called me a bloodthirsty guttersnipe. And Churchill was right; it was from the gutters of Vienna and Munich that I came.

"I pushed forward in 1938 thanks to the Munich Pact. Chamberlain returned to London proclaiming 'Peace In Our Time'. He was foolish. I grabbed parts of the Sudetenland and then the rest of the rest of Czechoslovakia. I had already annexed Austria. In German I was being called General Bloodless...

"In 1939 I gobbled up Poland and split it with Russia to keep Stalin happy and after dithering France and Britain declared war on Germany. Now I could take umbrage and push on despite the jitteriness of General Beck who thought Germany was not prepared for war. I fired him and spread the tale that he was queer like Ernst Rohm...

"Pope Pius XII and Beck plotted against me. They aimed to withdraw my troops from Poland and Czechoslovakia and restore democracy to Austria and Germany. But the Pope hesitated; he feared that denouncing me would lead to more persecution of Jews and a backlash against Catholics. I later learned that the sneaky Pope had hidden many Jews in his summer residence...

"The year 1940 was mostly wonderful. I named my train 'Amerika'. German women adored me, my speeches captivated them, I was almost a Messiah...

"I had neutralized Russia with the Nazi-Soviet Pact and gone further. Almost all of Western Europe was now under my control including France. But I worried about Rudolph Hess, he was acting strangely. I discussed him with Martin Bormann...

"I was becoming more flatulent...

Being me was not easy, I would ride the crest of emotional waves with speeches of things people wanted to hear but easy it was not. I would sweat a lot. I was taking many pills, many baths a day...

"Dr Morell was always taking my blood pressure. Being me called for iron will, thick skin and grit to uphold my persona and Goebbels' propaganda. My limping little minister believed that if you tell a lie often enough people will come to accept it until their consequences reveal the truth. Still, it wasn't easy living in my skin, with my mood-swings, cajoling, scheming and drug taking, all fuelled by the high-octane blood flowing through my veins as if pumped by Satan himself...

"I felt invincible. If I escaped assassination attempts it was by chance, by my unpredictability and not because of my bodyguards. There was an attempt in 1939. I was speaking at the annual meeting of the National Socialist Party in Munich at the Burgerbrau Beer Hall where I tried to overthrow the government in 1923. Many of my comrades that took part were there. I

43

normally began speaking at eight thirty but I started at eight p.m. I finished at 9.07 p.m. and left. A bomb had been hidden behind the rostrum set to go off at 9.20. It exploded killing several people. I had escaped by thirteen minutes by pure chance. The perpetrator was caught and executed. His attempt to kill me is remembered in Germany to this day on the 8th of November…

"I had to deal with my cabinet ministers. And a strange bunch they were, if I hinted of favouring a course of action they would put it into practice without my written order. In a way it suited me, I hated writing anything down: Goering, Speer, Goebbels, Frick, Bormann, Himmler, Ketal, Funk, von Ribbentrop and Hess, they and the others were flawed individuals who disliked and were jealous of each other. But flawed or not they were elements in my plan if Germany was to reach the communist-free Jewless utopia of my dreams…

"My most dislikeable minister was my foreign secretary Joachim von Ribbentrop, a pompous, arrogant man who 'bought his title, married his money and wormed his way into high office'. The British foreign office despised him, so did I – but he suited me…

"If Vienna was a city of neurotics in the early 1900 I am a good example. And it's mostly due to sex. My urges were few so I replaced my low libido with hate and destruction. Except for my early flings, for the rest of my life I seldom could perform as nature had intended. The result were feelings of inadequacy that called for compensation – dominating people, seducing an audience, hating communist and the raping of nations. The Versailles Treaty, France, Bolshevism and Jews were valid reasons upon which to vent my spleen of sexual inadequacy

"Linked though I was to many women, what held them in my orbit was the aura I displayed of drive, stamina and destiny. The injections of bull's semen I was getting from Dr. Morell served only to boost me briefly until I once again sagged…

"The irony was that if I had fathered a son in my twenties he was certainly half a Jew, a contradiction and betrayal of everything I stood for…

"Despite my anti-Jewish ravings I admired them. Just like tiny Britain, they, as a people of limited numbers were achievers with brains and ingenuity. I agreed with the Jesuit's belief that Jews were behind much of the world's disorders. I felt there were too many in top German professions...

"Today Germany, Tomorrow the World' was never my ambition. To conquer Western Europe, Russia, Britain and to control North Africa and the Middle East were the outer limits of my aims. I had an eye on South America but events would not allow it. Himmler was keen all for it. As for Japan, they were welcomed to the Far East and Pacific. I sought to usher in a secular and religious order in Europe through force. And in addition to wiping out the Jews, I aimed to supplant Christianity in Europe with a new Nazi Religion with me in place of Christ....

"My 'letter in the bottle' was an attempt to dissuade the actions of America so that my dream could be realised...

"Except for a few, when the end for me drew near most of my party comrades deserted me – but not my valet Heinz Linge. Even when I released him from his duties he remained loyal, he followed my very last instruction to the letter. I know, I was there in spirit to see it...

"I made mistakes, I could have won the war but I made mistakes. Declaring war on America was a mistake. I was a dummkopf thinking the Russians were soft, listening to my air chiefs who said the British radar system was crude and useless, of trusting my generals. In 1942 I made mistakes by overextending my troops while trying to capture the oil fields in the Caucuses, I made many mistakes. My stupid delays in 1940 let too many soldiers escape from Dunkirk...

"I had seventeen Field Marshalls and thirty-four generals. Some were good, some useless. I fired many.

"But it really wasn't their fault. It was me, I asked too much of them, too many soldiers died in Leningrad, in Moscow, in the Caucuses and in Stalingrad. Too many innocent people died in the war, I made mistakes...

"I'm thrilled that the Labrador senses me, I hope I don't scare him too much, I mean him no harm, it's my passive self who can't let go, he haunts me, he's the always ticking shadowy son of a bastard that was my father. He made mistakes and I'm the living but the dead proof."

SIX

Peter and Heather did not question the letter's authenticity. They could not read German but Hitler's signature was unmistakable, his script was chilling yet thrilling.

The Moores were an upbeat couple. A spring in the step, an eye to the future and a hardy laugh were always present. They had plans for a safari in Kenya and a few days in Kilaguni Lodge where the squirrels almost have human faces. Peter had been a bank manager and Heather a school head teacher. Four of her past students were the sibling rascals who became The Bee Gees.

Tall, lean and brimming with life Peter had not lost the spark of wonder. The simplest things brought him pleasure. Heather was the other side of Peter's coin – still seventeen at heart, genuine to the core, giggles by the score and perfectly in tune with her mate from early childhood. Of average height and with greying golden hair, one of her prides was the dimple in her chin. The couple only disagreed about kippers; Peter had to cook them outside the house. On this Heather had put her foot down. Neptune agreed, when Peter was cooking them the Labrador was nowhere to be seen. He liked catching the occasional fish that washed ashore near the lighthouse but the smell of kippers cooking was not to his liking. He would wiggle his nose; his ears would go back and away from Avoca he would wander.

The Moores were not given to act in haste. They knew the bottle and letter could alter their lives by exposing them to unwanted attention. They also knew that if their dog's find were genuine, offers of money would follow. This scared them because where money is involved people can be vicious, they had no wish to expose themselves to the avarice of others; they were solid Presbyterians in outlook. They valued reward based on effort; sudden, unearned wealth held no lure for them. They admired Margaret Thatcher's work ethic.

Two years earlier the Sunday Times had been duped out of money for the rights to serialize fake Hitler diaries by a forger that had been jailed. The media ridiculed the British newspaper and damaged the reputations of the 'experts' who deemed the diaries genuine.

Peter and Heather were anything but average in personal wealth, they had funds to last a lifetime and their modesty spoke for itself. Their only car, a blue Ford Escort did not beckon attention. They were down-to earth people whose feelings of self-worth needed no boost by the flash of material possessions. Peter's only indulgence was an average sized sailboat.

For years the couple had invested in US Treasury Bills at a time when no tax was due on interest earned by non-US citizens living aboard. Their assets exceeded a million pounds. They also owned an apartment building on the Douglas seafront, which provided a steady income. Their married children who lived abroad were professionals and the thought of them now or later coming into money on the shoulders of Hitler was unthinkable. The Moores were rigid in the belief that such money would forever be linked with evil and bring misfortune. Nor were they thrilled with the publicity that would follow if news of Neptune's find were known.

But the couple's easy persona did not obscure deep thought. They were fortunate and took nothing for granted. Their parents had been the first of their blessings. And of all the places to be born, for them, God had chosen the mystical Isle of Man, away from the hustle, bustle and stresses of mainland Britain, far from its tensions and threats from the IRA. They lived quietly in an island-world, British to be sure, but Manx at heart. Sound health was a gift they also never took for granted.

Although under the British Crown since 1827, the Isle of Man had its own flag. At one time held by Norway, Scotland and the Earls of Derby, Manx, a form of Irish Gallic had once been the island language. Some thirty miles long and fourteen wide at one point, the island differed from the rest of Britain. There were no foxes or squirrels and even the cats showed a streak of individuality – some had no tails due to a genetic twist. Sometimes appearing were Peregrine Falcons with their mysterious occult status which figured in the ceremonies of the island's secretive masons.

Before deciding what to do next the Moores had something else to consider. They opted to keep the bottle out of sight and think things through. No one but they knew about their dog's find. Smart boy that he was, Neptune could sense something brewing. He had brought objects home before but this one was different. He would need to keep his eyes and ears open and sniff for clues. It didn't escape him that treats were now on offer that seldom were before and that another chill had stirred him from his afternoon snooze.

For the next two days Peter and Heather did not mention the bottle to each other. Whatever about the turmoil that would enter their lives if news of it were know, their curiosity about the letter was much on their minds. If they mentioned the bottle it was only in whispers to Neptune whose response was a rapidly wagging tail. He knew the subject was the bottle and that it was in the liquor cabinet which for him was off limits. Weeks earlier he had knocked over a wine glass and he wanted no part of another tongue-lashing, he knew Heather could be a tornado if upset. Opened or closed he wanted no part of the wretched cabinet.

When the couple finally discussed the bottle their thoughts mirrored each other. They had German friends on the island so finding a translator was not a problem, finding a discrete one was another matter. They had both thought of the same person, Otto Schmitt, an old friend in his seventies who had once shared a personal matter with them.

After the outbreak of war and the fiasco of Dunkirk in 1940, the detention of German, Austrian and Italian nationals in Britain came into force. Otto was a German Jew but unlike other Jews in Britain when the war broke out he was not fleeing Nazism but teaching in Lancashire. As a low security risk he was sent to the Hutchinson Camp internment facilities on the Isle of Man which were basic but humane and where the living quarters were boarding houses. Men were housed in one section, women and children in another. In time the barb-wired camp became known as the artist colony due to the number of Jewish or other internees whose professions were in the arts or were academics such as

48

Otto. Prisoners of war were later sent to the island and mostly worked on farms.

Born in Munich in 1912, in 1933 at the age of twenty-one, the swarthy, blue-eyed, black haired Otto was studying for his PhD in physics at Oxford. After gaining his doctorate he remained in Britain and taught physics and maths at Stoneyhurst College, a Jesuit school in Lancashire. When hostilities broke out and internment began he was sent to the Isle of Man. He was then twenty-eight.

During his period of internment life on the Isle of Man was not bad for Otto and other internees. The fact that he had an academic background in Britain pre-dating 1939 and that he was Jewish also stood him in good stead.

His first work was in a plant producing medical supplies; it later involved teaching at a local school. It was in his early days on the island that Otto had met the young Heather and Peter. After the war he remained on the island teaching maths at a local college; there was nothing in war-torn Germany for him to return to. He had no siblings, his mother had died and he was never certain who his father was- but he did have more than a suspicion.

Peter and Heather agreed that Otto was the person to approach. A brilliant teacher with an amazing memory, they knew he could keep a secret and he knew they could keep one too. Theirs was a friendship that went back to a sad period in Peter's life when he lost his sister June. At the time Peter and Heather were nearly eighteen. Before long he was in the Army and June was serving with the Air Transport Auxiliary – a unit of woman flyers that would transport military aircraft from factories to air, bases throughout Britain. June had been killed when a plane she was ferrying crashed off the coast of Hove. Death had also been the fate of Britain's famous flyer Amy Johnson. In the course of transporting a plane from Blackpool to an airbase near Oxford in 1941, she had run into bad weather and engine trouble and had bailed out. Her plane had crashed into the River Thames but her remains were never found.

Neptune was stretched out on the living room floor while Peter and Heather were talking. "What do you think, Neptune," said Heather, "Is Otto the one to speak to?" The dog's response was a tap of the tail. That afternoon he had frolicked with a bitch and poor Neptune was worn out because the lassie had an also sexy sister.

SEVEN

Neptune was a clever fellow given to Heather by a girlfriend from Liverpool. A handsome animal with winning ways, his good deeds knew no bounds.

He descended from a line of Labradors whose role in life was to care for the blind. Part of a large litter, he had never trained as a guide dog. A swift learner, his human instincts were uncanny.

Good fortune was his fate in being spared a life caring for the blind, a job he would have done with devotion and style. Fortunate to have owners who lived in pleasant Port Cranstal, he was free to roam at will, then return to a loving family for food, shelter and the occasional TV show that featured horses and dogs. He loved the Grand National and was keen on the voice of Matt Monro and the song *Born Free*. Whenever it was playing on the radio or being sung on TV he would come to attention, his ears would lift and his head would tilt in approval.

He had the instincts of a guide dog and sharp intelligence as well. He had an inbuilt clock, he could master any task, seldom forget it and he was always eager to repeat it and to please. And he was wonderful with neighbours too; they were part of his extended family, part of his domain to look after, he also had a deep sense of social responsibility.

For all his smarts and chivalrous ways, Neptune would never know the significance of the bottle he had found. But for him waiting on the beach for high tide and the surprise it often washed in, or for the dolphin that might appear with whom he would play after swimming out to meet it, the bottle might have returned to the Irish sea with the ebbtide. He was the unlikely link between Hitler's wayward message to America and the present day. Or, perhaps, knowing that Neptune would find him, Hitler's supernatural ghost chose to visit the Isle of Man after his self-imposed years adrift in the glass coffin of his fancifulness.

Hitler's supernatural form loved the irony of it all, his best friend had been Blondi and now, forty-six years after his own death, who should rescue him from a beach but a dog on one of the British Isles, a dot on the map, part of the country he once yearned to conquer, a nation that had slipped through his fingers like its soldiers in Dunkirk and by the gritty skill of its aircrafts that spit fire.

But there was something Hitler may not have known that would have pleased him back in time. It involved an Alsatian belonging to his ambassador to Britain Leopold von Hoesch and the only Nazi memorial in Britain. It exists to this day in honour of 'Giro'. In 1934 'Giro' was given a burial in London with full Nazi honours. His remains and headstone are in the gardens of Number 9 Carlton Terrace, which, in 1933, after Hitler became Chancellor, was the headquarters of the Third Reich in Britain. 'Giro' died when he chewed into a high voltage electric cable.

In 1936, three years before the start of WWII, ambassador von Hoesch died in London. To honour him German soldiers were allowed to parade by his swastika draped coffin down the Mall in sight of Buckingham Palace. Widely regarded at the time as the country's best hope of improving Anglo-German relation, von Hoesch was replaced by the notoriously pompous, rude and disliked Joachim von Ribbentrop. Unlike von Ribbentrop, von Hoesch was not slavish Nazi.

The ebbtide had swept Hitler's bottle away from America and a high tide or fate had delivered it to the Isle of Man. Between the two, five decades had past, Hitler was dead but his aftermath remained, a never ending source of fascination for many in the evil genius of his character and the canvas of murders he painted in a life of destruction.

Neptune was loved in Port Cranstal and didn't need to be walked; he was mostly out on his own. One of his daily visits was to the lighthouse at high tide, that's where he might grab a fish or something of interest that swept in. When locals saw him on the beach they knew high tide was pending. School kids adored him. He was their friend, their playmate and guardian. When the bell rang and classes were let out, there he would be at the entrance of the school, his tail wagging, and his golden coat groomed, present and correct.

He would call at homes to see if occupants were well, or to visit their bitch if he sensed love was on offer.

And he wasn't just a man about town, a fisherman, a lover or guardian angel. He could multi-task too. If friends needed items from the shop, they would pop money in an envelope with a list, drop it in a basket and Neptune knew what to do as did Clyde, the jolly neighbourhood shopkeeper. In due course Neptune would return with the handle of the basket in his mouth, the shopping inside and change in the envelope if any was due.

Two of his pals were the unusual ninety-one year-old spinster twins Johanna and Erika von Schneider. Natives of Berlin but originally from Austria, the sisters were renowned dentists who in 1939 had a thriving practice in London that catered to the cream of British society as well as theatre and film stars. Benedict, their German born father had been a well-known physician in Liezen who often helped Jews. He had left Germany in his teens never to return or to see his family again. He had a deep dislike of Hitler, as did the sister's mother, the no-nonsense Austrian born Isabella.

Already in their forties when war broke out the sisters were sent to the Isle of Man. They remained on the island after the war and were friendly with Otto Schmitt whom they had first met in 1940 at the Hutchinson Camp facilities. Now less able to fend for themselves, Neptune would look in on them and do their shopping if need be. He would do extraordinary things.

One winter's night he was out answering natures call: he was in an open field sniffing, looking for a spot for his deposit. It was cold, the wind was blowing in his direction when he caught whiff of something unpleasant. Gas was wafting from the sister's neat bungalow fifty yards away. Up went his ears and tail. He immediately knew its origin, not the two bungalows nearest him, but the one further back belonging to the von Schneiders.

Off he went like a shot towards the bungalow. All the house lights were out. Neptune barked and scratched at the door. No reply. He ran to the windows and barked again. No reply. The smell of gas was severe, Neptune went berserk barking.

A young couple named Leo and Bette McShane dashed from their nearby bungalow in response to the commotion. They could smell gas coming from the sister's home. Neptune raced towards them. He went round and rounds in circles barking, his tail was going wild.

The McShanes reacted swiftly. Bette raced home to telephone for help. Leo rushed to the bungalow with a handkerchief over his nose and mouth. He banged on the door. When no response came, he didn't dither, he put his shoulder to the door and broke in. The smell of gas almost beat him back but he pressed on and so did Neptune who seemed to be everywhere at once.

The sisters were in the same room in separate beds unconscious, barley breathing. Neptune was super-active pulling at their bed covers with his teeth and paws, prodding them with his head. Leo flung open the windows then quickly poured water on the embers in the living room fire. Goodness only knows why the bungalow had not blown up.

By now other neighbours were on the scene getting the sisters out of the bungalow. Within minutes the ambulance and police had arrived, the sisters were saved thanks to the clever Labrador and the quick-thinking McShanes.

The next day Neptune was in the papers and on television all across the UK being hailed a hero as were the quick thinking couple who leapt into action. But Neptune was the star, a saviour from another planet, a super-dog from Neptune.

His heroics had taken place a year before finding Hitler's bottle. The Moores knew how the media would react if they ever got wind of Hitler's bottle and the fact that Neptune 'the hero' had found it. If they ever put two and two together they knew that the media's grip would be unbearable and that the rhythm of their lives would alter and not for the better.

EIGHT

Otto Schmitt lived in Ramsey, a town seven miles down the coast from Port Cranston. His once black hair was now grey, his Tony Curtis looks of youth had faded, but he still cuts a fine figure for a man of his age. Tall and erect he hinted of the fictional character Dorian Grey. One could easily imagine the handsome Otto of years passed, probably enhanced by the fact that his mother's Jewish roots were Safatic not Ashkenazi. In his twenties he was alluringly sultry to behold.

He was home reading the Manx Evening News of Saturday, May 4th 1991 when the telephoned rang. When he answered it was only with a trace of a German accent. He listened then replied:

"Yes, Peter, fine, tomorrow, Sunday at Avoca for lunch."

It was not unusual for an invitation from the Moores, but the tone of Peter's voice and the shortness of the call suggested that this invite had a purpose other than social. Nonetheless Otto looked forward to seeing his dear old pals, Peter and Heather Moore.

The last time he had seen them was in March at Peter's retirement party in nearby Douglas. It was a friendship dating back to the war years when Britain's future looked bleak. And oh what had transpired in the last fifty years thought Otto: A war in Korea, The Berlin Wall had gone up and was now down, Communism had collapsed in Russia, a Third World War had been avoided, the Kennedy brothers had been killed, Nixon had been forced from office, the Vietnam war had raged, Ronald Reagan had been President, British troops were in Ulster and a woman Prime Minister now sat in Downing Street. These thoughts swept through Otto's mind like the leaves of a calendar falling.

Otto was a Jew but not that you would know it from his looks or manner, anyone who knew him would agree. He never spoke of his faith or the Holocaust unless given no choice. The subject of money never crossed his lips and he rarely observed Jewish holy days. He was a puzzle that drew you in with his avuncular nature, his sense of the correct and the obvious devotion he displayed in his teaching which he still did.

In his social life Otto had many friends but few were Jews perhaps because there were few Jews on the Isle of Man. He was cerebral to the core with a passion for The Theory of Relativity. Energy equals mass times the speed of light squared seemed to be his only religions. $E=MC^2$ was one of his never-ending worlds of study, devotion and exploration along with the study of quantum physics and the theory of Dr Paul Dorak. The subject of 'infinity' and God was another of his loves, the same subject that had driven the German Georg Cantor mad. His theory fed into one Otto himself was working on by way of a mathematical equation: the belief being that if the empty space in the atoms of our bodies were squeezed out, the entire human race would fit in the space of a thimble. Is there any wonder Cantor went mad.

The Moores had to be careful how they broached the subject of the bottle with Otto. Despite their friendship Otto was a Jew who was lucky to be out of Germany when Storm Troopers were thumping them and the SS were shipping them to death camps. All this was considered when the Moores chose him as the best person to translate Hitler's letter. They felt their bonds were strong enough to leap the subject of Hitler and his treatment of Jews. They knew that if Otto chose not to help, that no hard feelings would result and that he would not mention the matter to anyone. Year's earlier he had taken them into his confidence and now Peter and Heather were confiding in him.

After the war several ladies on the island had their eyes on Otto. Although already in his thirties, he showed no interest in woman, his only focus was on teaching. When the ladies' overtures were ignored, whispers began that Otto was homosexual even though no evidence to support the claim existed. On reaching the ears of the Moores, Peter decided to have a word with Otto about the gossip.

It was a sensitive subject but Otto was glad that Peter had broached it and in the years that followed the Moores never repeated what Otto had revealed to anyone. Peter did not react to Otto's revelation, but there was more Peter didn't know that had nothing to do with Otto's secret of more than fifty years.

Given that he was beautiful while studying at Oxford, in addition to female admirers, a few male students and teachers were always yearning for his body. And Otto was tempted. Since his teens his sexual preference sometimes leaned towards men. In time he gave in to the temptation and began dabbling in the practice with two students and one professor. If this were not enough, he had a flip in desires and had begun an affair with an upper class female student related to royalty. No one at the time in Oxford suspected Otto was Jewish as nothing about him hinted of Jewishness and he had never been circumcised.

This was a period of inner turmoil for Otto, he was being pulled in different directions sexually. Added to this he was keeping his faith quiet because anti-Jewish feelings were common at the time. In the 1930s being Jewish gave rise to few applauds in the Briton. In 1940 The Right Club, an anti-Jewish group led by the Scottish MP Archibald Ramsay had a large membership composed of the British middle and upper classes.

One night in the dormitory showers Otto was set upon and raped by two students. The school hushed it up and when his Jewishness was discovered he was treated like a leper and left without friends. When the girl he was seeing heard of this and learned that he was Jewish and bi-sexual as well, she transferred to another university.

Otto's feelings of self-hatred and revulsion were overwhelming. He had been humiliated, socially cast adrift and made to feel worthless. Added to this, he had no idea of his true sexuality. Jewishness and sex had brought him grief, so he vowed never to have anything to do with sex again, He would keep his faith to himself unless unavoidable and devote his life to the study and teaching of physics and maths.

He only found peace while teaching in Stoneyhurst College. There, in Lancashire, he had found tranquillity in a world of Jesuit priests who had hired him despite the fact that he was

Jewish. After Otto secured his teaching post, Father Donald Stone, the headmaster of the college said, *As far as this college is concerned you're a qualified teacher who happens to be a Jew. Who you worship is your business, it has nothing to do with Stonyhurst College.* Not everyone at the college shared Stone's view but expediency prevailed.

NINE

The weather was nasty as Otto drove up the coast to lunch with his friends. Rain and wind were sweeping across the island towards the British mainland to the east. He was listening to BBC's Radio 4.

In their anti-US mode the BBC were still talking about the 1986 American bombing of Tripoli and the death of Colonel Gadaffi's adopted baby daughter. The selective nature of the station's female commentator seemed almost to justify the Libyan bombing of Pan Am flight 103 in December 1988. The events leading to the tragedy were well known.

In 1986 the US had bombed Tripoli after an explosive planted by Libyans in a West Berlin nightclub had killed two American soldiers. In the early 80s Gaddafi was making death threats to the US. After the nightclub killings the finger of suspicion pointed to Libya.

The Pan Am bombing had killed 270 people, most of them Americans flying to New York prior to Christmas. The plane had been blown up over the Scottish town of Lockerbie. President Reagan, who was in the last few weeks of his presidency and not well, was livid.

The fact that the carnage was caused by Libya, a country known to sponsor terrorists didn't seem to matter to the BBC. It was no secret that Libya were supplying the IRA with weapons and explosives to use against Britain.

Otto pondered what he was hearing. The swipes against America were familiar because many in Britain and in Europe were of similar views. Unlike the increasingly left-wing BBC and other critics, Otto had not forgotten that for all its faults America for some may have been rancid butter, but when push came to shove they were on Britain's side of the bread. And if Europe was free and rebuilt after the war America had been the key instrument of change.

Except for his traumatic experience in Oxford, Britain had been good to Otto, but he found that there were negative aspects of outlook towards America among some Britons that were pedantic in nature, envious underneath and superior in self-belief.

The rain was lashing down when Otto reached Avoca; the wind swept him from his car towards the bungalow just as Heather was opening the front door with a frisky Neptune in toe.

"Come in, come in," she said.

"What a day," said Otto. "God bless this house." Although the Catholic-type house blessing coming from a Jew was unusual it was well within Otto's character who was himself most unusual. After taking off his raincoat and greeting Neptune Otto headed to the living room and his favourite armchair.

"Something smells good."

Peter appeared from the kitchen with an apron round his waist and wooden spoon in one hand.

"Welcome, welcome," he said, "whiskey, gin, sherry, wine or beer, what'll it be?"

"Beer, a small one please."

The rain continued with no let-up and the tail-wagging Neptune was all over the place, in and out of the kitchen. After lunch everyone was relaxing talking about old times and catching up on each other's news. Choosing his moment with care, Peter dealt with the matter of the bottle.

Neptune was stretched out on the floor. Peter looked at him and smiled.

"Do you know what this rascal brought home?"

"Not a clue," said Otto as he reached for his pipe.

Peter went to the liquor cabinet, slid back the door, picked up the bottle and handed it to him. Neptune was unconcerned; no chill had come his way of late. Heather searched for Otto's reaction. Holding the bottle and peering at the swastikas Otto drew breath, a corner of his mouth curled but he said nothing. Neptune came to life and sat at Otto's feet at attention, his tail wagging proudly.

"Where did this come from?" Otto said to Neptune in a low tone of voice. The Labrador's tail raced, his eyes darting from Otto to the bottle and back.

"It washed ashore near the lighthouse," said Heather.

Almost in a whisper Otto said "Does anyone else know about this?"

"No one," replied Peter.

"Good… What's inside?"

"Have a look said Heather, it's a letter in German, we were hoping you would translate."

Otto reached for his glasses. With care he removed the bottle's cap, slid the rolled up letter out, removed it from the silver ring and began to read. His only reaction was another intake of breath. When his reading was done he slowly shook his head in the negative. Neptune's tail was now silent, Otto was thinking. Time stood still. After a pause Otto went to the window and looked out at the falling rain. Years earlier rain was falling while he and his mother were arguing, when she revealed a secret that might have links with the author of the letter he'd just read. He was fifteen then, it was a secret Otto dare not share even with his friends, so he was thinking.

Peter and Heather were quiet. Neptune looked at everyone inquisitively, his tail was at ease. Still holding the letter Otto returned to his chair and removed his glasses; he rubbed his eyes then replaced them. "This is what's written," he said. A deep breath preceded his words. He spoke the words in German then said their meaning in English.

4 July 1940.

Achtung Amerika!
ATTENTION AMERICA!

Unsere Stärke ist unsere Schnelligkeit und Brutalitat!
OUR STRENGTH IS OUR QUICKNESS AND BRUTALITY!

Eure Schiffe werden versenkt:

YOUR SHIPS WILL BE SUNK!

Eure Matrosen werden vernichtet:
YOUR SEAMEN WILL BE KILLED!

Europa ist nicht ihre Angelegenheit:
EUROPE IS NOT YOUR CONCERN!

ADOLF HITLER!

Nothing more was said and when the weather improved a pensive Otto drove home. He had much to think about as did his hosts.

Before leaving Otto said, "Hitler rarely wrote anything in his own hand. Can you remember what date Neptune found the bottle?"

"Last Tuesday, 30th April," Peter replied, "The day my curtain rods were delivered." Otto thought for a moment, then he added, "Do you know what date Hitler killed himself?" The answer was 'no'.

"It was April 30th, 1945. And did you know that his hair was completely grey when he was in his thirties and that his personal wealth was enormous?"

Earlier, when Otto removed the rolled up letter from its silver ring he never noticed the word Zenitram engraved along its outer rim, or maybe he did and chose not to comment. Otto hardly slept that night, an old ghost had returned to haunt him.

TEN

The Moores were not thrown by news that Hitler's was prematurely grey. What was running through Otto's mind as he stood at the window is what had them wondering. It was obvious that the letter had struck a nerve - but what? It didn't appear to have anything to do with his Jewishness.

After knowing Otto for years the Moores new felt an air of mystery about their old friend. But what could it be? They toyed with the notion of destroying the bottle and letter but soon came down to earth. What to do now was the question?

Otto was disturbed as he drove home, his teeth chomped down on the stem of his pipe. Reading the letter had awakened memories of a night involving his mother, a Jewess named Sarah who was then involved with a man of mystery. That night had brought a shocking revelation and scene, which had caused Otto to despair at his mother's way of life; it was something that had irked him for years.

Then, as now in his seventies, Otto didn't know who his father was. Since that night and for more than fifty years he had wondered, always hoping that it was not who he thought it might be.

His mother's admission came in 1927 on a night of heavy rain in Munich. Otto had by chance found his birth certificate in the flat he shared with his mother. He was fifteen years old. Up to that point his mother had said that his father was Carl Single, a Berliner who had died in World War One. The birth certificate gave no name of his father so Otto was a bastard; being one was bad enough, being a Jewish bastard was another matter.

Swaying and smelling of drink, his mother had brought home a man she introduced as Herr Wolff. Dark of completion with piercing blue eyes, he was sober and well dressed. Although he was only in his thirties his black hair was obviously dyed. Wolff wore a grey felt hat with a black band. Average of height with a stern, imposing presence, he also wore a black leather coat that hung below the knees. As he took it off he asked if there was mineral water in the flat. Young Otto assumed the man was Jewish. From the moment he laid eyes on Wolff he didn't like him. He had seen his face before but could not remember where. Otto never forgot the events of that night, it was the ugly scenario that often haunted him at night when it rained.

His mother and Wolff had gone to a bedroom and shut the door behind them. After a while Otto could hear the escalating volume of his mother's passion. Beside himself with fury, he burst into the room and pulled them apart as the mounted Wolff was about to enter his mother's bushy cushion of flesh. Outraged at her son's intrusion, Sarah, naked from the waist down, slapped Otto across the face and from frustration she asked Wolff to leave, which he did while still rigid but without comment. Only his eyes spoke of annoyance as he left the flat. Wolff had not said a word to Otto since he asked for mineral water.

Even now, in his seventies, Otto could still see it, his mother, wild eyed, half naked, stumbling, trying to remain upright, reaching for anything she could grab to stay on her feet. And how could he forget what followed:

"Who is my father?"

"I told you, Carl Single," Sarah screamed.

"My birth certificate gives no name."

"Where did you find it?"

"In a box in the closet."

"You bastard, why do you go through my things."

"I wasn't, I was looking for my school reports."

Now out of control Sarah slapped Otto again and again.

"Who is my father?" cried Otto while shielding his face from the blows with his arms. "Who is he?"

"I don't know, I don't know, I don't know."

"What do you mean you don't know, how many were there?"

" All I could get. They help pay the bills. He could be anyone. Wolff could be your father, it could be anyone."

"Who is Wolff", yelled Otto, his face flush red.

" He's in politics. He got us this flat. He's been good to me. He's not a Jew."

Days later Otto's eyed fixed on a photo of two men in the newspaper, leading members of the Nazi Party. One was Rudolph Hess; the other was Wolff who was wearing a grey felt hat with a black band and a black leather coat that hung below the knees. But his name wasn't Wolff, it was Hitler, a rising star in German politics who had spoken at the Nazi Party's first official rally in Nuremberg's main town square and who, while in jail, had written a book many were talking about – a book called *Mein Kampf*.

Other unpleasant thoughts came to mind for Otto the evening of his lunch with the Moores, like the night two Oxford students raped him. He thought how the slimy pair were still living and were, up to recently, pillars of British society until their past came back to bite them. One had left the country, the other; a former cabinet minister had attempted suicide when his secret way of life returned to haunt him.

ELEVEN

Peter had fought with Montgomery's Army in North Africa; he had survived the bloodbath of El Alamein with only shrapnel injury to a leg.

His manner being so easy, one would never have thought that he had been decorated with the Conspicuous Gallantry Medal. Praise however, was a crown Peter found hard to wear. He never talked about the war, he cared not to recall the blown-up, bullet holed bodies of friends and foe alike in the sands of North Africa, the landing beach of Normandy and the forests of Belgium. Unlike other Allied soldiers he had never returned to the Normandy beach where he landed on the north coast of France code-named *Sword*.

Rewind to the middle of December 1942. After El Alamein, having been lucky to get Christmas leave in England while still recovering from his injury and while travelling on a train from London to Liverpool, Peter had met and made friends with a ginger haired American pilot named Dennis McClendon. Based in Norfolk with the 8th Air Force and no more than twenty at the time, Dennis, a Second Lieutenant, could have passed for seventeen. It was a friendship between the Brit and Yank that had endured the passage of time.

Dennis was then beginning what eventually would be fifty-eight bombing missions. As far he knew only Joseph Heller, the author of *Catch-22* had, as a young flyer flown more missions although British airmen had flown many more. Dennis had defied the odds and survived all his missions without a scratch even though bullets from enemy fighters and shrapnel guns on the ground often hit his bomber. When the war ended his mother said he was a red head with an angel on his shoulder.

He had flown missions with men like the film stars Jimmy Stewart and Clark Gable, flyers who had faced the same dangers as other airmen. Stewart, a pilots and Gable, a gunner, were older than the average flyer's age of twenty-two. Gable, one of the stars of *Gone With Wind* was in his forties, he too had faced the high probability of death in bombers heavy with fuel and explosives called 'flying crematoriums'. Stewart, Gable and Dennis had angels on their shoulders but many others did not.

Dennis lived in Tampa, Florida. After the war he and Peter had kept in touch and in the 1970s they would often see each other in Britain. Dennis and his wife Vivian would travel to the UK to visit Jean, their daughter who was married to a Yorkshire doctor.

When the war ended Dennis made the Air Force his career rising to the rank of Lt. Colonel with postings in the Pentagon working in intelligence. The same age as Peter and retired, Dennis was much the same in outlook as his British buddy from the Isle of Man.

They would ring each other often and now it was Peter's turn to call but Dennis had beaten him to it. The McClendons would soon be in Britain to visit their daughter and newly born grandson, so the Moores arranged to join their friends in Yorkshire, and for the Americans to return with them to the Isle of Man for a long overdue first visit. During their stay Peter would take up the matter of the bottle. Like Otto, the McClendons were people in whom he and Heather could confide.

Peter was thrilled to hear that Dennis and his wife would soon be in Britain and that his friends had said yes to visiting the Isle of Man. They would be in Britain in days. He said nothing on the phone about Hitler's bottle, one never knew who might be listening.

From the early 1970s British Intelligence was tapping phones because the IRA was on the warpath, not only in Ulster but also on the British mainland. In addition to their killings in Northern Ireland, Irish rebels had planted bombs on the mainland that had killed and injured people in London, Gilford and Birmingham. In 1979 they had killed Airey Neave, the most famous British escapees from Colditz Castle, a politician and friend of Prime Minister Thatcher.

In 1984 the IRA had planted a bomb that would strike at the heart of the British government. A huge device had gone off in the early morning hours of 12th October on one of the top floors of the Grand Hotel in Brighton during the Conservative Party's Conference.

Weeks earlier an IRA operative had registered as a guest and planted the bomb in a bathroom. It was set to go off during the conference with the hope of killing Margaret Thatcher. It went off as planned killing three people, including a member of parliament and the wife of a Tory official; more than thirty injured people had been pulled from the rubble. Mrs. Thatcher had not been hurt but one of her ministers and his wife had been badly injured.

Ulster Protestant extremists were no angels either, they too were in the mix of the mayhem. They too killed in a cold-blooded way but the IRA were masters when it came to handing out doses of disaster. Marcus McAusland, a friend of Peter's and a former British Army officer had been shot in the head in 1972 not far from his home in Limavady near Londonderry, Northern Ireland. His body had been found in a ditch along a narrow road on which one-day Neptune would be found alone walking in the rain.

Since British Intelligence was bugging phone calls galore, Peter was taking no chances with talk about Hitler on the phone. If anyone could advise him what to do about the bottle from an American perspective, Dennis was the man to do it. Adolf Hitler's letter was addressed to the American people so it made sense that an American friend with military links was a good person to consult for advice.

TWELVE

Just as Otto's passion was Einstein's theory of relativity, so too did Peter have a keen interest. It was not on a par with the world of E=MC2 but one that also called for concentration.

Peter owned a thirty-foot sailboat called *Get Knotted.* He loved sailing her round the island's coast weather and winds permitting and he could tie all the knots seaman employ. Anyone who knew him would agree that Peter was a nut when it came to knots; there was something about them that threw down a challenge. Mastering the twists and turns in a knot's structure focused his mind and Hitler's missive had given him much upon which to concentrate. Such was Peter's mind-set after speaking with Dennis, so he unboxed his fibre practice-ropes to work on his knots and think about the day, month and year of Hitler's letter – July 4th 1940.

Having seen his knot-tying rituals more than enough, Heather raised her eyes to heaven as Peter began creating the knots that had to be mastered for a sailor to feel fit for nautical purpose. They featured all types of oddly shaped knots with peculiar names for a variety of uses both practical and decorative.

Bend Knots, for example, are those that attach two lines to each other end-to-end such as Sheet Bends, the Garrick Bend, the Fisherman's Knot, the Hunter's Bend and so on. The magician Harry Houdini would have known them all and so did Peter, but he had to practice tying them so as not to forget. While doing this he could focus on other things. It was an odd way to fix his mind on other matters but it worked for Peter. In his working life he had solves many banking problems while fiddling with his knots.

As he worked on the Sheet Bend his mind settled on 4th July 1940, a date half a century earlier when he was eighteen. So much was happening at the time and it was so long ago that it was silly to try and pull the events of that date from the cracks in his memory. It was clearly an impossible task, he had no idea what day of the week it had been but he did know that July 4th was

America's day of independence from Britain, he had heard enough of it from Yanks in the war and from his friend Dennis McClendon. The day of the week was actually a Thursday.

It was easy to recall that Britain was preparing for invasion, that the RAF was battling with the Luftwaffe over England and that soon he would be in the army. It was also easy to remember that operation 'Pied Piper' had begun: the evacuation of millions of children from cities to the countryside. The rest was a blur, so he would need to look the date up, consult his encyclopaedia, go to the library, and, as the saying on posters said during the war, 'dig for victory'.

Peter wondered what was in Hitler's mind around 4th July 1940 and what was taking place. Had his memory been able to zip back in time and live in Hitler's skin much reliving of that month would he have done.

Hitler was happy. Everything was going his way, the Channel Islands were his, hardly a shot had been fired, the islands were undefended so his troops simply moved in and took over. The British had failed to notify the Germans that the Channel Islands were now a demilitarised zone. In addition his bottle was by now in the Atlantic off the coast of Montauk Point hopefully having drifted to shore with the high tide.

In July the Luftwaffe had begun their first daylight raids over Britain but the RAF was posing problems for Air Marshall Goring whose job it was to destroy British air power. But the RAF was resisting, The Battle of Britain had begun. Despite this irritation Hitler felt secure. After all…

Britain stood alone, the chances of the US joining the war were slim, and even if she wanted to, she was not prepared for war. By the time she was ready Britain, Russia and North Africa would be his. And having zipped back in time and lived in Hitler's skin and remembered all this, Peter would have recalled Churchill's radio talk to the nation, his theatrical rhetoric confirming Hitler's view that the old bulldog who had called him a Bloodthirsty Guttersnipe was drunk when he spoke on radio. Some MPs in Churchill's own government shared Hitler's belief that with the help of drink he was detached from reality when they heard his radio address.

As he worked on his knots Peter remembered one of Churchill's radio talks to the nation. This he would never forget.

Let us brace ourselves to our duty and so bear ourselves that if the British Commonwealth and Empire lasts a thousand years men will say: This was their finest hour.

On hearing a translation Hitler would have said

Unsinn, Unglaublich – Nonsense, the fat fool was drunk. The Third Reich not Britain will last a thousand years, Britain is all but mine. In years to come German will be its language, there will be no Jews or monarchy in the Britain. I will be dead but so will the Jewish race be in Europe. By then America and Germany will have joined forces to keep the Arabs in their tents, the Muslims on their knees and all slant-eyed people in rice fields where they belong. My ghost will enjoy it.

Peter recalled the British warriors that brought a smile to his face, the 'Local Defence Volunteers' known later as 'The Home Guard' – male volunteers ranging in ages from sixty and over with seventeen year-olds thrown in. Formed when the threat of invasion was eminent, 250,000 had come forward in a flash. It was the first civilian army in Britain since Napoleon's threatened invasion of England in the early 1800s. Peter recalled one Home Guard unit armed only with spears. He smiled because of the television series *Dad's Army*, a comedy about elderly volunteers. When Hitler heard about them he too smiled because after the 'debacle yet miracle of Dunkirk' Great Britain was now scavenging for men that were anything but fit and able.

Still inside Hitler's skin Peter would have felt his joy when he heard that the British Navy had blundered. But they had not. Fearful that the French Fleet at anchor in Algeria would fall into German hands, Churchill ordered that it be attacked. In the process more than one thousand French sailors had been killed. Hitler was overjoyed, he saw it as an error from which a feast of propaganda against Britain would flow. Some did but Churchill knew what he was doing and what its short-term effect would be - and that it was worth it. The two-faced French Nazi collaborator Pierre Laval, leader of the Vichy government was irate but nothing came of his rage.

Churchill announced that Britain regretted the loss of life and hoped it would not affect Anglo-French relations. At home however, the raid on the French ships restored hope and confidence after the hiding British troops had taken at Dunkirk. As important was the fact that this bold act convinced President Roosevelt that Britain meant business and would stop at nothing to win the war.

Outraged at the loss of French lives, Peter may have remembered that the new Vichy Government had severed relations with Britain, and that they had played both sides of the fence, one day helping the French Resistance, the next day being in league with their German friends. They had stripped naturalized Jews of their citizenship and imposed a death sentence on French servicemen who joined a foreign army because 400 French troops had died when a U-Boat torpedoed a ship carrying them to Britain.

As Peter worked on his 'Trick and Fancy Knots' he didn't need to dig deep to recall one of the greatest British embarrassments of the time, Edward and Mrs. Simpson: the Duke and Duchess of Windsor. In order to get the Nazi-friendly couple out of sight, Edward had been appointed governor of the Bahamas. Hitler had a big laugh over this too. But he wasn't laughing when the Democratic Party chose Franklyn D. Roosevelt as their candidate to run for a third term as American president.

"Done!", Peter called out to Heather. All his knots had successfully been tied and much had run through his mind in the process. He would wait to see Otto and Dennis before the future of Hitler's bottle was decided.

THIRTEEN

Otto was home in his armchair filling his pipe with tobacco. He thinking about Hitler, Germany and Europe in the 1930s; Oswald Mosley's British Union of Fascists and America were also in the mix of this thoughts.

In 1932 he was in his first year at Oxford but few knew or even cared how a poor German Jew of dubious parentage had managed to secure a place in such a high seat of learning, so recalling the decade with his sharp memory was not difficult.

How could he forget Germany's civil disorder, its rampaging communists and the terrible depression in Europe that rendered millions jobless. How could he forget how the Nazis had bullied and cajoled their way to power and the turmoil they created exploiting social ills.

How could he forget Germany's leaders, the slippery aristocratic Chancellor Franz von Papen and the elderly, crusty president Paul von Hindenburg. How could he forget the war Hitler had brought to Europe, the scores he had killed in death camps, the secret police, all in the name and for the good of Germany, which he led into oblivion. How could he forget the stain he had brought to Germany, the Nazi Party's pillaring of Jews and the Storm Troopers' bloody street-fights with communists. And how could he forget the secret link he had with Mr. Wolff, the man who was really Adolf Hitler, the man with a scorpion for a heart who rose from the streets of Munich and grew into a killer.

He had met Wolff again after the Munich night of rain in 1927. Despite the episode of their first meeting and the fact that they were Jews, Wolff had been good to him and his mother. Maybe Wolff was his father – there was a possibility. An example of how he helped would soon come.

When it was evident that Otto was bright with a promising future it was Wolff who had secured a scholarship for him at Munich University from which young man had emerged with honours in Physics and Mathematics.

Wolff had again come through with a scholarship, this time for him to study at Oxford for his PhD so for Otto the 1930s were unforgettable. Those years were fixed in his mind, an uncomfortable blend of memories and emotions side by side. What a strange contradiction this had been to live with. And all the time the possibility existed that Hitler might be his father, that Hitler might be the man whose seed sparked the miracle of life that Otto in his youth reflected and enhanced in the form of black-haired, blue-eyed handsomeness.

He didn't know if he should hate Hitler or be proud that the man who had helped him and might be his father was a demon with ambitions on a mission to excel but from brutality. This was the inner conflict Otto had lived with for years.

How could he forget the Nazis' treatment of Jewish traders long before von Hindenburg appointed Hitler Chancellor, or the way they kicked Jews in the streets, humiliated and hounded them and treated them like vermin.

He remembered that even before these anti-Jewish scenes the Nazi Party had increased its members in the Reichstag to form the second largest party after the Socialists. And how the decade's economic gloom had played a role in swinging votes to the Nazis, and how the rise of Nazism had sent shock waves through Germany's stock market.

Otto recalled the uproar at the opening of that Reichstag when Nazi deputies appeared in uniforms, which was illegal for civilians, and the brutal Jew-hating riots in the streets of Berlin that followed.

He recalled Hitler's hatred of the Versailles Treaty, proclaiming that he would build a conscript army contrary to its terms. Linked to this thought Otto remembered that the French had already started building a line of defence along the French/German border called the Maginot Line.

He recalled that in Vienna thousands of Nazi sympathisers had demonstrated against "All quiet On the Western Front"- the film about Germany's role in World War One.

It came back to Otto that in 1933 unemployment in Germany stood near five million and that three million in Britain were out of work, and that due to Germany's dire economy, that its war debts were suspended. And that the banks in Germany had closed because the Dana Bank had collapsed, and that banks in France and New York had to lend Britain millions because it too was in financial tatters. All this and more came racing back to Otto's active mind.

He recalled Nazi deputies in the Reichstag demanding Germany's withdrawal from the League of Nations saying they would sterilize some races to ensure 'Nordic' dominance', while at the same time, Hitler was telling journalists that he was a democrat. Otto remembered how the press reacted when Hitler made this claim, and that soon after the Austrian born Hitler had been granted German citizenship.

And how could he forget the 'Battle of Cable Street' in London's East end when Oswald Mosley's fascist Blackshirts with police escorts tried to march and insight racial hatred but where stopped by local Jewish and Irish residents. And how could he forget how the battle had stopped the British fascist movement, and how two days later Mosley had wed the scandalous Diana Mitford at the Berlin home of Joseph Goebbels with Hitler as guest. How could he forget Evelyn Waugh's comment about Diana when he wrote: "Her beauty ran through the room like a pearl of bells."

And how could he forget that if the name of Germany were not tarnished enough, how two men in America with German names were in the news and in the eye of murky episodes. The first was the aviator Charles Lindberg who was centre-stage in what was then called 'The Trial of the Century', a trial that would blight his name. The second was Bruno Richard Hauptmann, a German born carpenter, an illegal immigrant living in New York who had escaped from prison in Germany.

Hauptmann had been tried, convicted and executed for the abduction and murder of Lindbergh's baby son, a conviction based on thin evidence. He had gone to his death professing his innocence.

The Hurst newspaper empire had offered Bruno's family riches if they could get him to confess but Hauptmann had refused. Lindberg, although a hero to most Americans was also considered to be a weird character due to his obsession in unlocking the secrets of eternal life. Well known for his pro-Nazi anti-Semitic racist views, he had been given a medal by Hitler but Lucky Lindy, as he was known, had not walked away from the trial with clean hands; some thought he was involved in his son's death. At the time of the trial in 1937 Otto remembers thinking that here again were people with German names who were up to their necks in sordid affairs that many felt typified all Germans.

Otto recalled that in 1932 millions in America were jobless, that Roosevelt had been elected president, that Japan had occupied parts of China, that von Hindenburg had sought re-election, that Hitler had run against him and been defeated but that he had come second making him a future contender for the chancellorship of Germany.

He remembered Hitler being blocked from the post by the serving chancellor von Papen and of Hitler's refusal to serve under him.

The past ran riot in his mind, Otto recalled the Nazis party's gloom after losing seats in a national election but that von Papen had resigned after failing to form a government, and that Hitler refused the offer of the chancellorship if it meant joining with other parties as von Hindenburg wanted. Then came a day in January 1933 - a day so firmly fixed in Otto's mind.

After weeks of intrigue involving bankers, army officers and right-wing politicians, von Hindenburg, who months earlier had said a Hitler cabinet would mean a party dictatorship had changed his mind and appointed Hitler Chancellor of Germany. This timely twist had resulted from the near collapse of Germany's government; the country was on the brink of civil war with its daily street battles between Hitler's Nazis and German Communists.

Apart from Hitler, there were only two other Nazis in his eleven-man cabinet, William Frick, a former police officer and Hermann Goring, a WWI aviator and former drug addict. The rest were right-wing Nationals who believed they would soon tame Hitler and his wild men with brown shirts and swastika armbands.

Many in his cabinet considered Hitler a rabble-rouser, a forty-four year-old high school drop-out and wartime corporal. They cared little for his wild speeches that brought audiences to their feet and his air stabbing fascist salutes, and the chanting's of 'Seig Heil'. How wrong they were, thought Otto.

How could Otto forget that after becoming Chancellor, Hitler had denounced the Treaty of Versailles and that his brown shirts had marched by torchlights to the cheers of thousands. But that the communist weren't cheering, they had spilled into the streets demanding a general strike.

Only weeks earlier Hitler and his followers were demoralized when support for their cause seemed to be waning. It was then that von Papen, plotting his return to power arranged for Hitler to meet Kurt von Schroeder, a Cologne banker. Swiftly, in a matter of only one week von Hindenburg agreed to accept not only Hitler as chancellor but also to install General Werner von Bloomberg – a Nazi sympathiser - as Defence Minister in order to win support of the army for the new government.

Hitler had always refused to accept anything less than the chancellor ship. It was only good fortune that the failure of von Papen and von Hindenberg to secure parliamentary rule had dropped the chancellorship in his lap.

At the time, as now, Otto knew that Hitlerism was born of the middle classes longing for order while also fearing Bolshevism, greedy bankers and shifty industrialists. He knew that what they put in place were the seeds of World War II and a clinic in killings and destruction on an unimaginable scale by a warped, bellowing exponent of the master race and his eager followers.

FOURTEEN

From the day of Neptune's find Hitler's passive voice was knocking on Heather's mind, returning her to the days when the Luftwaffe was bombing Britain's airfields, cities and ports.

More and more her thoughts were with her sister Blanch who, during the war was nursing in a London Hospital. Blanch had lived through bombing raids and one near miss in the heart of the city on which a bomb struck a dancehall she and a friend had intended to visit but had cancelled the night of the bombing.

Heather still had Blanche's letters from the war, among them the one in which she said how she and her friend June had slipped through the fingers of death at The Café de Paris. A bomb had crashed through the cinema above the dancehall killing more than thirty patrons below. Another letter recalled how Blanch had sheltered beneath the Clapham South tube station during a raid; "Wave after wave of bombers kept coming, bomb after bomb whistled down and the ground shook" Blanch wrote.

Not wanting to reveal all Blanch never wrote that down the road from her hospital at Balham High Road, at a point where two underground tunnels intersected and 600 people were sleeping, a bomb had hit killing sixty-eight of them. And that afterwards those sheltering in a nearby station were aware of a 'ghost 'train that slipped quietly along the track at midnight clearing the debris of the bombing like shoes, bits of clothing, handbags, toys and other personal items.

Reading the letters was distressing for Heather at the time and still was. She and her family were safe on the Isle of Man while Blanch was exposed to dangers day after day. It was an especially worrying time for everyone on the island who had relatives or friends on the mainland where ports were being struck like London, Liverpool or Portsmouth. And, of course, Heather was worried about Peter who by then was in the army in North Africa.

These events had faded from her memory until Hitler's bottle came calling, rekindling thoughts of her sister, and how Blanch had survived the Blitz and what fate had in store for her.

Up to March 1940, Blanch had written only of one raid on London. What followed were stories of escalating raids that came daily for weeks, some involving hundreds of planes that somehow looked majestic in the sky.

Airfields and convoys in the channel were also being hit, but Britain was responding. Outnumbered in aircraft and pilots and with its army depleted after Dunkirk, Britain was fighting back the only way it could, by air, and Hitler didn't like it.

The pesky RAF had struck several German cities including Berlin, a raid that had angered Hitler and shocked Germany's populous who had been told this would never happen. Berliners had been shaken by the raid that followed the Luftwaffe's accidental bombing of London - their intended target had been an airfield. Churchill had ordered the Berlin raid as revenge for the one on London. Bombers had raided Berlin in two waves and all had returned safely. This irritated Hitler no end because other bombers had struck Hamburg at the same time. The RAF was also active over the skies of England in The Battle of Britain, they were shooting down more planes than they were losing. But the Luftwaffe kept coming.

After hearing the translation of Hitler's letter, Heather could not stop thinking about life in 1940 Britain, about what Blanch had gone through in London, and of the madness in Hitler's mind at the time. She could not stop thinking about the man who seldom wrote anything down in his own hand, and of his script, which she had now seen.

In September 1940 Heather had turned nineteen and had qualified as a teacher, a 'reserved occupation' , a profession she undertook on the island throughout the war with dedication and skill.

Britain's back was against the wall, an invasion seemed likely, the country was not prepared, its army and generals seemed listless and Churchill was being scrutinized by US president Roosevelt. His ambassador to Britain, Joseph P.

Kennedy, who disliked Britain as much as Charles de Galle thought that Britain didn't stand a chance against Germany.

Despite a military presence, the brutal side of war did not reach the Isle of Man. At the time Heather felt guilty in not sharing the hardships others were enduring on the mainland like her sister who was at the centre of it all. Blanch worked at the Woman's Hospital in Clapham, south London and shared a flat with two other nurses in Hightrees House, a building on Nightingale Lane near the hospital.

What to do with patients during a raid was a matter of carry on and pray. Opposite the hospital was the entrance to the Clapham South tube station where people would shelter during raids even though the government had forbidden the practice. Londoners took no notice because public shelters were not always near and mostly overcrowded.

One raid referred to by Blanch was an attack on Clapham Common, the oval-shaped park ringed with anti-aircraft guns that overlooked her hospital. She wrote that when sirens signalled an impending raid everyone not involved in delivering a baby or on an urgent medical procedure would rush to the tube for shelter. Those that stayed behind had to pray that a bomb didn't hit the hospital or nearby vacinity. She wrote that bombs were falling all around the Clapham area.

Behind blacked out hospital windows, dim lights and the din of anti-aircraft fire, Blanch and a doctor named Blunt were ready to deliver twins to a lady name Sharp. The delivery table rattled, the lights flickered, the mother was pushing, the equipment shook, searchlights were crossing the sky and just as a bomb struck nearby, out popped a baby girl followed by a boy.

Blanch wrote that on that night she experienced one of the most exciting, frightening, rewarding and thought provoking events in her life; that two lives were being lit while one street away on Hazelbourne Road, two were being doused, and others, like her own were being spared. She came to the conclusion that whether it be through war or otherwise, the tree of life bares sweet and bitter fruit – a never-ending truth in the tapestry of life. It was later that same night that sixty-eight people were killed at Balham High Road nearby.

Lived over the bombing of Berlin and the grit of the RAF who were destroying German aircraft and crews at a high rate, Hitler burst into a flatulent rage and said he would destroy London. He tore into Goering for the Luftwaffe's failure to command Britain's skies.

Heather remembered that from this point forward in the summer of 1940, Hitler began blitzing London. And how every evening scores of planes would drone over the capital and how Londoner's were now in the crossfire of a bloodthirsty disaster. Other raids during the Blitz also stood out in Heather's mind.

It was late afternoon when swarms of bombers began a raid on East End ports. In minutes the docks were ablaze; hundreds of people had been killed and injured in Hitler's overture to the Blitz. More was yet to come.

His most savage attack occurred on a spring night in early 1941 after weeks of bombings. It was a moonlit night in which the heart of the city was nearly crushed earning Hitler Churchill's apt epithet of Bloodthirsty Guttersnipe. The onslaught of high explosives shook Londoners who by now were hardened by the raids, 1,000 civilians had been killed and many more injured. The East End of London was on fire, hell on earth had come calling courtesy of Hitler and Herman Goering's Luftwaffe.

The Nazi High Command had described the raid as reprisal for the RAF's bombing of residential quarters of German towns including Berlin. Britain answered back. Bomber Harris would soon give the people of Dresden a taste of what hell was really like.

Although other major cities with ports had been hit with massive damage and loss of life, it was London that had taken the brunt of the Blitz including the House of Commons chamber and the Houses of Parliament. Some 20,000 Londoners had been killed or injured.

Heather remembered the night when London's heart was nearly crushed because her sister had again been spared. And also because after living through the Blitz Blanche's life had been taken in a Liverpool car-crash by a draft-dodger who slammed into a taxi in which she was a passenger. What the Germans could not do with bombs, a drunk had done with a stolen car.

As Heather relived the past, Neptune wandered in, sank at her feet, wagged his tail, and wondered why she looked so sad. He didn't know that Hitler's bottle had prompted echoes from the past and that the Guttersnipe's ghost had come knocking on Heather's mind.

FIFTEEN

As a former Air Force officer Dennis and his wife Vivian could avail of free military flights to any country their planes were flying to if space was available. The Air Force had bases in Britain and planes flying in and out of the country so free 'military hops' were always available to the UK.

They would use the flights to visit their daughter Jean in Yorkshire. The catch was that flights could be destined to one of many US airbases in Britain and once there reaching your destination was up to you. In the McClendon's case it was to Pateley Bridge, in Yorkshire, a lovely English town with pubs, bowling greens and quaint, stone bridges. Their flight was landing at a base near Coventry whose airfield had a long runway, which was needed for landing the aircraft they were taking which was huge. Since their flight was arriving on a Saturday, Tom, Jean's husband would drive from Pateley Bridge to the airbase and meet them.

Returning to the States posed a problem too, the same conditions applied in reverse, Dennis and Vivian were never sure if their return flight would take them back to Florida let alone Tampa where they lived. But the savings were considerable and time was of no matter, they were retired, the trips were an adventure with the added pleasure of seeing their daughter and her family.

The flight they were taking this time offered an unexpected bonus, Dennis would see Coventry again albeit from the air. He had been in the city after the Luftwaffe had demolished it in November 1940 during a brutal raid that Dennis had heard of, read about and seen its effects on the newsreels before visiting the city in 1942.

Fifty years had passed and Coventry was back on its feet so Dennis was anxious to see its rebirth – it was burned-out rubble when he last set foot in the city. Always a man with an interest in churches, he was shocked to see the damage inflicted on the city's famous Cathedral during his last visit.

The McClendon's flight from Florida had been wonderful. They had flown on an eight Engine Boeing B-52 Stratofortress which had a range of 9,000 miles and wingspans that went on forever. Except for the crew and one Major General on board, they were the only passengers.

As the Boeing crossed the Welsh coast and began its descent to the midlands, one of the crew came back to say that they would soon be landing at a USAF base south of Coventry and that a good view of the city could be seen from the left side of the plane.

Dennis recalled the shambled city he had seen in 1942. These thoughts spiked a mixture of emotions that he had never put aside because he too in the war had caused death and destruction to people and cities. These were not new thoughts to him, only affirmations of truths that hide so that sanity and duty can prevail in wartime.

He had been a bomber pilot flying out of county Norfolk. By December 1942 he had flown missions to Berlin, Hamburg and Cologne. Scores of the planes in his squadron had been damaged on missions and were being repaired. The cloud cover over targets in Germany was terrible and since no missions could be flown he had a few days leave. Joe Mazella, a navigator and buddy from New York had suggested that they visit Coventry and see up close what the bombs had done and how the city was coping. It was an odd place to visit but he and Mazella had made the trip.

Dressed in their smart uniforms they arrived in Coventry on a damp, misty day near Christmas. What Dennis and Joe saw left them speechless and almost ashamed because they too were doing the same to German civilians, people no different to those of Coventry.

Had they been in the city on November 14th, 1940, they would have known what it was like when bombs were falling. But they weren't in Coventry, they were civilians in America. The last thing on their minds was bombing people.

"What on earth must it have been like?" Dennis asked his friend. Mazella had no answer. Only those who were there could reply. The bombing was Hitler's revenge for the British raid on Munich on November 8th, a sacred day in the Nazi calendar on which party officials were gathered to remember those killed when Hitler tried to overthrow the Weimar Republic in 1923. Although the damage had been minimal the raid was an embarrassment to Hitler.

As the sun was setting on the evening of the Coventry strike, hundreds of Junkers 88s were starting their engines on the north coast of France. Most were carrying incendiary bombs that would light up the city for the bombers that would follow.

The target was Coventry, an industrial city with factories working on Rolls Royce engines in order to give Spitfires and Hurricanes the advantage needed in the sky-battles over England. Coventry was in for a hiding like never before – Hitler had ordered it personally.

His astronomer had said that any bombings on the 14th of November should be codenamed 'Moonlight Sonata' because a full moon would be lighting up Britain, so Moonlight Sonata it was.

There was a full house at the Rex Cinema for the first showing of 'Gone With The Wind'. At seven p.m. the initial warning sirens began, people started rushing to the public shelters. Minutes earlier the Civil Defence Controllers had received an urgent message: *Air raid Yellow Raiders approaching your area.*

People were hurrying to the shelters beneath the General Post Office in the city centre near the cinema. In the distance but growing louder the drone of bombers could be heard. The Civil Defence's sirens were wailing and ground searchlights were sliding across the moonlit sky. Then the Junkers appeared, pulse after pulse of them, all members of the orchestra that were eager to play their Moonlight Sonata instruments of death on Coventry.

First to explode were incendiary bombs and dozens of parachute mines. They were dropping on the tight, city centre and its half-timbered houses with winding lanes and surrounding factories and houses. They were lighting up the city, setting the stage for the necklace of high explosives yet to adorn the city's neck. This was the Guttersnipe's payback for the bombing of Munich on a sacred day.

Dozens of buildings in the compact area of the city were being blown apart. There had already been twenty raids since the summer and the debacle at Dunkirk six months earlier. The Battle of Britain was now raging and Coventry, like all industrial England was on high alert, its people resigned to taking it on the chin but nothing they had lived through would prepare them for this. Night workers had just arrived at factories; day workers were at home, black blinds drawn across their windows. Most were listening to the radio when the sirens began, they wailed across the city where incendiary bombs were already falling, lighting up the city. Owen Owens, the city's department store was ablaze as were roofs in the city centre.

After the incendiaries had struck, bombers zeroed in on the flames with heavy explosives. The city shook from end to end. The air was filled with the crash of guns, the whistling of falling bombs and the chilling flash and bang of explosions. The sky was a tapestry of planes with vile cargoes to release.

The Home Guard or any able body rushed at the flames with buckets or stirrup pumps but were beaten back, overwhelmed by the heat's intensity. Planes were coming without a break. By now anyone in Coventry that had been bombed before knew that this raid was like no other.

The aircrafts droned on without a break, dropping their bombs then breaking off to return to their bases and refuel, reload and return to deal more death, more havoc, more destruction, all courtesy of Adolf Hitler, the Bloodthirsty Guttersnipe, the dead man who forty-six years after his suicide still spoke, but not at one of his rallies, not on radio, not in newsreel, now his ghost pulsed like his bombers of 1940 from a bottle on the Isle of Man.

It was this relentless blitz on Coventry that made the raid so different. In the cathedral men was throwing sand over the nave and chancel to douse the flames. The oak ceiling was ablaze; the roof's lead was melting. Firemen were trying to save the city's loved medieval cathedral but even with the help of others they were powerless; the water mains had been shattered. No more could be done to save Coventry Cathedral.

The flame's intensity had forced people out of their hiding places. A bomb had exploded dropping the end of a house on a shelter trapping everyone below. With bare hands people removed bricks and rubble to try and reach them. They eventually found the occupants, some warm, some cold, but all dead.

By midnight the end of the raid was in sight. What remained was chaos, rubble and destruction. When morning came a few Luftwaffe lurked over the city surveying their work. Of the 500 bombers that raided Coventry only one had been shot down. The rest had returned to France safely.

When the raid was over the people of Coventry complained that the city was undefended but this was not the case, it's anti-aircraft guns had run out of ammunition. But it could not be denied that both they and aircraft sent up that night had not been effective, neither had met with success. It was left to wardens and policemen to shout the news into shelters that the raid was over. A shattered population emerged into a city crushed beyond recognition. Some 600 people had been killed.

Looking out of the Stratofortress' window Dennis remembered the stories he heard of the vans filled with bodies, one piled atop the other and the blood trailing from the back and sides of the passing vans. And Dennis knew that bombs from his B-24s and B-17s had done the same to people in German cities.

SIXTEEN

Wolf's Lair was Adolf Hitler's Eastern Front field headquarters. Situated in East Prussia in the Gerlitz Forest Hitler spent more than eighty days there between 1941 and 1943; the Berghof in Bavaria is where he spent most of 1942. Wolf's Lair contained eighty buildings, fifty bunkers, a cinema, a casino, a power generator and 3,000 soldiers. An airstrip and railway station was near.

Nazi propaganda in 1941 gave the impression that Hitler was in good health and totally in control. Not so, he was a stressed hypochondriac suffering from escalating aliments. He was hardly sleeping; his stomach troubles and mood swings were frequent, he was taking spates of pills, he was also self-administering enemas daily. A vegetarian diet was giving him foul smelling breath and if he flashed a sunny disposition it was due to doctor Theodor Morell who was injecting him with crystal meth and other addictive drugs.

Dr Morrel, a heavyset man in his late fifties fell somewhere in character between a Dr. Dirty and Dr. Frankenstein. He, like Hitler had anti-social table manners, his body odour was lethal and he was considered by many to be an opportunistic quack. He was injecting Hitler with an amazing array of drugs daily which his boss became addicted to. Despite taking sleeping pills, Hitler was spending his nights pacing up and down in his quarters usually listening to Wagner's music. When he did sleep, his dreams were disturbing.

The summer of 1941 was warm in East Prussia and Wolf's Lair's air conditioning had broken down. Operation Barbarossa, the code name for the invasion of Russia had begun and was progressing reasonably well but Hitler was a troubled man. The siege of Leningrad was no going according to plan. Late one night he was pacing from one side of his bedroom to the other. Blondi, his Alsatian was down on the floor lying on her side panting from the heat. Hitler was fuming and worried, the war was not going as well as he wished. He was thinking: 'That Jew Roosevelt is trouble.'

His letter in the bottle to the people of America had not worked, a year had passed since its release in the waters off Montauk Point. He knew that any number of things could have happened to it. If it had reached America and been found it might have been taken to be a joke. And if it had reached the notice of the authorities the public had been denied news of its existence. Hitler paced the floor fanning his face with a folded map while speaking to himself. He was white as a sheet and looked like a ghost. At one point he doubled up from stomach pains.

Roosevelt had been elected President for a third time. *SCHEISSE - SHIT*, said Hitler. After Germany invaded Russia the previous month Roosevelt had said:

The Nazis are international gangsters engaged in blatant 'piracy' for world conquest. He said he would help Russia in any way he could.

BASTARD shot out of Hitler's mouth as he walked up and down fanning himself. Roosevelt had signed a Lend Lease agreement with Britain. Letting them military equipment and paying for it after the war had been Churchill's idea - a breach of the neutrality act Roosevelt had signed in 1935. He had justified it by saying that he was lending a neighbour a hose to put out a fire. *Lies* thought Hitler.

For Hitler this was another example of self-serving Jew hypocrisy. *The old Dutch Jew can't wait to get America into the war.*

Roosevelt stood by while his banker friends as well as German and American industrialists financed the Third Reich. It was they who had helped transform Germany into a nation bent on conquest through war which was fine because after the self-richest glow of ridding the world of Hitler had cleared, the business of America was business and war was always good for business.

Roosevelt had frozen German and Italian assets in the US and even though America was not yet in the war, their soldiers had landed in Iceland. Hitler was furious and now, in Wolf's Lair, well after the event, thinking about the landing still enraged him. In response he had ordered the Luftwaffe to bomb Iceland but the raid had virtually gone unnoticed.

Hitler's mind was troubled. He had not won the battle for the skies over Britain and was now trying to starve her with his U-Boats. They were sinking ships with aid but he had less than forty subs, only a third of which were in the Atlantic at any given time. Not enough had been built in the run-up to war but more would soon be available.

He had invested huge resources in the defeat of Russia. His army was doing reasonably well but success was not the case with his Italian allies. Mussolini, as he had always suspected was a clown with an appetite for sex, often juggling fourteen women at a time, sex was where his mind always seemed to be. While El Duce's trollops were dropping their panties on command, his army in North Africa were throwing up their hands in surrender. They were inept in the Balkans too. In 1936 the Italian army with modern weapons had conquered Ethiopia, but even then they needed mustard gas to complete the job against Africans with primitive weapons.

Because of Mussolini, Hitler's military and political plan for the Balkans was failing. His aim with their help to take over the government of Yugoslavia had been foiled; he had to send troops to the Balkans, to North Africa and Crete to bailout the Italians. The plan had been to use Crete as a base for the Luftwaffe to strike North Africa once the Italians had taken the island. But they had failed, again he had to do the job that they could not, this was a use of men and equipment he had not planned for, all because of the useless Italian Army.

Another reversal dealt with the Judas behaviour of Rudolph Hess. This, to Hitler, was a sign that within his ranks were those who felt the war was already lost. Hess, his once loyal friend who had helped in the writing of *Mein Kampf* and the financing of the Third Reich through German and other industrialists and banks had cracked. The dagger of betrayal digging in his back ran through Hitler as he remembered.

Hess had broken his ankle while parachuting into Scotland with a false and fanciful 'peace offer' and he was now in the hands of the British. German radio had announced that he was suffering from 'hallucinations'. Hitler vowed that if he ever got the traitor in his hands a piano wire round his neck would be his punishment. Another 'bastard-word' shot out of Hitler's mouth as he walked up and down fiddling with his moustache and fanning himself. In the meantime Blondi continued lying on her side panting with her tongue protruding.

Another problem dogged Hitler. His giant ship 'Bismarck' had sunk HMS Hood, the pride of the British fleet only to be sunk by the Royal Navy after a three-day chase that ended in a gun battle. When news of the Hood's sinking reached Britain the country fell silent and Hitler rejoiced. But spirits were lifted when the Royal Navy sent the oil-leaking Bismarck to the bottom of the ocean.

Some things were going wrong, others right, parts of his master plan were working. Although few in number his U-Boats were sinking allied shipping. His merchant ships were armed and active. There was other good news. In May his planes had again bombed London and his panzers were powering into Russia - so far mostly so good in his quest to crush Stalin's army.

His plan to rid Europe of Jews was also working: they were being rounded up and sent to death camps. In Paris the Vichy French police had arrested 1,000 Jews and handed them over to the Gestapo. His army and French collaborators were stealing their money, their treasures and even the gold from their teeth to finance the war and line their own pockets. Others too were earmarked for the same treatment as Jews. That was the sunny side of the equation, and then there was the dark bulge on the other end.

He had invaded Crete but his plan for a coup in Iraq had failed. With the help of British troops, Iraq's pro-German government had been forced to surrender. The oilfields had been secured by British and Russian forces and to Hitler's chagrin, Iraq would now provide a land-route for the supply of materials to the Soviet Union. Added to this, an active Nazi Fifth Column in nearby Iran had also been dislodged. These reversals were driving Hitler mad.

As if Berlin and other cities had not been bombed enough, the Russians had carried out their first raid on the capitol. *Scheisse!* said Hitler, the words spewing from his twisted logic. It was fine for him to pulverize Russians from the air but out of order for them to respond.

Hitler was irate; his brain was in a quandary. In Iceland one of his weather ships had had been seized yielding data on the master coding machine 'Enigma'. The British at Bletchley Park could now decipher German naval coded messages as other vessels with Enigma codebooks would also be seized.

In Egypt the former German world heavyweight boxing champion Max Schmeling had been captured by the British and in the US Marlene Dietrich had given up her German citizenship. These propaganda coups were helping the western allies and demoralizing the Nazis. As far as Hitler was concerned more things were going wrong than right. Had he been Mussolini he would turn to sex for relief, but this was not the case with Hitler, coming to attention with a woman when it mattered had mostly been a problem for him in life unless the woman were Jewish.

A staff officer at Wolf's Lair had acquired a print of *Citizen Kane*. Even though subtitled - and unlike the other officers at the screening, Hitler grasped the essence of the story and identified with the industrialist Charles Foster Kane whose first word in the film before he died was Rosebud - the name of his boyhood slay. Rosebud represented the time when Kane was young, happy and at peace with himself, which was the case with Hitler for a spell after his father died and he could do as he pleased.

Hitler retired that night with all his cares spinning in his mind. He had taken four sleeping pills - 40mg in all, he had never taken that many at one time.

His mistress Eva Braun was not with him. She was tucked away in his remote retreat in the Bavarian Alps, few people knew she existed in his life. She was years younger than him just as his mother was much younger than his father.

Before Eva, the woman in his life was Geli Raubal, his niece by way of his half-sister Angela. Geli had committed suicide in suspicious circumstances. Eva, no wallflower, had tried suicide twice but had failed like Unity Mitford. Hitler's women were inclined to do themselves in.

But there was more to Eva than subservience. Vivacious and assertive, she often complained that her man didn't always rise to the occasion. Despite his disapproval she smoked and sunbathed in the nude. A lively woman with a zest for life, Eva loved parties and dressing up and once posed for a photo dressed like the American minstrel singer Al Jolson with her face blackened. It was a shocking image for Hitler because Jolson was Jewish and Eva's blackened face did not conform with his idea of racial purity.

Preferring his woman to be dumb, Hitler often said, *Intelligent men should choose primitive, stupid women.* Above all Eva was a friend as was his Alsatian Blondi. At the time and in his wildest dreams Hitler would never have imagined that years after his death a dog named Neptune would retrieve his bottle and spirit. His supernatural ghost was on the spot when it happened forty-six years later.

The code names of military operations spun in Hitler's brain as he tried to sleep; names like A-Day, Mercury, Sea Lion, Barbarossa and Eagle's Nest. Thoughts of his heavy guns jump into his mind, those monsters he hoped would crush Russia but were so vulnerable to air attack. He needed to sleep, to think of soothing things but not his generals, they irritate him. Some were aristocratic and intelligent, some mediocre and some simply stupid. What many had in common was a habit of second-guessing him, of testing their will against his. They made demands on his energy and time, they gave him stomach cramps, and they were always vying to be in charge of his incoming mail. They also mostly disliked and were jealous of one another - a condition he encouraged by creating competition between them.

What should he think then to help him sleep? Yes, that's it, his faithful friend who loved him without conditions, Blondi, who thankfully was with him there on the floor panting with a water bowl near his head and a big, electric fan spinning in his direction.

He thought of being away from the cares of the war, of being in his Bavarian retreat, and of Blondi and Eva. He thought of stroking and playing with his dog, of being tranquil and of Blondi and Eva being happy because he was with them. These were pleasant thoughts, which, coupled with the pills, forced Hitler into a state of troubled sleep with haunting echoes of the past.

His father was the first to appear through the haze of forced sleep, his customs officer father, Alois Schickelgruber Hitler, the man of dubious parentage who made something of himself, who ruled with a heavy hand, who badgered the resisting Adolf to aim for a career in civil service, who mocked young Adolf's artistic ambitions.

It all came back through the haze, his father, a man with a temper that flared for no reason, who thrashed him when he talked back, or when he was late for meals and whose death released him from a flood of tyranny. His father, the bully who shaped him, who made him a resentful and moody boy strongly attached to an indulgent mother. A mother so closely related to his father that a special dispensation from the church was needed for them to marry - a mother who always called her husband uncle - and a mother whose death was a blow to him.

These and other thoughts reminded Hitler of his failed life as an artist and of the son he may have even though he never wanted children or thought himself capable of their creation, and of his relatives in America. And of one in particular, William Patrick Hitler, a treacherous man, the son of his half-brother Alois Hitler Jr.

SEVENTEEN

The haggard-looking Hitler was awake in bed. Blondi remained stretched out on the floor with her eyes closed. In years to come Neptune will strike the same pose at the feet of Peter and others.

Hitler tosses and turns but his brain is too active. He's thinking, thinking, thinking. Badgered by concerns, his mind rewinds to how he came to be in such a lofty yet vulnerable position. How from humble beginnings he now has such powers. How people in Britain, America and elsewhere hiss and boo when they hear his raspy voice on radio or see him in the newsreels, and of his worries swing to the beat of events.

He's back to one of the scenes that shaped his character as a boy. His father is slapping him around, saying he'll never amount to anything, he's yelling at Klara, his wife, saying it's her fault, that she pampers the boy, she ties his shoelaces, she peals and sugars his apples. In a fit of anger his father turns to a photo of Christ on the wall and bellows that he's had three wives and that this one is the worst of the lot, that she's a peasant who would starve but for him, *Why did you give me leave to marry this woman?* Klara's humiliation still clings in Hitler's memory.

Gustav, Ida and Otto, the three older siblings he never knew who died in infancy come to mind – and then Edmond, his younger brother who perished from measles - and then Paula - his younger spinster sister who for years he's helped support and whose name is now Wolff not Hitler at his insistence. His older half-sister Angela also enters his mind, she's the sibling he's closest to, his housekeeper in Berchtesgaden. Even now, years later, powerful as he is, determined as he is, driven to his destiny as he is, Hitler still cringes when he thinks of his father, a bastard at birth in every sense of the word, a prolific fornicator in or out of marriage, the man whose angry sperm made him and many others.

Hitler continues restless in his bed. His hair is not slicked across his forehead as normal, its ruffled and needs dying again, his narrow moustache has lost precision. He's unshaven, the stubble of his beard is pure white though he's only fifty-two. In this moment he's not the conqueror we have come to know, he's the man who's rarely out of bed before eleven in the morning due to the eighty pills he takes to get him through each day. He's a man with a swollen early morning belly from the two pounds of chocolates he eats almost daily with constipation the result. He's a man with rotting teeth and gum disease who dreads dentists, a man who cannot sleep because the walls of reality are closing in, because his mind is not at ease.

He never wanted children fearing that offspring would not rise to his expectations, fearing they would not reflect the blond, blue eyed Aryan look of perfection. His eyes are blue, his complexion dark and once upon a time his hair was black like scores of Jews. The last thing he yearned for was a clone. A uniformed reflection of himself is all he needed. Stories of his life would forever fill the pages of history, Hitler, the man whom God had sent to save Germany. For this he would forever be remembered together with images of his earthly form. He was certain that in years to come his ghost would return to witnesses the sweet landscape of Germany's greatness that he had sculpted and the Jewless state of Europe he had striven to erase. And yet the possibility existed that he had a half Jewish son who looked nothing like an Aryan.

His parents were a poor example of what marriage was like so coupling was not for him. A woman drained a creative man's energy - keep them around at arm's length was his modus operandi.

Hitler's eyes role in his head, then they close but he's wide-awake. He's lying on his back. His left arm raises then folds across his chest. He breathes deep, irregular breaths. His chest heaves but still no sleep will come. He is clueless that his bottle is drifting off the east coast of Nova Scotia and Halifax.

His thoughts stumble back to his tenth birthday in 1899. The next decade lay ahead but the end of one century and the start of another is beyond him. One year at a time was all he could handle. What was I doing then, what wrung of the ladder to my destiny was I on thinks Hitler through his sleeplessness.

He's home in a village near Linz, a small town east of Braunau where he was born and christened in a Catholic Church. His school grades are poor. His father is a stout man of sixty-two who keeps after him to do better in school, to prepare for a career in the civil service, this is a bone of contention between them. His father, his father, his father, he keeps returning to his father, the man gives him no peace. Would pride fill his father now or would he continue to be a bastard?

Fearful of the reaction he tells his father that he wants to be a an artist. His father berates him with the thunder that terrifies his mother and little sister Paula, with a blast that calls him a dreamer. It was this battle of wills that made young Adolf a person to dominate and not be dominated. With a sigh of weariness Hitler rolls on his side. Blondi lifts her head and looks at her master.

He's now fourteen, his father is dead, and Adolf has quit high school. He spends his time in idleness, sleeping late, drifting around Linz, going to the opera and museums and dreaming about becoming an artist. He's besotted by a Jewish girl named Stephanie but too fearful to approach her. He's invisible to her.

Working for someone and submitting to authority fills him with revulsion. With his father dead there is no one to tell him what to do, he does as he likes, his mother's attempts to get him back to school or to find work fall on deft ears. These teenage years free of responsibilities and knocking around with his opera loving friend August Kubizek are the happiest in his life.

With money from his mother, in 1906 he ventures to Vienna to study the picture gallery in the Court Museum but he spends his time mesmerised by the city's architecture. With money from his inheritance he returns to Vienna to take the entrance exam at the Academy of Fine Arts but he fails the test and returns home to his sick mother who dies of breast cancer in 1907. Her death is a blow; he's seventeen years old. With nothing to keep him in Linz he sets out to live life's journey in Vienna leaving his half-sister Angela to care for little Paula.

He had not known poverty as a boy but had grown up in a middle class home where he had only slight contact with Jews in a region of the Austro-Hungarian Empire in which ethic Germans felt betrayed by the unified German government of 1891. They had not included German regions of the Hapsburg Monarchy in Austria. It was not Jews that irked him at the time, but the country's multi-cultural leanings and the growing presence of slaves in Austria, which the Hapsburgs seemed to favour over people of German blood. His mother's doctor had been a Jew and Hitler liked him.

Reflecting on his wilderness period he relives the five years he spent in Vienna after his mother's death, the first of which he was least proud of. He had fritted away his inherence. The few affair he had proved an embarrassment, he had caught VD from a girl who was a slavish Calvinist. These years saw him making a meagre living from odd jobs, leading a vagabond life, living from hand to mouth and painting water colours. If he sold one it was often to or with the aid of a Jew who worked on commission. He had little money, no future, no hope, a state of being that continued until 1913 when he was twenty four and when service in the Austrian army was pending.

How could he forget the hostiles he had lived in during those soul-destroying years. One incident remained vivid in his mind. It was winter. The hostile was rat-infested, he was sleeping elbow to elbow with Vienna's poorest. It was the dead of night, the dormitory was freezing, the beds were old and shaky, having been slept in mostly by down and out men who had come and gone and were now mostly dead, killed by poverty and despair under the leaky, hypocritical umbrella of the Hapsburg Empire.

That night still haunts him. His bed was dirty, it smelt of urine, bed-bugs abounded, life-weary men in nearby beds were snoring, breathing deeply and breaking wind into soiled mattresses. Stomachs grumbled, cats wandered at will. The odour was terrible. Even now, years later, the stinky hostile smell of yesterday's humanity still linger as Hitler lies on his side in his clean Wolf's Lair bed. Then on that freezing night came the dragon, the huge rat that jumped on the foot of his bed and ran up his body to bite his ear. Just thinking of it makes Hitler shutter in his bed from a chill on this hot summer night in East Prussia. Rats and cats still make him jumpy.

In those days nothing was going right for him, the shadow of his mother's death followed him day and night. Only forty seven when she died, her Jewish doctor had done everything to save her but to no avail, a raging breast cancer had reduced her to the size of a doll and killed her. When she died she was only a head on a pillow.

His rejection from art school still hurts. The Academy thought little of his drawings. His one big hope was gone like the mother who truly loved him. . They said his sketches lacked imagination, that he should forget painting and be an architect. But that was not possible, he has not finished high school and was poor at maths. He didn't hold Jews responsible for the Academy's rejection, it was the faculty professors, especially the pompous fool from North Germany, Christian Griepenker, the others would have passed him but not Griepenker.

What flowed next from Hitler's Vienna years was his growing dislike of communism and its Jewish fathers, liberalism and the Hapsburg Monarchy. He remembers how he delved into politics and refined his 'Eternal Jew', ideas – perceptions that see Jews as rats, like the one that jumped on his bed. To him Jews are increasingly symbols of chaos, exploiters, degraders of a nation, bandits of racial purity, proof of their supernatural ugly face.

A hidden chapter of his life returns to him. In a tavern he meets a stunning Jewish woman named Sarah Schmitt. She had a fetching quality, she looked Spanish, and was easy to be with. Older than him, she had bought one of his sketches. He was twenty-four with poor sexual encounters to his credit. Sarah was his first meaningful one. The second with another Jew followed soon after. They were Jews therefore beneath him so he had no trouble performing. It was with equals or those above him in social status that his manhood failed. With Sarah and the other Jew he had risen and exploded on queue. There was something about the texture of their skin and the whiff that rose from between their legs that ignited him. Six weeks later Sarah announced her pregnancy and eventually a boy appeared. His given name was Otto like the brother he never knew. Sarah had been seeing other men so he didn't know if Otto was his. But Sarah had been honest and this he respected and never forgot.

To avoid military service with the Austrian army he had moved to Munich in 1913 then travelled to Liverpool where he lived for six months with his half-brother Alois and his Irish wife. While in England he had visited Blackpool and marvelled at the architecture of its three piers. The experience would later trigger his plans for Blackpool after he had conquered Britain.

Now it's 1918, he's twenty-nine, it's the end of World War One. He's been a military dispatch rider with a Bavarian Infantry unit. He's fought and nearly died, become a corporal, he's been a good soldier and earned the Iron Cross.

Wounded twice and temporarily blinded by gas he had spent months recovering. He was sure that fate has chosen him to rescue Germany from the Jews and Bolsheviks who had conspired with France to install the Versailles Treaty with its brutal demands. He had survived the war with the certainty that this was his preordained destiny. There was something supernatural, something beyond belief in his certainty - he could taste it. The sleepless Hitler had more to dwell upon – his climb to power was with him to relive and keep at bay his demons of the night.

It's 1919, the war is over, and he's still in the army, with them he's found a home. They send him to spy on the German Worker's Party but he joins them instead. Their name soon changes to The National Socialist Workers Party: The Nazi Party - his rise within them is steady. Through various means he's soon party chairman. It is now that he discovers a talent he never knew he had, a gift for persuasive oratory, an ability that make him the object of attention, a person whose ideas ripple and resonate and demand attention.

He given the party a new symbol, a swastika and the arm-extended greeting of 'Heil'. The swastika had come to his notice as a pupil of the Benedictine Order. He uses it as a symbol of Aryan superiority and is soon leader of the movement. The result is that Party membership grows. These reflections lift the spirits of the sleepless Hitler in Wolf's Lair.

His mind skips to the early 1920s and his quest to unseat the German government who increasingly are paying reparations from WWI. In Berlin liberal attitudes abound in cabaret nightlife with Negro music, homosexuality, drugs and lesbianism. Convinced that the Weimar Republic is poised to collapse, he fails to overthrow the government in a coup and is jailed for five year but is released in less than one.

In prison he dictates *Mein Kampf* to his friend and fellow prisoner Rudolph Hess. After his release and his Nuremberg rallies and his creation of the SS and his brutality and speeches and luck he amazingly becomes Chancellor in 1933. And now, in 1941, here in Wolf's Lair, on another sleepless night, and except for Britain, he has all of Western Europe and part of the east in his grip. But nothing is certain yet.

Hess has betrayed him. His generals are troublesome. He does not command the Atlantic. Britain is resisting. Roosevelt is a threat. Russia is not defeated. Berlin is being bombed. North Africa is not secure, nor are the Balkans. The Italians are hopeless, nor can he count on Spain. Salazar of Portugal is anything but neutral, the whereabouts of his bottled letter is a mystery and every so often he wonders if he has a son and if he's still in Britain. And in addition to all this Japan is stirring up America.

EIGHTEEN

Hitler's alliance with Italy and Japan was odd, their efforts often uncoordinated. They worried him but for different reasons. Mussolini's military were sluggish, gritless and unreliable. Japan's was different, they were highly motivated and ruthless, as they had proved in Manchuria and China in the 1930s. By 1941 their expansion in the Asia-Pacific region had been so vast that conflict with the US was inevitable; all this fed Hitler's fear that Japan would ignite America into war.

He didn't trust the Japanese. They would smile, bow and pledge all manner of things with no intention of honouring them; like him they told others what they wanted to hear. To trust Emperor Hirohito and Prime Minister and the head of the army General Tojo Hideki was unwise, but what choice did he have - an eye on them had to be kept.

It wasn't only Hitler that was watching Japan's military exploits, so too were others in Asia and the Pacific. America was watching her like a hawk.

In early 1941 the Japanese foreign minister had travelled to Rome and Berlin and it didn't take a genius to conclude that a union was in force between Germany, Italy and Japan.

If Japan was on the warpath in 1941 it was not a sudden impulse but part of a plan going back many years, just like Hitler's aims were clear in *Mein Kampf*.

In the 30s Japan was already planning its attack on Pearl Harbour and Hitler knew what would follow - war with America - a scenario he didn't relish. It was the reason for his letter in a bottle to America - he and others were aware of Japan's aims.

By the 1930s Roosevelt knew Japan's thirst was to conquer the Far East as well as key Pacific islands. In the 20s American Colonel Billy Mitchell was convinced of Japan's aims, certain that in addition to China and French Indochina, that their eyes were also on Burma, Malaysia, Borneo, Indonesia, the Philippines and many Pacific islands.

Mitchell, an advocate of air power and a thorn in the side of the US military had predicted the Pearl Harbour attack in the early 1920s and again at his Court-Martial in 1925. He was in trouble for disobeying orders and insubordination. Well ahead of the time, few believed him.

Even before becoming Chancellor in 1933 Japan had Hitler's attention. He knew their aggression could spark conflict in the Far East and Asia as well as the Pacific, none of which might suit his plans in Europe and beyond. But he recognized that they were enterprising little people always seeking to master new technology. He respected their motivated soldiers; there were advantages in having them as allies. When the time was right they could hit Russia from the east while he attacked from the west. Unlike Italians, a Japanese trooper would fight to the finish rather than surrender.

Examples of Japan's forward thinking and drive were two things they did in 1931. The first was to televise a baseball game, something that not even America - home of baseball - had done. The second was that their troops had made bold moves into China's Manchuria region and parts of Mongolia. In these adjoining regions to Russia and the landmass of China to the south the earth was fertile and rich in raw materials.

The governor of Manchuria had ordered his garrison not to retaliate but Japan had not held back, they had pushed on capturing a key city. This in turn had sparked an international incident which had taken a call for peace by America to halt. The peace failed to hold.

Six years after the 'Manchurian Incident' came the occupation of Shanghai, confirming the widely held belief that Manchuria was a first-step leading to an all-out Japanese invasion of China.

Herbert Hoover, who was near the end of his Presidency had sent forces to the Far East to join British and other friendly powers in protecting the foreign population of Shanghai.

In 1932 the Japanese had signed a non-aggression pact with Russia, but had stabbed them in the back the following year and

Hitler had not forgotten their double-crossing ways. Japan's boldness grew. They said they would quit the League of Nations if condemned for its actions in Manchuria. The League did just that and Japan carried out its threat. In 1937 they had pushed further south into China where the 'Rape of Nanking' had taken place. Japan was active in the Pacific too.

Enter a mystery. Since 1937 a theory has grown that on her round the world flight during which Amelia Earhart and her navigator disappeared, that she may have been spying on Japan and was on a photographic mission to monitor their activities in the Pacific. It is known that she was short of fuel after leaving Lea, New Guinea where she had stopped to refuel. Some say she landed on the Marshall Islands and was taken prisoner. Others think she crashed in the Pacific, her aircraft was never found. What really happened will probably remain a mystery but there may be a link between Japan's activities in the Pacific and her disappearance.

With Hitler in control of Western Europe in 1940, Japan was again on the move militarily. In September she had invaded Indochina and troops from Australia had arrived in Singapore to reinforce the garrison. Japan answered back. They had warned Britain about their actions in the southeast and frozen British and US assets in their country in response to similar moves against them. There was no stopping Japan.

Thousands of troops had entered Saigon the capital of Thailand, they could now use it as a springboard to attack Burma and Singapore. At this point America and Britain denounced Japan's aggression and even the isolationists in the US congress agreed that enough was enough.

In March 1941 Japan and Russia had again signed a non-aggression pact that removed military threats to their borders. In June, by which time Germany had attacked Russia, Hitler demanded that Japan attack the USSR. Tojo considered it but only agreed to bolster his forces along Russia's borders. Anxious Hitler had urged Japan not to attack America.

In the summer of 1941 a Churchill broadcast warned Japan that its aggression must stop. Under pressure at home and from the Pacific, the Prime Minister of Australia demanded from the

British that its troops be relieved from Tobruk as they were needed in the Pacific.

Japan was deadly serious in its quest to dominate the vast Far East/Asia area as well as the Pacific, but not keen to tangle with Russia. They were not foolish like Hitler who had already engaged Russia's vast Army. The Japanese were reckless but not when it came to a fight with Russia; Hitler could only hope that America was not one of its targets.

Japan was only one of Hitler's worries while he was in Wolf's Lair. His letter in the bottle had not worked but another message did arrive for America, Japan's attack on Pearl Harbour, a strike that would trigger an explosion of US power on a huge scale, a response that would end with the dropping of two atomic bombs, a weapon Hitler's scientists had been working on for years.

All these worries from the present were haunting the sleepless Hitler. In time they would roll up in a ball and become his newly freed supernatural ghost after death.

NINETEEN

Ten days after speaking with McClendon, Peter and Heather travelled to Yorkshire and met their friends as planned in Pateley Bridge. A week later the two couples were on the Isle of Man.

Neptune had stayed with the von Schneiders. In no way uncertain that his owners would return he had a whale of a time as did the sisters who were happy to have the company of their guardian angel.

Having heard so much about Neptune, Dennis and Vivian were charmed to make his acquaintance, as was he to meet them. Any friend of his masters was a friend of his and he showed it with a flair of bonomi that was his trademark.

Vivian, a slim lady with streaks of grey in her hair thought Neptune was great; her liveliness was only topped by a wicked sense of humour. Also grey on top, Dennis, the once flaming redhead looked in fine shape to deal with his remaining years of life. Laid back but sharp, little escaped his piercing blue eyes.

The couples were back on the Isle of Man several days before the Moores said a word about Hitler's bottle. Their guests were staying ten days so no rush was called for, everyone needed time to rest after their trip from Yorkshire via car and ferry.

In life everyone has a secret and Dennis was no different. It was nothing to be ashamed of, in fact the opposite was true. Nevertheless, a slight embarrassment of riches may have played a part in Dennis' reticence to reveal all. But he felt he owed it to his friends. Like Heather and Peter, Dennis and his wife were down-to-earth folk not given to displays of wealth.

Soon after the war, when Dennis was twenty-seven, his father confessed to a pre-war indiscretion from which a son had ensued. The result was that Dennis had a seventeen year-old half-brother named Warren Ward who lived with his mother in Corpus Christie, Texas. By 1949 Dennis's mother had come to terms with her husband's fling and had forgiven him after he had served a lengthy spell in the doghouse.

When Dennis met Warren they became good friends. Warren was no ordinary fellow; he had a very high IQ. After University, he worked in the oil business and by the age thirty-three had amassed millions and was on the board of one of the largest utility firms in the US southwest. The boy from little Corpus Christie - 'the sparkling city by the bay'- had done well for himself through his own initiative.

Now in his late fifties, Warren's achievements spoke for themselves. In addition to his many interests, he was also consultant to The United States Department of Energy and Commerce, his expertise being in global oil and US utilities. Acting on Warren's advice, Dennis had invested wisely and was more than secure financially. Another string to Warren's bow was his link with former president Ronald Reagan, they were good friends dating from the time Reagan was governor of California.

The time had come to deal with the matter of the bottle and the best place to start was where its story began at the beach near the lighthouse.

Spring had sprung. It was late in the afternoon, the days were growing longer. Peter and Heather had been showing their guests the island, driving here and there, pointing out places of interest including the world's only working water wheel. Everything was new and exciting to Dennis and Vivian. Neptune was in the back of the car sitting between his new friends. A visit to the beach was next on the agenda and soon they were there. Neptune sniffed around the water's edge but nothing of interest at first grabbed his attention. Suddenly he raced to the spot where he made his find and sat, tail wagging, his eyes fixed on his friends.

The two couples strolled along the beach looking at the lighthouse, drinking in the views, listening to the sounds of the lapping Irish Sea and watching the birds that seemed to hang suspended in the air just as baby Adolf had hung suspended between Aries and Taurus in the Zodiac at his birth. The birds hung there, near motionless, frozen against the sky. Peter was giving his guests a little talk on the history of the keeperless lighthouse when Neptune barked twice to draw attention.

"What does he want?"

"To show off, he comes here every day," said Heather to her friends in answer to their question.

"Really?"

"Yes, he looks for things that wash up on the beach."

"Well I'll be damned," said Dennis with a chuckle.

"He fetched something home that worries us," said Peter.

"What is it?"

Neptune's tail was racing, he seemed to know what was being said.

"A Nazi bottle with a letter inside."

Dennis' jaw dropped, Vivian swallowed hard. Out of nowhere a Peregrine Falcon swooped overhead and landed at the top of the lighthouses. Its eyes were on Neptune. It sat there, mystical in stature, like the black bird in the film Maltese Falcon. Only Neptune noticed him.

"Who's the letter from?" said Dennis.

"Adolf Hitler."

The McClendons froze on the spot then drew breath. Neptune barked again. Vivian's eyes narrowed and Peter fumbled for a cigarette. Virtually together Vivian and Dennis said:

"No Kidding?"

"No kidding," replied Heather. "He found it April 30th, the date in 1945 that Hitler killed himself."

No one had noticed that Neptune had slipped away, a chill had returned to him. The Falcon's eyes followed him until he was out of sight. It then flew off, he too had felt the chill and not for the first time. It was all very spooky and supernatural.

During the short drive home Dennis wasn't thinking about Hitler but of two friends and the sneaky Japanese.

TWENTY

Sunday, December 7th 1941 was a day Dennis would never forget. It was the day Pearl Harbor and other Pacific bases where attacked, a day that nearly wrecked the US Navy. It was also the day that silenced the isolationists in congress. No longer could they mock Billy Mitchell's prediction in 1925 of the strike by Japan. Few believed him then just as many in the 20s felt that Hitler and his Brown Shits were only street thugs and not to be taken seriously.

Recalling the attack did not trigger the anger Dennis felt in 1941, his thoughts were with two friends. One had died during the Pearl Harbor raid, the other days later: Kevin Alexander and Colin Kelly Jr. were their names.

In December 1941 Dennis was nineteen and Kevin, a sailor in the US Navy was eighteen. From boyhood Kevin's dream had been to join the navy, he was thrilled when he learned that his first ship would be one based at Pearl Harbor. He had been one of 2,400 sailors killed when his ship was sunk during the air attack. In recalling the day of the strike Dennis could still see the joy on Kevin's face when he announced weeks earlier that he going to beautiful Pearl Harbor.

Then there was Colin Kelly Jr. In 1932 the nine year-old Dennis had met the seventeen year-old Colin whose ambition was to qualify for West Point and train to be a pilot. Dennis had met Colin in Madison, Florida during the summer holidays, his father knew Colin's dad. Even at his tender age Dennis could see what a serious teenage Kelly was. Colin made it to West Point, became a bomber pilot and by the age of twenty-five he was already a Captain in the US Army Air Force.

Before the assault on Pearl Harbour Japanese activity had increased in the Pacific so Colin's Bomb Group were ordered to Luzon, one of the Philippine islands. After the December 7th attack Japan's movements had stepped up in the Pacific. Kelly had been killed on December 9th when his bomber launched a raid on the battleship Haruna. With his plane a focal point of enemy fire, Colin had shown valour and skill in placing three direct hits on the Haruna, but on route to his home field Japanese planes had beset his bomber and set it on fire. It crashed in the ocean.

Colin had been awarded the Distinguished Service Cross posthumously. But all that had happened years earlier and this was now, May of 1991, soon Dennis and Vivian would see what washed ashore on The Isle of Man.

They waited anxiously. Vivian fiddled with her watch and Dennis asked for a drink. Hitler's bottle stood behind the Johnny Walker in the liquor cabinet. Neptune was milling around, he knew what was coming next. The chill that had run through his body at the beach was gone but not a distant memory, only a reminder that there was something about the bottle he didn't like.

With the drinks now before them Dennis and Vivian waited for the bottle to appear but this was not the case. Peter and Heather had decided they would first say what concerned them, which they did in detail.

Dennis lit a cigarette. Neptune lay on his side, his eyes closed, his tail tapping the floor with a steady beat. He had felt something but dismissed it. When the Moores had said their piece Peter produced the bottle and handed it to Dennis who was sitting by his wife. Peter then handed them its letter and translation.

Dennis and Vivian examined everything without comment.

"Well I'll be damned," whispers Dennis.

"So what do we do with it?" said Peter in a low voice.

"Let us sleep on it," Dennis replied.

After everyone had retired, Neptune went to the kitchen for a drink, his left hind leg was bothering him, he had developed a limp.

TWENTY-ONE

All was quiet in Avoca. Peter and Heather were asleep but Dennis and Vivian were awake in their bed whispering about what advice to give their friends; Hitler had invaded their minds.

Neptune was sleeping on the living room sofa and dreaming after having limped his way to bed. His dreams were normally about the beach or fish, or dolphins or bitches. But not tonight, it was about the bottle that was causing him concern, altering his mood and starting to unsettle him. Now he had a limp.

There was much to justify what he was sensing. The bottle had a sinister history. All whom it had come into contact had met with misfortune. More and more Neptune's antenna was receiving signals from the telepathic spirit of Hitler's supernatural spirit. It was there pulsing them out from the bottle that was standing behind the Johnny Walker in the liquor cabinet. Neptune's cold, wet nose was twitching as a mild current ran though him.

The bottle had begun claiming victims while Hitler was alive. The first were the crew of the U-Boat sent to deliver it to America. After the sub was clear of the Montauk coast, Captain Schulhart had surfaced to give the crew air as German subs early in the war had no snorkels to vent in air. From that point in the early morning hours of July 2nd 1940 his U-Boat had never been heard from again.

Neptune was making muffled woof sounds. Behind closed lids his eyes were moving rapidly following the movement of the bottle as Peter handed it to Dennis earlier that day, his tail was tapping the sofa anxiously. He could smell fish and sea – feel wind and rain – and sense the essence of events from the past but not their detail.

The first person to spot the bottle in the Atlantic was Carl Erickson, a 30 year-old schoolteacher from Julianehab, a town on the south coast of Greenland. On July 18th 1969 – twenty-nine years after the bottle's release in the Atlantic, Erickson was fishing for cod along the Grand Banks in a small, open motorboat a few miles from Greenland. It was late afternoon; it was warm and muggy and starting to get dark. Clouds were gathering, rain was on the way but Carl was prepared, he had a large, green golf umbrella.

There was thunder to the west. Seconds later there came a flash of lightening. Carl had caught as much cod as he wanted and with the weather changing he knew that shore was the place to be. It was getting windy. He revved up the boat's motor and headed for land steering with the tiller. He could just about see the shoreline. It began to rain so Carl steered with one hand and held the opened umbrella over his head with the other. The wind was blowing harder now, the waters were getting choppy, his boat was rocking.

For twenty-nine years the tides, currents and winds had pushed Hitler's bottle northeast up and around the coast of New Foundland. It was now bobbing in the Grand Banks with Carl's boat heading its way. Another clap of thunder came, this one closer than the last. It cracked like a whip, fingers of light flashed across the sky

Carl's boat past within feet of the bottle. The first thing he noticed as he churned by was something red on its top and sides so he returned to where he spotted the object for a better look. As he approached he shut down his boat's motor. His craft was now pitching from side to side.

It began to rain harder and as Carl looked for the object in the water his boat began to drift. He looked in all directions but to no avail. The rain was now pelting the top of his umbrella and with the wind blowing the rain was sweeping sideways, Carl was getting soaked. As he was putting the hood of his jacket over his head he heard a tap, tap, tapping on his boat behind him, and when he looked down there was the bottle waiting to be rescued. It had appeared like a ghost knocking on his door.

He retrieved it from the water and when his eyes fixed on the swastikas he was startled. In the war German soldiers had shot his two uncles after being forced to dig their own graves. The pair, who were twins, were zealous members of the pesky Norwegian resistance. Their fate came rushing back to Carl.

It was obvious that the bottle did not hold liquid but what if anything did it contain?. It was natural for Carl to wonder but now was not the time to delve so he placed the bottle on the floor of the boat. With his vessel collecting water he had to get ashore. Carl started his motor and headed towards the coast, which was close but hard to see due to the rain and gathering darkness. He was still steering with one hand and holding the handle of the open umbrella over his head with the other. Suddenly there was another clap of thunder.

It would be the last sound Carl would ever hear. A few seconds later a bolt of lightning caught the tip of his umbrella not only killing him on the spot and bursting him into flames, but also ripping his boat apart and returning the bottle from where it came but without a scratch. But that's not the end of this episode and the forty-eight hour span in which it took place, there was something preordained or supernatural or down right freakish about it.

In the late hours of the same day, 18th July 1969, in the State of Massachusetts, Mary Jo Kopechne would drown in Chappaquiddick Island when Senator Ted Kennedy, who was with her in a car drove it off a bridge. He had been drinking all day. On the 20th of July, the astronauts Neil Armstrong and Buzz Aldrin, two of Apollo 11's three-man crew would set foot on the moon, a truly out of this world event that remains beyond belief. Streaking through outer space, their spacecraft was nearing its objective as lightning was killing Carl Erickson.

Ted Kennedy's actions to save his own life would forever cast a shadow over his character and, like his brothers John and Robert before him who had been shot in the head in 1963 and 1968, a tumour in his skull would take Ted Kennedy's life in 2009. From man or fate or God for their misbehaviour they all got it in the head.

Another unfortunate soul to cross paths with the bottle was Michael O'Leary, a businessman from the village of Gregnamanagh in Ireland. In the summer of 1981, twelve years after lightening had killed Carl Erickson, he too would meet his maker. O'Leary, a man in his sixties was out on his boat, he was sailing near Loop Head by the mouth of the Shannon Estuary when he spotted the bottle drifting off the coast of County Limerick. While trying to pull it towards him with the curved handle of an umbrella, he suffered a heart attack, toppled into the Atlantic and drowns. His body was found three weeks later near the coast of Kinsale in county Cork. Ten years later the bottle would wash ashore on the Isle of Man.

Neptune was sensing something that was telling him to steer clear of the bottle. The next morning at nine o'clock the phone rang and Peter answered. The call was from a policeman Peter knew.

"Peter, sorry to call so early, I have bad news."

"What is it?"

"A pal of yours is dead."

"Who?"

"Otto Schmitt."

"When, how?"

"He drowned in his bathtub after suffering a stroke."

For the rest of the day Neptune was unsettled and stayed away from the liquor cabinet. His limp was more pronounced but due to the shocking news no one noticed.

TWENTY-TWO

In his youth Hitler had helped him but now Otto may have been one of his victims like Erickson, O'Leary and the crew of U-Boat 29. All had crossed paths with his bottle and its supernatural spirit. Otto had died not knowing if Hitler was his father. It's one of the paternal mysteries that persists in the Hitler family because no one can say if Hitler's mother was the niece or cousin of her husband Alois. During their marriage she almost always addressed her husband as uncle.

By January 1942 the tide of the war was turning. Hitler's mood swings were increasing as were his medications. Dark clouds were gathering but he refused to face reality. It was only a matter of time before his lunacy would end with the loss of millions of lives, huge numbers being innocent civilians caught in the crossfire of his madness. But Hitler pushed on. Driven by demons of self-belief, he didn't care how many died. Maybe, in his twisted logic, his aim in life was to kill as many people as he could in pursuit of unreachable dreams. He had once said: "Even if I cannot conquer I will drive the world to destruction." In the vineyard of life he was, indeed, a poisoned fruit like no other.

He was in Wolf's Lair when Japan attacked Pearl Harbor and he knew it would bring America into the war in Europe. It confirmed his belief in the summer of 1940 that the Japs would bring him grief, and that whatever action they would take against America would be without his knowledge.

What do Hitler and Mussolini do when Pearl Harbor is attacked? Do they consider every angle? No! They make an amazing mistake. After four days, on December 11th, and with no obligation to do so, they declare war on America. By the end of 1941 Hitler had many problems, America was now added to the list.

His troops in Russia were in trouble. Weakened by the fight to take Leningrad they were being hammered on the Moscow Front. In a brutal five-day battle the Red Army had retaken towns and villages, thousands of soldiers on both sides had been killed, hundreds of Nazi tanks had been captured or destroyed. Sub-zero weather and stubborn opposition was giving his troops hell so plans to take Moscow had to be put aside and shifted to Stalingrad in the southwest from which better news was to come. The city had been seized and this was important to Hitler because Stalingrad had been named after his arch-rival Joseph Stalin. Hitler's Sixth Army was now within striking distance of the real prize, the oilfields in the Caucuses.

Since the Russian recapture of Rostov, their position along a 1,000 mile front had altered for the better, now they had momentum and were showing their amazing mobility and grit in frigid weather. Hitler's generals were now being subjected to his verbal abuse.

In "The Battle of the Atlantic" his navy was doing better. With 200 subs now available, U-Boats were sinking supplies to Russia, Malta, Egypt and India. They were also sinking ships with aid from America and having a field day torpedoing fuel tankers near the New York coast that were nicely silhouetted against the city's lights. Germen submariners were calling it: 'The Great American Turkey Shoot'.

January 1942 was a wake-up call for Hitler, alarm bells were ringing galore - he was livid - Churchill and Roosevelt were driving him mad. He was banging tables, kicking furniture and talking to himself in the wee hours of the morning. Only drugs, Wagner's music and Blondi were keeping him on the right side of sanity.

Churchill had been cheered after his speech to the US Congress. It was only a matter of time before America would sling her hook round his neck. Winston's speech had made full use of his oratory skills. He quoted Abraham Lincoln, spoke of his American mother and acknowledged the storm of applause with his famous V sign. One senator said the speech was electrifying. Nor was Hitler happy when the American press wrote that Churchill had a rapturous response when he mingled with crowds outside the congress building.

The Churchill/Roosevelt duet was close and often edgy but it would also yield dividends. A more than symbolic event had taken place on the day of the speech, the result of a plan timed to coincide with Churchill's address; its aim being to leave Hitler in no doubt that America was fully committed to Europe's liberation. Several thousand US troops had landed in Ulster and were there even before Churchill had taken to the rostrum in Washington to speak. The landing had been kept secret, but Hitler knew about it quickly from his IRA and other spies in Northern Ireland.

They were the first American troops in Europe since WWI when their forces arrived in France to help the Allies. Sir Archibald Sinclair, the Secretary for Air had welcomed them. He told the troops: *Your safe arrival marks a new stage in the war. It's a gloomy portent for Mr. Hitler, nor will its significance escape the Japanese military.*

Hitler knew that Britain and America agreed that the defeat of Germany took priority over Japan's. This meant that almost the full force of America would be thrown into his defeat.

Bad news continued for the Fuehrer. Almost every South American country had agreed to break ties with the Axis powers and nations globally had affirmed their opposition to Germany in the 'Declaration of the United Nations'.

In the meantime Japanese troops had taken Manila and landed on Borneo and other islands. They were also bombing Singapore and pushing into Malaya with Singapore their objective. British forces were being shot at from every direction but the invaders were meeting opposition.In some places Japanese reinforcements were swarming in like ants. They were landing in other locations using boats armed with machine guns, all forms of transport were being brought in overland, Allied forces were in retreat and civilians were fleeing from Singapore's north shore.

Japanese troops had opened another front by landing on the Solomon Islands and New Guinea: they were now threatening Australia. Within weeks, Singapore, the British military base once considered impregnable would surrender.

A reinforced Afrika Korps was achieving tactical surprises. Due to the demands on the Russian front, North Africa had become a lower priority when it came to fuel and equipment, even though its loss would expose Europe to invasion from southern France, Italy and Greece. Nevertheless there was good news for Hitler from the region thanks to the great General Erwin Rommel.

In January the Afrika Korp was advancing in the Western Desert. From their starting point in Libya, Rommel's tanks had swept east towards Egypt. Benghazi was now under threat, the British were losing the tank-battle.

The extermination of Jews in Europe was near the top of Hitler's agenda in January 1942 - the plan to step up the gassing of Jews had been approved.

When Herman Goering dropped the remark that such-and-such was 'The Final Solution', alarm bells rang. He was actually referring to the provision of brothels for foreign workers. Coincidentally, the Gestapo's Reinhard Heydrich, who relished the thought of killing Jews, was using the same words. Speaking to government officials he admitted that the words referred to 'the Jewish Problem' and involved plans for the extermination of 11,000,000 European Jews.

By January 1942 the Nazis had killed thousands of Jews haphazardly. The aim of the Final Solution was to kill them in camps built for that purpose. The decision to implement the plan had been made; Every Jew in Europe that the Nazi's could get their hands on was now potentially a dead one.

No longer was Britain alone, nor Nazism unopposed. In January 1942 Hitler's mind was being concentrated wonderfully and his drug use was rising. He didn't give much thought to Otto, the son that might be his and who, unbeknownst to him was safe among friends on the Isle of Man. Other thoughts weighed heavily on Hitler's mind; among them a plan to hurt America that was as silly as his letter in bottle with the added feature of being farcical in all respects.

TWENTY-THREE

Operation Pastorius was one of Hitler's most audacious plans and, like his decision to declare war on the US after Japan attacked Pearl Harbour - one of his silliest. It began on June 13th 1942 when he sent stupid saboteurs to America. His plan was to set America aflame. It was similar to the aims of Churchill's 'Special Operations Executive' but there the similarity ended.

The Operation was named after Francis Pastorius who led the first German settlements in America in the 17th Century to what is now Germantown, Pennsylvania. To this day the largest ethnic group in America deriving from a single country are German-Americans.

On the dinghy bobbing towards the beach near Amagansett, a village in Long Island, New York, sat a team of four jittery Germans sixteen miles from Montauk Point near which Hitler's bottle had been released in July 1940. They had many targets in mind including Pennsylvania Station, New York City's water supply as well as its power plants and bridges. Jewish-owned department stores like Gimbals, Sterns, Wanamaker and others were also on their hit-list. A few days later another U-Boat delivered a second team of saboteurs to the east coast of Florida.

The New York operation started badly when the U-Boat was nearly discovered near Amagansett. From that point forward every step of the mission was a failure.

It's leader, thirty-nine year old George Dasch was an unlikely saboteur. Prior to the war he had been a waiter in America with a shady past including arrests for running a brothel. He had been recruited by the Nazi secret service upon his return to Germany before Japan attacked Pearl Harbor. Joining him where Richard Quirin, who had lived in the US before the war and Ernest Burger who also once lived in America and had served in the US National Guard. The fourth member of the team was Heinrick Heinck. All spoke English.

The four men had been sent to 'sabotage school' where they learned the basics of terrorism. They read American magazines, practiced slang and the singing of the Star Spangled Banner. Key to their training was bomb making and use.

On reaching America they were to lie low before starting operations aimed at disrupting the US war machine. Their instructions were written in invisible ink on the back of handkerchiefs and their cover stories varied.

When they reached shore in Amagansett and slipped over the side of the sub that June morning they were totally unprepared. Everything went wrong. As they made their way along the beach Dasch came upon a loan coastguard named John Cullen. Burger, Heinch and Quirin were out of sight burying boxes of explosives behind sand dunes. Dasch told Cullen that he was a fisherman and might have got away with it had not one of his team called out in German from behind the dunes. Reacting to the event Dasch panicked and pressed cash into Cullen's hand. Outnumbered and armed with only a flashlight, Cullen, no fool, wisely played dumb and waved the Germans on their way.

The men hurried off but the alarm was quickly raised as Dasch and his scruffy team headed for New York by train. When they arrived in Manhattan they bought suits and made themselves presentable.

British files are critical of the Americans for doing too little to catch the saboteurs. They also revealed that the operation had been undermined from the start when one of the men drank too much at a dinner in Germany prior to the mission and said he was a spy.

When the second team landed in Florida they wore only bathing trunks and German military caps, thinking that their dress would be enough for them to be treated as prisoner-of-war and not spies if they were captured. The leader of the team had been a Brooklyn meatpacker before the war. It would not take long for him and his team to be picked up and jailed as spies.

Despite the poor efforts to catch the New York saboteurs, Dasch lost his nerve. A week after arriving by U-Boat he was living in Washington D.C. at the Mayflower Hotel from which he rang the FBI to give himself up.

At first he was not taken seriously and deemed a neurotic but his story was believed when Dasch produced a briefcase with $84,000, a huge sum at the time. The remaining spies were swiftly rounded up and put on trial. With piles of cash at their disposal and not knowing what to do next, the Germans had taken advantage of their situation by shopping, going to nightclubs and procuring prostitutes.

Dasch argued that he had planned to betray the mission from the start, that not only had he disobeyed orders by sparing John Cullen, but that he had also given the name he planned to use as part of his cover. He also claimed that a German cigarette packet was deliberately left on the Amagansett beach. All but two of the spies from both U-Boats were found guilty and sentenced to death. Six were electrocuted but Dasch and Burger were spared because they had given themselves up. After the war they were deported to Germany.

At his trial Dasch described how even the short journey from the U-Boat to the shore had fallen into farce as a mist had descended and they had paddled in circles. The failure infuriated Hitler who refused to risk another U-Boat for further missions. Much of his attention was now on developing long-range weapons.

Had Operation Pastorius successfully infiltrated American society, Hitler aimed to send more spies. No evidence exists that meaningful sabotage was ever carried out in America in WWII. And it is likely that none of the talkative spies like Dash and Burger knew a thing about Hitler's relatives in America.

TWENTY- FOUR

Otto's death was a shock. The night he died vibes were pulsing from Hitler's bottle and Neptune was receiving them, he was sensing something ominous the hour of Otto's death.

At one point he was wandered around limping and scratching on bedroom doors. With guests in the house Heather was embarrassed and Neptune was told off. "Not one more peep", she said. The Labrador cowered and spent the night on the kitchen floor, his tail between his legs. This time his limp was noticed but Heather said nothing to Peter until morning.

When Peter told Heather about Otto she shed tears for the friend she had known and admired for years. The Moores had planned to take him and their guests to dinner but had not told Dennis and Vivian that Otto had translated the letter. They planned telling them the day they learned of Otto's death. He was gone now, drowned in his own bathtub. Who, they thought, would have imagined such a dreadful tragedy-Neptune knew in advance. He was most unsettled at 1 a.m. According to the police this was close to the time Otto drowned. The time was known because Otto, who was about to step into the bathtub when the attack struck was still wearing his treasured Benrus watch. It wasn't waterproof; he would not have exposed it to water and was probably removing it from his wrist when his heart gave out. It was then that he fell into the filled bathtub.

The watch's partly undone strap was still on his wrist when Otto's house cleaner found him, suggesting that he was removing it at the time of his heart attack. The Benrus had stopped at 1.07 a.m.; it could not have stopped at 1.07 p.m. because Otto was teaching a class at that hour, he would have noticed and rewound the watch. It was not until later that Peter and Heather connected the coincidence between Neptune's behaviour, his limp and Otto's likely time of death.

When Dennis and Vivian surfaced that morning they knew something was wrong. What with their whispering about the bottle during the night, Neptune's behaviour and the early morning phone call they had slept very little and were primed for bad news when they heard of Otto's death.

Having been strongly reprimanded, Neptune was now in the doghouse and stayed away from the liquor cabinet, throughout the day he did not make his usual trip to the beach. His limp persisted and was now noticed by all.

Given the tragic news, the matter of what to do about Hitler's bottle was put aside but the Americans had considered options they would take up with their friends when the time was right, one of them involved Dennis' half-brother Warren.

Peter spent the day informing Otto's friends and speaking to his lawyer to enquire what funeral arrangements Otto had made in his will. Cremation without delay is what he wanted after a simple service. Years earlier Otto had asked Peter to be executor of his will.

Within two days Otto was cremated and like so many Jews in Europe in World War Two, his body went up in smoke, as had the fisherman from Greenland, the Irishman from Gregnamagh and to some extent the remains of Adolf Hitler outside his Berlin bunker.

On the day of the cremation Neptune was in a filthy mood, perhaps his way of showing sorrow over Otto's death, a pal who often bought him treats like the big bones from the Ramsey butcher whose name was Mr. Butcher.

In the meantime Hitler's bottle stood at attention behind the Johnny Walker with more tales to tell to the increasingly tuned in but fearful Neptune. It had more to tell about its journey even before the fisherman from Greenland was unlucky enough to spot it.

At Otto's funeral Heather was distraught until she met a lady friend at the service who was bursting with news about a budding romance between a mutual friend, a widow, and a man who might now figure in her life. Delivered in a hushed voice, the news gave Heather a lift. Gossip between women about romance is what toys are for boys, thought Peter. In her nightly phone chats with her friend in Liverpool, romance involving widow friends was a subject on which they could speak endlessly.

TWENTY-FIVE

It was a glorious day. The two couples had been milling around the sun-drenched island. Now they were home, drinks were ready to be summoned. Hitler's bottle continued standing behind the Johnny Walker in the liquor cabinet.

Neptune was home lying on side near Peter having a lazy afternoon after visiting the beach for the first time since Otto's death. He was not his usual self but he was better and his limp was gone. Avoca would not have the pleasure of his company when the liquor cabinet door was being opened - he was out of the house like a shot. No one noticed the link between the two events.

Time had passed quickly, the McClendon's would soon be returning to Yorkshire so the subject of the bottle was back on the agenda. They had five options to suggest and had written them down so their friends had something to refer to. They had thought hard about the issue, it was a matter that had to be handled with care. They knew that Otto was the only one other than themselves who was privy to the bottle's existence and that the secret had died with him.

The first of the options was that Moores might contact the Ministry of Defence and say that they were in possession of historical objects from WWII that they were willing to give to the nation under certain conditions. If they showed no interest, the offer had been made.

The second option mirrored the first but the offer might be made to the US Defence Department, the opposite number of the British Ministry of Defence.

The third option was that they leave the bottle to the nation in a will.

The next option was that they might leave the bottle to their children to keep or dispose of provided that they did not profit from the bottle or its contents in any way. Peter and Heather had made this point clear to their friends: they did not want their children stained by money derived from Nazism.

The last option was that through them the matter might be taken up with Dennis' half-brother Warren, a well-connected man that Dennis had already told the Moores about.

Peter and Heather had not been idle in thinking what to do with the bottle, some of the McClendon's options had been thought of by them so they were pleased that their friends were of a similar mind.

News that Dennis had a half-brother that was close with Ronald Reagan was a surprise. The thought that a bottle Neptune had found might come to the attention of a former US president was hard for them to take in.

In the meantime Neptune sat well outside Avoca in the shade tapping his tail on the grass. No fool was he; if the bottle was pulsing telepathic arrows his way, he was hopefully out of range to receive them. He hoped.

TWENTY-SIX

The Moores had yet to grasp the link between the bottle and Neptune's behaviour. Delving into matters dealing with the supernatural was beyond them at this point.

By the end of 1942 Hitler knew that he and his allies were losing control. Attempts by his army to seize the oil fields in the caucuses would end in November though his U-Boats remained a force. As for the Japanese, their navy could no longer match America's.

Hitler's boast that German cities would never be bombed had been exposed. In February Arthur Harris had been appointed RAF Commander. Hitler soon learned that Harris and Churchill could be surgically ruthless. If the Luftwaffe kicked a Britain city in the teeth and killed 500 – Harris would hit back with a vengeance. He and Churchill were warriors, do it to me and I'll do it to you only bigger, better and harder. They were just what Britain needed, two gladiators with the vengeful instincts of the Mafia under orders from the Godfather.

In March Bomber Command launched a savage raid on the Baltic shipbuilding port of Lubeck. Tons of explosives and incendiaries had been dropped, half the built-up area had gone up in flames. Hitler's left hand was starting to shake from the onset of Parkinson's disease. But the raids were costly for Bomber Command, their losses were terrific. Nazi pilots could be deadly. Heinz-Wolfgang Schnaufe, a Luftwaffe night fighter pilot was known as 'The Night Ghost of St. Trond' after his unit's base in occupied Belgium. In 164 sorties he downed 121 British and Commonwealth bombers and may have caused the Allies 500 lives. He survived the war only to be killed in a road crash at the age of twenty-eight.

German intelligence felt that the RAF was using a device that helped bombers concentrate over a target swiftly. Suspicions grew when all Lubeck's firebombs had been dropped within minutes of one another. They were right, the fire fighters had been overwhelmed.

Harris was bombing German-controlled industries in France and Calais' gun emplacements. They were being truck daily by 4,000-pound bombs carried by the new Lancaster Bomber. RAF fighter planes were also multitasking, not only were they escorting bombers, they were also shooting planes down.

Nor was the war going well for Hitler in the Mediterranean. Mussolini had let him down again. Escorted by the Royal Navy, a convoy with supplies and outnumbered by Italian ships had battled through to Malta. Cruisers and battleships had attacked the convoy but despite their numbers the attack had been beaten off. Hitler despaired.

While this was taking place Hitler's killers were deporting Jews to Auschwitz for execution. It was not the finest hour for the man who once said:

I was born and will forever be a Catholic.

Perhaps as God's reprisal, bad news kept bringing Hitler grief.

By March Allied convoys with aid were reaching Russia but with difficulty as air attacks were being launched from Norway. But the U-Boat base at St. Nazaire had been left ablaze after British commandos stormed ashore from a destroyer and crippled the only dry dock on the French Atlantic side capable of taking the battleship Tirpitz. Commandos had also destroyed a radio station near Le Havre. First by air, now by land, the British were infiltrating Fortress Europe with hit and run raids.

Enraged by the Lubeck bombing, Hitler ordered attacks on British targets. The first was on Exeter followed by raids on Bath, Norwich and York. The RAF had replied by wrecking the Baltic port of Rostock with bombings spread over several nights.

Hopping mad, Hitler heaped abuse on his air chief, demanding that every British city be gutted. But with the loss of planes and pilots so severe, and with the Russian Front growing in demands, the pointless raids stopped.

Hitler kept up with Japan's war from the Berghof. Even before Singapore had fallen he knew that the US had struck bases in the Gilbert and Marshall islands. In April they had brought the realities of war home to the people of Japan just as the RAF was doing it to the jittery people of Germany and occupied countries.

B-25 bombers from the carrier Hornet had bombed Tokyo, a strike that had done little damage but had shocked the Japanese. As in the case of the German populace, they too had been told this could never happen. Hitler could hardly believe that Tokyo had been bombed. Long before Neptune felt them 'a cold shiver' ran through him too.

Even before the Tokyo raid the Japs had tasted defeat. Their naval aircraft had been beaten off in Ceylon; they had tried to repeat their stunt on Pearl Harbor but had failed. When they attacked the base guarding the western entry to the Bay of Bengal the British were ready. But they had taken Bataan capturing thousands of Allied troops in the process. In Burma however, the allies had destroyed important oilfields thereby preventing them from falling into Japanese hands.

After the Philippines had fallen earlier in the year General Macarthur had said: *I shall return.* His appointment as successor to Britain's General Wavell as Chief of Allied Forces in the Pacific said it all. America was now boss in the Pacific, soon they would also be running the war in Europe much to the displeasure of Churchill who, for all his brilliance and skill always thought of Britain in terms of an Empire second to none never to be ruled by others.

In May more bad news for Hitler. The Russians were foiling his summer offensive and raining on his parade, a huge battle was underway: the Red Army was trying to retake Kharkov. The opposing armies were locked in fierce, hand-to-hand fighting. Both sides were pouring in men and equipment at a frenzied rate.

Wave after wave of Hitler's most modern tanks were being hurled back, hundreds had been lost. His spring offensive had opened with an onslaught by tanks and dive-bombers on the Soviet lines along the Kerch peninsula in the Crimea; everything hung in the balance as the battle raged.

In May the RAF had destroyed 200 factories in Cologne. One raid especially infuriated Hitler; more damage had been done on the city than in previous attacks. One thousand planes had dropped 2,000 tons of bombs, four times more than the Luftwaffe had dropped on London in April 1941. Cologne was being wrecked. May had also seen the end of the Axis air raids on Malta. Added to all this, the greatest number of US troops to date were arriving in Northern Ireland.

In the Battle of the Coral Sea both the US and Japanese navies had claimed victory in one of the most unusual sea clashes ever. Not one shot had been fired at an enemy craft by an adversary's ship. The vessels had acted as launch pads for their carrier-borne aircraft; the ships had never even seen each other. The result was that the Japanese had been prevented from landing in the Solomon Islands and New Guinea. But the victory was costly. Although American losses had been high, they nonetheless dealt Japan their first serious defeat since Pearl Harbor.

Not all of May was bad for Hitler. Rommel's push was driving the Allies back. Across the sparsest desert in Libya and full moon his panzer divisions had attacked. The Eighth Army was in trouble, Tobruk and its strategic seaport would soon fall with thousands of troops captured. In a clever manoeuvre, Rommel had switched tanks from north to south and turned the British southern flank.

The arrows of bad and good fortune kept whistling towards Hitler. In May he was forced to admit that a Soviet offensive around Kharkov had pierced his defences, but in the US along the east coast, fuel tankers were being hit by U-Boats at will. One tanker had been torpedoed at the mouth of the Mississippi River in the deep south.

The struggle in Russia continued in June but German Panzers were making headway in their drive to seize the oil fields in the Caucuses. And in Prague, Reinhard Heydrich, Hitler's architect of the 'Final Solution' had been ambushed when two rebels attacked his car with a bomb. He died days later from blood poisoning in his wounds. The results were fierce reprisals: two hundred people from a village were shot; others were taken to death camps. For good measure, in France, all Jews over the age of six were ordered to wear the Star of David on their clothing in public.

Hitler's head and health were in a whirl. Japan was casting her net wider and wider by threatening Australia. In the 'Battle of the Convoys', Italian ships were being sunk in the Mediterranean by the British navy. A further irritant for Hitler was Churchill. Despite his age, he was popping up in one city after another while his double, George Fowler, an obscure stage actor with an uncanny resemblance was appearing elsewhere. This time Winston was in Washington for talks with Roosevelt. When the talks ended FDR announced:

"Our aim is the earliest concentration of allied power on the enemy. America is not training three million troops to play tidily-winks with Germany. We will pen the German Army in a ring of steel."

On his own by choice on the Berghof patio Hitler was irate when he learned that General Eisenhower was to command Allied forces in Europe. Another Jew! In his mind Jews were everywhere: - Roosevelt, Churchill and now Eisenhower. In his West Point days Eisenhower's fellow cadets often referred to him as 'That Dirty Swedish Jew'. Hitler knew it in the 30s via Jew hating pro-Nazi German-American friends.

By early June Hitler knew that Japan's future was bleak. In the Battle of Midway the US Fleet had damaged Japan's navy beyond repair; their attempt to grab Midway Island and use it as a post to attack the Fleet had failed. The Yanks had sunk four of the carriers used on the Pearl Harbor raid with the loss of only one. After Midway, Hitler knew that the game was almost over for Japan, that allied forces would now take to a full offensive.

There was, however, better news for Hitler. With the 8th Army routed by Rommel's advances in Libya, Axis forces were again across the border into Egypt. The British were giving ground; naval bases at Alexandria and Cairo were now under threat. In Russia German forces were also on the move, they were breaking the Red Army's grip of Sevastopol, it had been the Soviet's third defeat of the summer. Troops from both sides had perished in huge numbers, the losses on both sides immense.

Adding to Hitler's anxieties was his ever changing fortunes in North Africa. After many defeats, The 8th Army had beaten back Rommel. For days both sides had thrown everything into the battle but this time the British had held at El Alamein and struck the Axis flank. German troops were now moving westward in retreat, trying to regroup - but the Afrika Korp was not finished. They were soon on the offensive pushing east. In the meantime the US Air Force, which now flew from England, were night bombing German bases in Holland while the RAF was carrying out daylight raids on the Ruhr industrial area.

Mistaken orders by the British Admiralty in July had helped the German navy decimate a convoy of merchant ships heading to Russia. The thirty-three ship convoy had been allowed to sail despite reports of a German fleet off Norway's north coast. Only four of the convoy's ships had survived the attack.

With criticism rife, a parliamentary motion in July censuring Churchill for his handling of the war had been defeated. Hitler was certain the motion would be carried and that Britain would lose heart and give up. In fact Churchill had engineered the censure motion knowing that his oratory skills would best his critics.

In July Bomber Harris issued a stern warning in a radio broadcast heard in Germany. He said to expect US and British raids day and night. He promised to scourge the Third Right from end to end and that the US would be joining the raids in great numbers.

Unhappy with his army's record in the desert, Churchill flew to North Africa in a filthy mood. He fired some generals and appointed others like General Alexander, who was now made chief of Middle East forces. General Montgomery was now to command the 8th Army; both men had distinguished themselves at Dunkirk.

Montgomery had not been first choice to command the Eight Army but Lieutenant- General William Henry Gott, a forty-five year-old officer who had risen in rank beyond his abilities. Shortly after his appointment Gott had been killed on his way to Cairo when the unarmed transport plane he was on was shot down by the fighter pilot ace Emil Clade. Montgomery, who replaced him had not even been considered for the job, at best he had been an opportune after-thought.

All was not gloom for Hitler in Fortress Europe. In August the biggest Allied landing on Mainland Europe by British, Canadian,

American and Free French forces had been at the Port of Dieppe on the coast of France. It was a disaster.

Operation Jubilee was a raid ordered by Lord Mountbatten at the suggestion of Ian Fleming who was then an intelligence officer with the Royal Navy.

Dieppe had been a test for the full-scale invasion of Europe, an attempt to test techniques and equipment for landing from sea. The greatest loses had been over 1,000 Canadians killed and 2,000 captured. Added to this victory the Germans were advancing on Stalingrad. And still not to be forgotten, Jews were now being rounded up in occupied France.

While this was taking place Churchill was again on the move. After his trip to North Africa he popped up in Moscow for talks with Stalin and US envoys. It was the first time Stalin and Churchill had met; the subject of their three meetings was the destruction of Nazism. The first two meetings did not go well, Stalin was in a nasty mood constantly asking when the Allies would launch a second front and relieve the pressures on his army. One of the US envoys attending was Averill Harriman, a former banker who had been involved in the financing of Nazi Germany in the 1930s. A final private meeting between Churchill and Stalin over dinner and copious drinks proved more fruitful. Churchill flew back to London the following day in a Liberator bomber with a monumental hangover.

TWENTY-SEVEN

July 4th 1940 was a Thursday, it was a lovely sunny day along America's northeast coast, a day to fly the nations flag and celebrate Independence Day. By now Hitler was certain that his bottle had drifted to shore at Montauk Point and had been found. He was sure the country's isolationists would be screaming to Roosevelt to stay out of the war in Europe and abide by the Neutrality Act he had signed in 1935.

The bottle had much to reveal even before Carl Erickson of Greenland found it and was killed by lightening. July 4th 1940 and what followed were secrets held by the bottle but the only living creature who could sense them was not eager for hints of the insights - Neptune was steering clear of the bottle.

Since the 4th fell on a Thursday, workers in America were keen to stretch Independence Day into a long weekend. Tom Buckridge and Bill Clay, the keepers at the Montauk lighthouse had this in mind; they had tended to the lighthouse since the late 1920s. In their fifties and unmarried they happy to be living in the two-story keeper's dwelling which stood to the side of the reddish-brown lighthouse with its seventy-eight foot octagonal tower - the views were wonderful.

Like most lighthouses the one at Montauk Point stood on a hill. From its vantage point on a clear day parts of Connecticut and Rhode Island could be seen as well as nearby Gardener's Island on Gardeners Bay beyond which lay Long Island Sound.

Tom and Bill had replaced a father and son who had been fired after colluding with liquor smugglers from Canada during America's period of prohibition, a time during which Joseph P. Kennedy, a future American ambassador to Britain in the late 1930s was very much involved. Throughout most of 1920 to

1933, he was bootlegging whisky with outlaws while practicing his hypercritical brand of Catholicism.

Tom and Bill had a stand-in for the long weekend and no ordinary chap was he, Tom's thirty-two year-old nephew Ralph Hatton, a newly ordained Jesuit priest who was soon to start teaching in New York. Ralph was a jolly fellow with greying hair, a man with a sharp mind that was often torn when decisions had to be made for which he might need to account.

Keen on lighthouses since his boyhood, Ralph's summers had been spent with uncle Tom in and around the Montauk lighthouse learning the job including the workings of its lights, its radio contact with ships and coast guard and the all-important weather bureau updates. He knew so much about the workings of the lighthouse that just for fun he took the required test and qualified as a lighthouse keeper at the age of twenty-one.

On reaching twenty-two and after his schooling at Fordham, it was a shock to his family when Ralph announced that his true vocation was in religion; he wanted to be a Jesuit and devote his life to teaching. His parents had always assumed that he would follow a career in medicine like his father but they were nonetheless pleased.

Following Fordham University Ralph had joined the Jesuit Order. As part of his training leading to ordination he had spent 1935 teaching American history in Ireland at the Jesuit's Clongowes Wood College in Country Kildare, the same school James Joyce the author had attended as a boy. More than fifty years later, an impulse would lead Neptune to Clongowes Wood College.

Ralph's love of lighthouses never waned so when Tom asked if he was willing to fill in for the weekend he quickly agreed. He needed permission from his superior but since he had time coming after ten years of hard work and study, and he was qualified for the job, he received permission to be keeper of the lighthouse for the long 4th of July weekend. The pay, or course, would go to the Jesuit Order.

The 4th of July was beautifully sunny at Montauk Point. Ralph had been in and around the lighthouse tending to his duties. When time permitted he would listen to the radio because like most Americans he was anxious to know what Hitler was up to. Now that Paris had been occupied, everyone knew Britain was next on his menu. The Luftwaffe had 2,800 aircraft ready for deployment, sixty-five percent of them being bombers. On the 20th of June Churchill had said to the House of Commons: *Now that the Battle of France is over, the Battle of Britain is about to begin.* Three weeks later on the 10th of July Churchill's prediction become a reality.

The waters off Montauk Point were calm. With the sun still above the horizon Ralph took an evening stroll to the water's edge and sat on a rock with his bare feet dangling in the lapping ebbtide waters.

The rock on which he sat was one of several clustered together with gaps between each. As in years to come Carl Erickson would hear a tap, tap, tapping on the side of his boat, Ralph also heard sounds but they were clinking sounds. Something was clinking behind him.

The sound was coming from behind the rock on which Ralph was sitting. Then he spotted it, a black, square sided bottle with a red cap hitting the rock in rhythm with the lapping water. Swastikas on its sides caused Ralph to draw back, a shiver ran through him as he fished the bottle from the water - he didn't know what to make of it. True to his Jesuit training he decided to think before acting. He made no attempt to open it. For the next few days he thought deeply and found himself faced with the same dilemma that Peter and Heather Moore would confront half a century later.

To mention the bottle to anyone other than the authorities was not wise. His Jesuit mind jumped to overdrive with questions: Is the bottle genuine? What good can come if its existence is known? What if other similar bottles are bobbing in American waters and have been found? If one or more have been found and the authorities know of their existence why has it been kept quiet? These questions were impossible to answer.

It was too much for Ralph but after a few days he knew what to do. When his uncle returned from his weekend break, and without saying a word about the bottle to anyone, Ralph borrowed a rowboat and using a fishing trip as an excuse, at ebbtide he returned the bottle to the Atlantic. In past years his fishing trips had been barren of results, he hardly ever caught a fish. On venturing out uncle Tom smiled, then he cast his eyes to heaven.

After lowering the bottle into the Atlantic Ralph flung his fishing line in the water with the hope of breaking his fishless spell. Within thirty minutes he had landed three luscious cod. Tom was shocked at Ralph's catch but happy for his nephew who, in true Jesuit tradition showed no sign of humility.

The war ended, the years passed and in 1978, age seventy, Ralph, by then a Monsignor, was in Rome working for Vatican Radio recording programmes for the Catholic English speaking world. For thirty-eight years he had said nothing about the bottle to anyone. Increasingly of late however, he was feeling guilty at what he had done with the bottle. He kept asking himself the question: What if it contained something that might have saved lives? The question was starting to haunt him. He had to confess.

He had an old friend in the Vatican named Albino Luciani, a priest who had requested Ralph's services from the Provincial of the Jesuit Order in America.

From his living quarters in the Vatican Ralph rang Albino's internal number and his friend's secretary answered. He put Ralph straight through to Albino. Ralph asked his friend if he would hear his confession, he said that something was weighing on his mind. *Of course, come to my quarters tonight at nine o'clock,* said Albino.

At 9.15 p.m. Ralph confessed to Albino. His friend made no judgements and gave no prayers for Ralph to say or pennants to do.

That night, before midnight, the 28th of September 1978, Albino Luciani, aka John Paul 1st, died in his sleep. He had only been Pope thirty-four days.

Only God knows if knowledge of the bottle had anything to do with his sudden death. Ralph died two days later. Like Albino Luciani, he had no known health problems. And just like Albino, who knows if the bottle had anything to do with his unexpected demise, and if it played a role in the deaths of Carl Erickson,

Michael O'Leary, Otto Schmitt or the crew of U-Boat-29 in July 1940. It was all very spooky.

TWENTY- EIGHT

Hitler had mostly stayed at the Berghof in 1942. By September his troops had reached the Volga north of Stalingrad having driven through Soviet lines. They had taken a naval base on the Black Sea with the oil fields in the Caucuses their objective. In Poland the SS were clearing the Warsaw ghettos of Jews, Himmler had ordered that they be killed. The walled enclave that contained them had already been destroyed, its Jews sent to death camps and gassed; others had killed themselves by staying in burning buildings or jumping from roofs.

In a twist of fate a U-Boat had torpedoed 1800 Italian prisoners of war, scoring a direct hit on the British ship Laconia. In 1942 the Allies had already lost five million tons of shipping; in June alone one ship was being sunk every four hours, worse still, 400 more subs would soon be in service.

In the middle of September the RAF made its 100th raid on Bremen. Together with the Soviet Air Force, but at great cost, they had caused huge damage to the oil fields at Ploesti in Romania.

On the island of Madagascar off the southeast coast of Africa, British troops had occupied the chief port near the capital. Vichy-French partisans were crumbling, they had pulled back after British ships appeared off the coast. A few shells from the ships was all it took for the capital to surrender. The island's location was strategically important, it enabled control of the Mozambique Channel used by convoys as a rout to the Middle East, Russia and India. U- Boats had already sunk ships in the island's wide channel.

By late September the Soviet Army was defending Stalingrad house-by-house. The offensive against Russia's industrial strength had turned into a battle of attrition - a huge struggle was underway. The Russians had been driven back into the city within miles of the Volga, clinging to every house, defending every factory in the face of dogged air attacks. Among the rubble and twisted steel hand-to-hand fighting was at play. The city was no longer recognizable - it was a cloud of burning, blinding smoke, dogs were rushing to the riverbank in the hope of crossing to escape the earth-shaking upheaval.

In October Hitler decreed that occupied countries must make up the food shortage caused by the Allied blockades. In Norway arrests and executions were increased following anti-German resistance and in Stalingrad, German troops had started new offensives. Something else concentrated the minds of the Fuehrer and his henchmen: a commission to investigate war crimes had been formed by the Allies.

In the Pacific Japan was far from finished. Two US destroyers had been sunk near the Solomon Islands. Despite the loss of many sailors, the sinkings had done little to alter the Yank's pace. Their resources were limitless; US factories were churning out weapons twenty-four hours a day. The business of America was business and business was thriving.

The Allies kept pressing. The RAF was inflicting ruthless damage on Genoa in its biggest raid on the Italian city; round the clock raids were taking place. Now under the command of Montgomery, The Eight Army had begun an offensive along the coast of El Alamein. And in Britain a taskforce led by General Eisenhower was set for an invasion of Morocco and Algiers, a thrust in North Africa into which Churchill had talked the US into with the underlying motive of not losing Egypt, the Suez Canal and India from the British Empire. More bad news for Hitler: in Stalingrad his army had begun a fresh assault but it had stalled despite the 60,000 German troops involved.

October was a turning point for Hitler. He went mad over the Allies bombings of Milan. In reprisal Canterbury became the latest cathedral city to suffer raids. The Luftwaffe came in two waves, a short one at dusk, then another at night. Tons of bombs had been dropped causing great damage and casualties. And, as if not already locked in battles in Russia, Hitler suffered a blow in North Africa; a victory of attrition had unfolded. General

Montgomery had beaten Rommel's Army at El Alamein albeit with great losses.

When Montgomery gave the order to attack, in the midst of which was a youthful Peter Moore, 900 guns thundered at 9.40 p.m. The Battle of El Alamein had begun.

Under shelter of ground and air support, the better-equipped Eight Army had struck on two fronts. Behind them had come heavy armour ready to exploit enemy lines. It wasn't easy, the Afrika Korp was tough, but the Brits had persevered. The battle sank Hitler's hopes of occupying Egypt, of controlling the Suez Canal and of seizing the rich oil fields of the Middle East beyond the Red Sea. It marked the end of Axis expansion in Africa and exposed Southern Europe to invasion.

General Rommel was in Germany recovering from illness when the Eighth Army attacked. His replacement, General Stumme, suffered a heart attack and died when the battle began. Rommel rushed back to find the British eating into his defences, taking prisoners and smashing his panzers but no matter what he tried the British stopped him.

On taking command and using a cricket term Montgomery said, *We will hit the Afrika Korp for six.* And that's what his troops did! The enemy were soon in retreat with thousands captured, half of them Italians who had only excelled in battles against ill-equipped Ethiopians years earlier.

Montgomery's forces were British, Greeks, Australians, New Zealanders, Indians and Free French. When the victory was announced Church bells rang throughout Britain and for good measure, Tobruk, with its important seaport had also been recaptured.

There was more bad news for Hitler in November. His army had been routed near Stalingrad; the Russians had smashed through German lines so swiftly that fleeing troops were shot in the back: 70,000 had been killed or captured. Cut off from supplies and with winter drawing in and with unsuitable clothing, Hitler's troops were freezing to death, gone also was any hope of seizing the oil fields in the Caucuses.

Other events were coinciding. German soldiers had landed in Tunis while in France, German and Italian troops had begun occupying Vichy southern France. In Geneva, no longer were there doubts that the Nazis were killing Jews. Hitler's pals in Switzerland let him know that contacts in Geneva were certain that war crimes were taking place. America knew about it too but the State Department was withholding the information. In this wheel within wheels of contradictory spokes, American Jews were falling into two camps. Some wanted Roosevelt to do more to save European Jews while others, led by Rabbi Weiss preferred keeping a low profile fearing that the war would be called a Jewish war. Hollywood screenwriter Ben Hecht was one of the first to expose the horror of the Holocaust in Europe. Along with the actors Paul Muni, Edward G. Robinson and others from the world of movies they called for more action to save Europe's Jews.

Early in November the greatest number of ships ever assembled for a single operation landed troops in Vichy-French North Africa. It was preceded by clandestine activities featuring American General Mark Cark and leaders of the Free French in Algeria whose duplicitous mode rarely allowed their left hands to know what the right was doing. Outside this loop of intrigue was the leader of the Free French, General Charles de Gaulle - and for good reason, he was an obnoxious, interfering, self-centred nuisance.

As US troops stormed ashore, paratroopers landed on airports in Morocco and Algeria. By nightfall all objectives had been taken, the resistance of Vichy collaborators had collapsed. They had no wish to clash with the invaders. The Americans had handled the matter diplomatically. General Eisenhower said: *France is not America's enemy.*

With a force of 140,000, the invasion marked the start of an Allied push aimed at trapping Axis forces in a pincer movement. British divisions soon joined the action. Beaten and humiliated by Montgomery's Army, the Afrika Korp was already being chased west to Tunis - the Yanks would not find them easy to deal with. Their newly trained troops took a nasty beating but eventually recovered.

The war in Europe soldiered on. Despite heavy losses Allied air strikes on occupied lands continued. In December the biggest raid ever crashed down on Holland targets. In Stalingrad the Russians were bashing the enemy and in Albania, rebels had killed hundreds of Italian troops.

By December the British were advancing down the Mayu Peninsular pushing the Japanese back into Burma. In league with troops from India, progress had been slow due to the mountains, the jungle and the criss-crossing of fast streams. The object of this push - the first real British offensive since the Japs conquered Burma was its total occupation.

1942 ended with the Allies condemning the Nazis for their slaughter of Jews in a declaration read by governments in Moscow, London and Washington. The statement accused Germany of; *Putting into action Hitler's repeated intention to exterminate the Jews of Europe.* It warned that: *Those responsible for these crimes shall not escape retribution.* The condemnation did not escape the notice of Hitler and his gang. But they were not the only killers at work - another murderer was on the loose in London. He had danced with Blanch, Heather's sister at a club in Leicester Square on a night in early 1942.

TWENTY-NINE

Another murderer was at work in 1942. He was called The Blitz Blackout Ripper. By February he had strangled and mutilated almost as many women as Jack The Ripper fifty-years earlier. Using blackouts as cover, he attacked prostitutes in and around the Piccadilly area of London's West End.

Winston Churchill described the era of the Blitz as Britain's finest hour; the country had shown grit over a long period against great odds. That was one side of the coin - the other was very seedy.

Using darkness as cover, an ugly element surfaced from the city's underbelly: the criminal class and other shady people who in normal times would think twice before breaking the law for fear of being caught. But this was war, the police were older, less physically able, bombing raids were daily, who knew about tomorrow never mind tonight, the streets were in darkness, so what the hell, the pickings are good, the risk is low, let's do the crime.

The war was heaven for criminals; some were deserters from the army like Mad Frankie Fraser who, when the war ended said he would never forgive Germany for surrendering. For career criminals like Billy Hill and Wally Thompson the Blitz and blackouts were "The golden age of crime". Jimmy Day for example would pray for sirens and the cash registers left open by shopkeepers when warning sirens sounded.

These hoodlums played by different rules while their fellow citizens were suffering, having their homes destroyed and often dying from bombings. Some of the gangsters were crooks from the continent who had fled to Britain to avoid military service and the Nazis.

Using darkness and confusion as cover, these men and often women indulged in criminality when the nation's energies were fixed on survival and some of the police were inexperienced or too old for the military. Many a person was stabbed, shot or murdered never seen again in the confusion caused by the Blitz.

Black marketers, pickpockets, muggers, every calibre of law-breaker was active in Britain in the Blitz especially in London. Prostitution was thriving, blackouts were ideal for women to ply their trade with servicemen and others – they were often called 'Piccadilly Commandos'.

Another element of the same nature was at play, as in the case of Paris after the Nazi's occupation in 1940: Britain and London in particular had become sex mad. It was not unusual for normally reserved women of all ages with high libidos to drop their inhibitions and live for the moment. Morals of all social classes and points of the nation's compass fell with abandon during blackouts, at times in public air raid shelters.

A man that used blackouts to commit the ultimate crime was Gordon Compton, a thief and killer who preyed on women in London's West End. One of his near victims in February 1942 had been Blanch Delaney, Heather Moore's sister.

Loath to bring her family more worries, Blanch never disclosed her scrape with the killer, she took the episode with her to the grave. Nor, at her insistence, did the police ever release her name for fear of being labelled a woman of ill repute.

Compton, a tall, handsome man of twenty-eight targeted almost any woman but prostitutes were his preference; they were easy prey and always had money on their person from the night's work. Blanch, of course, was not a 'lady of the night', she was a decent girl in her twenties who worked as a nurse, an important 'reserved occupation' in wartime.

She had met Compton at the Club Trocadero near Piccadilly Circus on a foggy night in which there was no air raid. The Café de Paris near Leicester Square was a stone's throw away and her favourite place for dancing, but it was rubble after being bombed in 1941 with the loss of thirty-four lives. Immediately after the raid and before help could arrive looters had swept in and helped themselves to dead people's possessions, they even cut off fingers for rings.

The assault on Blanch had taken place on a night she had attended the Trocadero alone as most of her girlfriends were not free. Having been on duty at the hospital for three weeks without a break Blanch had a day off and needed a lift. She had travelled to the club by tube, having taken the Northern Line from Clapham South to Leicester Square.

Wearing his RAF uniform, Compton, whose manner at first had been polite asked for a dance and bought her a drink. He had taken her home by cab, which was a treat, taxis were expensive and hard to come by in blackouts but he managed to find one. *Hightrees House, Clapham,* Blanch told the driver and off, slowly went the taxi through the mist and darkness of Piccadilly Circus with only dim, shaded headlights to mark the five-mile journey.

It was after midnight when they reached Clapham. Blanch's roommates were working the night shift at the nearby Woman's Hospital. Her flat's number was nine on the ground floor at the end of a long corridor. The five floor building was quiet, its wide passageways dimly lit. A few feet from the entrance of her flat stairs led down to the basement. All the building's windows were covered with dark drapes as no lights could be shown at night.

Blanch thanked Compton for the nice evening and for bringing her home and said good night. He asked for a kiss and she complied with a peck on the cheek but there was a strange look in his eyes that was new. He then began fondling her. She pushed him away and turned to open her door but he grabbed her from behind wrapping his left arm round her neck. She struggled to get free but could not. With his arm round her neck she could not cry out, she could hardly breathe. Wildly, Compton dragged her down the stairs to the barely lit basement level, his grip was so tight round her neck that Blanch fainted and fell to the floor at his feet.

Thank God for Mr. Jenkins the building caretaker who came upon the scene while making his rounds, but for him Blanch might have been killed. Compton was rifling through her purse when Jenkins appeared. Taken by surprise, Compton bolted up the stairs and was swiftly gone across Clapham Common under cover of darkness as the caretaker revived the badly shaken Blanch.

In his haste to flee Compton had dropped his very distinctive gas mask, its unique number would give the police a valuable clue. At this point in his spree Compton had already murdered four women. First he had strangled them and then mutilated their bodies. All his victims had been prostitutes.

Privately educated, Compton was a habitual liar who had been fired from jobs and drifted from part time work to casual labour. He had married the daughter of a London club owner but the union had failed. After that he had joined the RAF, his duties being with ground staff.

In February his first victim had been forty-year-old Connie Kramer who was not really a prostitute but would not say no if money was offered for sex. She had quit her job in London and was travelling home to Liverpool the following day. Compton had picked her up in Regent Street, strangled her in a doorway, thrown her body in an air raid shelter and emptied her handbag. Clues led the police to suspect that the killer was left-handed.

Two days later the police were called to examine another corpse near Leicester Square. The body was of an almost nude woman, the victim of a horrible attack. Mary Scott had sustained shocking injuries after strangulation. A tin opener and broken mirror had been used on her body. The pathologist felt that a sex maniac was at bay targeting females of any social class. London, a city already hardened by the prospect of daily bombings and an active criminal class was now gripped by a new terror.

Compton struck again the following month. This time it was Doreen White, a prostitute with a flat near Victoria Station. The police found a stocking wrapped round the neck of her mutilated body. Fingerprints of a man's left-hand on a gin bottle were found. It was clear that in addition to robbing his victims, the killer enjoyed inflicting injuries on their bodies.

Another slaying followed in Sussex Gardens, Paddington, a popular haunt for women who sold themselves. Millie Emanuel, the wife of a musician had been strangled with a scarf. Her near-naked body had been ripped open. When her husband found her body he had two shocks, he had no idea how his wife had been spending her evenings. The police said that her injuries were caused by a razor blade wielded by a left-handed man. The press were now describing the case as the 'West End search for mad killer.'

The police's first real lead came when Blanch Delaney reported that in February after the body of Connie Kramer was found, an RAF man in uniform she had met at the Trocadero had tried to choke her. Fearing publicity and worry to her family she had not reported the attack despite the pleas of her building's caretaker and friends.

May Davis, another near victim also came forward. She had been attacked in her Paddington flat the same night as Blanch. Screaming and kicking, she had driven the man away. In his rush to flee Compton had left the belt of his RAF coat. The police acted quickly. The number inside the gas mask dropped after the attack on Blanch and belt led them to cadet Gordon Compton who was arrested in North London at RAF Hendon. It was over for him when he signed the fingerprint authorisation documents with his left hand.

As he was languishing in Brixton jail on remand, another prostitute he had tried to strangle made herself known. Sadie Clark described his eyes. *They were very wide apart, a sort of light green, they were blazing like a madman's,* she said. Blanch Delaney, May Davis and Sadie Clark all identified Compton as the man who had attacked them.

Souvenirs of his killings taken from his victims were found among Compton's belongings. The jury quickly found him guilty and Albert Pierrepoint, the famous hangman performed the deed at Wandsworth prison in June 1942.

But a question remains. In October 1941, before Compton's first known murder, the body of Bette Black, a Soho prostitute was found in a bombed out building in Pye Street near St. James tube station. The police felt that someone who was left-handed had strangled her.

Was she the fifth victim of Gordon Compton? If so, he would have equalled the grisly record of Jack The Ripper by using the wartime blackouts to bring terror to the West End just as The Ripper had used London's fog of fifty years earlier to terrorise the East End of the city.

In the months that Compton was murdering four women and perhaps a fifth, Hitler's killers had sent at least one million Jews to their deaths as well as many others. Nor were the Japanese shy about slaughtering people. The Rape of Shanghai in the 1937 was but one of their war crimes. Nor had Mussolini been timid about killing Ethiopians with mustard gas.

There was no comparison between the killings of Compton and those of Hitler and his gang, but Compton's victims, living or dead would not agree.

THIRTY

The McClendons were returning to Pateley Bridge the next day. At the outset of their visit who would have imagined what would follow: the sight of Hitler's letter and the sudden, shocking death of Otto Schmitt.

Despite Hitler's evil life, Dennis and Vivian felt privileged for the insight they now had of his thinking when he seemed an invincible force and Western Europe was his. Few could claim to have read words written in Hitler's own hand. Even *Mein Kampf* had not been scribed by him but dictated. In 1937 Carl Jung, a handwriting expert had analysed Hitler's script and wrote that it included characteristics of a man with female instincts. One can make of that what one will. If true his feminine side was a bitch in boots.

Neptune was nearly back to normal. But the supernatural wolf within him cared little for the mind games being played by the pulsing bottle and for the mental pushing around to which Neptune was being subjected. The wolf was urging Neptune to pull himself together, to buck-up, to be a man, to act like the wolf he once was. He was urging the Labrador not to be afraid of the bottle and the spook inside that was sending telepathic darts. The wolf had sprung from his lair to remind Neptune of his linage and Neptune was listening. But neither he nor the wolf could begin to know that the name Adolf means 'noble wolf' and that Hitler used the pseudonym Wolff early in his career to keep a low profile and to avoid recognition. He had even made his sister Paula change her surname to Wolff.

Neptune's intuition that evil was poised to strike came at the hour of Otto Schmitt's death. More than a hint of the bottle's past was with him but not its details. That world between his ears that lived through sounds and smells knew nothing of the Jesuit who had heard the bottle clinking behind a rock and how he pondered what to do, and how, after much thought, how the priest had returned it to the Atlantic to live out its deadly future.

Nor would that world between ears have known the guilt felt by the Jesuit years later at the Vatican. Or of his confession to the Pope, or how The Pontiff had died the very night of hearing the confession having only been Pope briefly. And what followed would also have been unknown to clever Neptune: the sudden death of the Jesuit himself.

Nor would Neptune know of the lightning that had killed the fisherman Carl Erickson, or of Michael O'Leary's fate when he toppled off his sailboat. Or even of Hitler himself, how some of his body had gone up in smoke after he was dead, just like Schmitt, Erickson, and O'Leary who, unlike most Catholics had opted for cremation in his will just as Jews had been cremated but not by choice while still living. Or, for that matter, of the long past disappearance of Captain Schulhart and the crew of U-Boat 29 after the bottle had been released by the sub near Montauk Point. Or, in addition, the fate of another U-Boat with a very strange number that, while surfacing to re-charge its batteries had skimmed Hitler's floating bottle by accident or maybe by design in the vastness of the Atlantic Ocean.

Neptune knew nothing of all this, but he could sense the bottle's past and Hitler's supernatural spirit. Urged by the wolf within him, Neptune dug deep for courage. He would spend the night on the living room sofa not the kitchen floor as he had been doing. No one knew why his friendly bearing had changed, no link had been made between the bottle, his demeanour and Otto Schmitt's death.

His tail motionless, his chin on a cushion, his limp gone, his ears on guard, Neptune settled on the sofa. Half opened, his eyes were on the liquor cabinet. His eyelids grew heavy but he fought off sleep. He was anything but at ease, he was primed for a brain-wave from the bottle. His throat was dry so he went to his bowl in the kitchen for a drink. With his ears primed, his body in defensive mode, he oiled his way back to the sofa.

He knew that Dennis and Vivian were leaving in the morning. Their bags ready for travel, they had retired early. He didn't know why they were leaving but he knew two members of his pack would soon be gone. He likes them and he knew they liked him, why else would they stroke him and speak in low voices and slip him treats under the dinner table.

When Neptune retuned to the sofa he fell asleep quickly and began to dream, but his sleep was troubled; his nose twitched, his ears were on alert and his tail was tapping the sofa. The sound it made was like the sounds hitting the fisherman's boat near Greenland, the bottle's tapping sounds.

Neptune was dreaming of a bitch he had mounted and another he'd serviced; it had aroused him. A growth with a glowing hue appeared between his legs like a crimson lipstick rising from its lair.

Then something eerie happened, rapid, rattling, clinking sounds began coming from the liquor cabinet. Neptune's ears jumped to attention. He sat up quickly displaying a weapon that pointed to the liquor cabinet as if primed to fire. His eyes were fixed on the source of the sounds. Something was happening, the sounds of bottles trembling, hitting one another but not in anger. The sound was of clinking like the clinking of the bottle hitting the rock at Montauk Point. After a while they stopped and Neptune fell asleep – but his sleep remained disturbed.

Dennis and Vivian flew away the following morning heading for Manchester where their daughter Jean would meet them. Peter, Heather and Neptune saw them off at Ronaldsway Airport.

Neptune was anxious when his friends were about to depart. The weather was not good for flying, a steady rain was falling, the sky was a blanket of lead. His eyes were on the prop-driven plane as it lifted into the sky and slowly disappeared from view heading southeast.

From his window seat on the plane Dennis' thoughts drifted back to the ghostly World War Two Liberator bomber with the hopeful nickname of 'The Lady Be Good'.

THIRTY-ONE

Neptune heeded the wolf but Blondi needed no boost, fearless in all respects, the big Alsatian was always near his master Adolf Hitler.

By the end of 1942 the mixed fortunes of Hitler's military preyed heavily on his mind, his stomach cramps and medications were increasing. Dr Morell was applying leaches to his temples to reduce his tensions. Blondi could sense Hitler's agitation, his lord and master was a worried, anxious man with more and more pressures to deal with. The war was not proceeding according to plan in Russia and North Africa.

Blondi's eyes followed the Fuehrer pacing the floor in his Berghof quarters in the small hours of the morning. As usual music from the gramophone filled the room with the sounds of Wagner. His thugs were now killing Jews in great numbers, no longer was this the open secret it had been. Hitler knew that he had to win the war or his future would be bleak, hence, mixed with other concerns, his agitation, sleeplessness, high blood pressure, constipation and stomach cramps: all the triggers to his ever growing Parkinson's Disease.

How had these killings of Jews come about in a civilized country like Germany? One of the many steps leading to their slaughter had been approved and triggered in 1938, the same year that *Time Magazine* had elevated Hitler's world-status by naming him 'Man of the Year'.

Hermann Goering sat behind his huge desk in Berlin signing papers happily. The former flying ace of the First World War and head of the Luftwaffe, the second most powerful man in Nazi Germany was putting the final touches to a plan that would help solve the Jewish Question. Acting on orders from Hitler and building on the racial aims of the 1935 Nuremberg Laws, he was signing away the remaining rights of German Jews that would leave them destitute.

In 1938 the Nazis had been urging Jews to leave Germany. In fact pushing them out, isolating and cutting them off from the economy. Little by little they were facing crippling laws, like having to register property. No matter their size Jewish owned firms had to register with the government. Regulations restricting the professional class were already in force: the licensing of Jewish doctors, lawyers and architects was unlawful.

Gold, silver and valuables had to be surrendered and Jewish firms had to be run by Aryans. The result being that Jews desiring to leave Germany were cast adrift financially, left penniless and unable to leave the land of their birth. These measures were at odds with the original aims of the Nazi government to rid itself of Jews by dumping them elsewhere. With little or no money to resettle, Jews were at the mercy of the Nazis state.

Not all Jews wished to leave the country, most had been born in Germany, it was their home. Some had fought and died for the nation in the first war, others refused to believe that they would be restricted from owning property.

By 1938 Hitler's intentions towards Jews was well known and long before expressed in *Mein Kampf*. But the world looked the other way. Having already passed the Nuremberg laws - its aim being racial purity and the lowering of Jews to non-citizens, there was no question what Hitler had in mind, it mattered little to him what the world thought.

Obsessed with 'Lebensraum' - the acquisition of living space in the East for Germans of Aryan blood by aggressive means - steps were being taken to push Jews out of Germany. Emigration offices had been opened throughout the land and in Austria after its annexation. Adolf Eichmann, who was hanged in Israel for war crimes ran such an office in Vienna.

Deporting Jews swiftly, by the middle of 1939, only one third of Austria's original 180,000 Jews remained. Not all countries were accepting them, the world had virtually turned its back on the plight of German Jews.

Up to 1939 America had admitted less than 100,000 Jews. Britain had let in 80,000 including 10,000 unaccompanied children. Leery that permitting Jews into the Middle East would damage the shaky relations it had with Arab states, few were allowed into British controlled Palestine.

The plight of the Jews was of such magnitude that in order to discuss the matter, in 1938 Roosevelt called for a meeting of thirty-two nations at Evian, France. The world knew that laws had been passed to deprive Jews of their livelihood and remove them from competitive roles in Germany's economy. To the dismay of anti-Nazi groups, the Evian meeting closed without deciding on a policy to help. Only the Dominican Republic agreed to accept Jews.

Historians have questioned whether Hitler's plan to deport Jews was based on knowledge that the doors of other countries would be closed to them. The answer is that he probably did know. Be this or not the case, the fact remains that most Jews could not leave Germany. This also applied to Jews trying to leave occupied countries. With no place for them to go, Jews were caught in a web with no way out. Many had slipped east to Poland and Russia believing they would escape persecution; the result being that they were trapped in remote areas, rounded up in ghettoes and sent to death camps.

At first the Nazis had a 'preferred-plan' that would forcibly relocated European Jews by sending them to the island of Madagascar off Africa's east coast. Some say the plan was originally a British idea. Whoever thought of it first Hitler liked it immediately. Once implemented, he hoped that Jews could be lanced from sight through large-scale expulsions to Africa or other colonies.

Although his generals were highly dubious and though he was mad, after the outbreak of war in 1939 Hitler was sure that victory over France was certain and that colonies like Madagascar would fall under his control and that the plan could then be implemented. He was bullish that a quick peace treaty would also be reached with Britain, that they would cave in quickly and that the Royal Navy and French Fleet could then be used to ship Jews to Madagascar.

Initially the plan was to remove all Jews from Europe. But some felt that Jews from Poland and Russia were a source of militancy and should be used as hostages to control American

Jews, and that Madagascar should be a land to resettle Jews from Western Europe only. Hitler agreed that removing four million Jews from the west was more practical and easier than sending them from the east as well.

The plan entailed taking over Madagascar from the Vichy French with the SS governing the island by force. Nothing in the plan considered the treatment of the island's native population. The Nazis would want the world to think that they had given 'autonomy' to the Jews in Madagascar, in truth they would be strictly controlled.

The plan fell apart after the Battle of Britain. The hope of using the British navy to ship Jews was gone, it was clear that the war would last much longer than expected. In time British and Free French Forces would invade Madagascar driving the final nails in the plan's coffin. It was at this point that the Nazis shifted into high gear to solve the Jewish Problem with their mass killings in gas chambers.

In August 1938 options were few for most German Jews. Many parents ensured that their kids escaped to other countries knowing they might never see them again.

Three months later on November 9th came Crystal Night, The Night of Broken Glass, a pogrom that saw Jewish property and businesses destroyed in Berlin and other German cities, 30,000 Jews were arrested and deported to camps, many were murdered. The world stood by as Jews were stripped of their rights, treated like animals and sent to gas chambers. At the stroke of a pen Hermann Goering had removed almost all their rights. In the cross-fire of all this at the end of 1938 *Time Magazine* would elevate Hitler's stature in the world.

What Blondi was sensing from Hitler was his growing anxiety because the Fuehrer knew that if he didn't win the war there would be no place for him to hide. His only option would be suicide. But, at least for a while, his dark mood was lifted with thoughts of better days - the 1936 summer Olympic Games in Berlin.

THIRTY-TWO

Prior to the 1936 Winter Olympics in Bavaria Hitler had yet to annex the country of his birth and return it to where many German-Austrians felt it belonged. But he had not been idle reclaiming ethic Germans elsewhere. The Nazi party had already taken control of the coastal Free City of Danzig; in addition the Germany Army had waltz into Germany's demilitarised Rhineland with not a peep from France or Britain. Hitler had taken a chance and won – his arch enemies had neither bark nor bite.

Growing up in Austria Hitler had contempt for the House of Hapsburg, an amalgam of the Austrian Empire and the Kingdom of Hungary. There were tensions resulting from the Hapsburg's policy of Slavic integration which seemed to favour them over ethnic German-Austrians like the Hitler's; in Vienna for example less and less German was being spoken.

As far as young Adolf was concerned Slaves were a mongrel race whereas ethnic Germans were pure. And the same racial impurities applied to Jews who comprised ten per cent of the Austrian population, much more than the one per cent in Germany

When the heir to the Austro-Hungarian throne was assassinated in Serbia, Hitler said that it was thanks to the "hand of eternal goodness" as it was he, Archduke Franz Ferdinand who had promoted greater outreach to Slaves. Following WWI, the First Republic of Austria had come into being after more than 600 years under the Hapsburg Dynasty.

That July day in Vienna in 1936 as the Olympic Torch passed by the mood of the people in the street turned nasty, there was yelling and shoving. As tempers grew the police struggled to control the mob and many were arrested.

The citizens of Vienna had been whipped into a frenzy. A few Jews had dared venture out to watch the Olympic Torch pass by. So successful was the Nazi's scheme to foster anti-Semitism in Austria that the mere presence of a Jew was enough to spark disorder. Austrian Nazis were bent on keeping Jews away from what most ethnic Germans believed was a symbol of Aryan superiority – the Olympic Torch itself- which is what they had been told.

To this day the International Olympic Committee describes the relay of the torch as an age-old tradition going back to ancient Greece, a symbol of global peace. In fact the torch relay idea first came from Hitler's Olympics organizer Carl Diem who helped turn the Olympics of 1936 into a propaganda coup for Nazism. And even now, in the Berghof, in late 1942, the thought of this triumph lifted Hitler from his sombre mood.

The torch relay from Olympia to Berlin was Hitler's way of linking Nazi Germany with the ancient Greeks who he claimed were the Aryan ancestors of the Third Reich. By way of fabrication, he described the torch as a spiritual bond between the fatherland and the sacred places of Greece founded by Nordic immigrants 4,000 years earlier.

To give the torch greater spiritual significance, propaganda minister Goebbels created a ceremony that claimed the torch was a relic of an ancient Greek tradition. A conveniently supplied high priestess used a parabolic mirror to focus the rays of the sun to light the torch while pretty Greek girls in short white skirts were hired to sing ancient chants accompanied by equally ancient instruments.

The spectacle was pure theatre, the Nazi's Olympic organizers had hijacked the Olympic dream by claiming   the girls were vestal virgins whose role was to protect the sacred flame. This too was fabrication: vestal virgins were a Roman not Greek tradition.

Some 3,000 runners had taken part in carrying the torch nearly 2,000 miles between Olympia and Berlin, the athletes passing through Bulgaria, Yugoslavia, Hungary, Austria and Czechoslovakia –all the countries Hitler aimed to occupy or control in his expanding Third Reich.

When the torch reached Berlin, homes were flying Nazi flags next to those of the Olympics. In Berlin Stadium itself the rostrum was decorated with a huge German eagle grasping the Olympic rings. The symbolism was obvious: the Olympic games had fallen victim to Nazism, its rings clutched in the eagle's claws.

How could such an assembly of thugs host games meant to foster peace?

Germany had been awarded The Games before Hitler came to power in 1933. At first he said that Jews and Freemasons invented the games, that they were nothing but Yiddish theatre that could not be hosted in an Aryan country ruled by him. Goebbels viewed them differently, seeing them as a vehicle for propaganda, a way of promoting Germany's image worldwide.

Hitler altered his thinking when he realized the value of The Games after the winter Olympics in Bavaria. The spectators, athletes and journalists that came and took part were so impressed with the organisation and friendliness of the people that their suspicions of Nazi Germany were set aside.

Captivated by the success of the winter Olympics, France and Britain failed to oppose the summer Games and ignored Germany's military build-up. But the polished look of the winter Games did not hide the reality of Germany under Nazism.

German Jews had slowly been banned from many aspects of life in their own country by way of the Nuremburg laws the year before and the further restrictions that followed; the US and British Olympic teams came close to boycotting The Games in protest. The organizers of The Games replied that they had Hitler's word that Jews would not be excluded. This too was a falsehood: Jewish athletes were not allowed to train.

During the winter games in Bavaria signs saying 'No Jews or dogs' should have been removed but they were left near the Olympic village and seen by members of the Olympic committee. Hitler promised that they would be removed for the summer Games. The humiliation was only temporary for Herr Hitler, the opening ceremony made up for his loss of face.

In 1936 at the same time as the 'No Jews or Dogs' signs were appearing in Bavaria, in most of America's southern states as well as some in the north, a similar, more inclusive sign was in evidence in front of hotels, rooming houses and other places of residence. It read: 'No Negroes, No Jews, No Catholics, No Dogs.'

As Hitler was being driven to the stadium thousands of Brown Shirt Storm Troopers lined the route. As he entered the arena 100,000 people raised their arms in the Nazi salute shouting 'Heil Hitler!' Teams from every competing country then past him and many, including France, but not Britain, gave the Olympic salute with one arm raised out to their side. From a distance it looked like the 'Nazi Salute' . The German crowd cheered.

Exactly on cue the Olympic torch was run into the stadium and when Hitler announced the opening of The Games the Olympic fire was lit. This was followed by a German weightlifter taking the oath symbolically on behalf of all the competitors. He, mistakenly – it is said – held a flag bearing a swastika instead of the Olympic rings. By then the symbols of the Olympics and Nazism were so entwined that few people noticed. The Games provided a spectacle that stunned the world and left it in such awe of German power that it was too late to oppose Hitler.

Given the stunning success of the Olympic Games and the unstoppable rise of Germany that followed, is there any wonder that *Time Magazine* named Hitler 'Man Of The Year' in 1938? These reflections lifted Hitler's spirits and gave him the strength to continue vandalising Europe and killing Jews. As he looked back on the past he felt anything but finished. Another flame of hope stirred his soul like the bountiful 1936 Olympics, work on his Wonder Weapon, the V1 Rocket. Its development had started in 1937 on the Baltic Sea island of Peenemunde. Mr. Churchill knew all about it.

The Nazi scientists Klaus Riedel and Werner von Braun had been working on the rocket. In Hitler's mind the V1 would do what the Luftwaffe had failed to do – terrorize Britain into surrender. In short order the V1 was followed by the supersonic V2. Both were pilotless bombs launched against Britain near the end of the war. Hitler hoped that they would turn the tide of war and that work at Telemark in Norway using heavy water and uranium would soon yield results and lead to the first atomic bomb. The hope was never realized thanks to Mr. Churchill's 'Special Operations Executive' and the efforts of the elite Norwegian Commandoes - but it very nearly was.

Aimed at London during the Normandy invasion from sites along Europe's coastline, over an eight-month period , V1 and V2 rockets killed nearly 9,000 Britons, injured thousands and destroyed more than 30,000 homes.

One of the last V2s to land on London shortly before Hitler committed suicide was devastating. Fired from The Hague, it landed on a block of flats in Whitechapel at 7.21 p.m. on March 27th, 1945, killing 134 people. At about the same time another V2 struck Elm Grove in Orpington killing Mrs. Ivy Millichamp. The rocket could penetrate shelters, there was no defence against it. When they were overhead and their engines stopped, those on the ground could only take cover and pray.

THIRTY-THREE

The McClendons took off for Manchester at eleven a.m. on Man Air Flight 666, a two-engine Saab-Fairchild with fourteen passengers and four crew. Why the airline had chosen 666 as flight numbers is a mystery. Neither the McClendons or Moores had absorbed their significance at check-in when Dennis paid for the tickets. It's not that they were ignorant of the belief that the numbers symbolized Satan, it was simply that the sadness of Otto's death still lingering and with everyone busy saying their goodbyes the numbers went unnoticed. And if Neptune was ill at ease when his friends took off it had nothing to do with the three sixes. Or did it?

The last thing Dennis said before leaving is that he would phone on arrival. The flight was a short one, about 100 miles, the only concern was the weather; rain was moving east from Ireland ready to sweep across the Isle of Man and the British mainland. Mist was gathering and it was muggy.

It was drizzling when the plane took off; the aircraft seemed to struggle to get off the ground. During the war Dennis had often laboured at the controls to get his bombers airborne. He had many interests, one of them being military aviation. A tale that had captured his imagination was that of The Lady Be Good, the nickname of the US Liberator that had vanished in 1943 while on a mission to Naples, Italy. The bomber and her crew were on Dennis' mind as flight 666 lumbered upwards reaching for the sky.

The Lady Be Good had taken off from an airfield near the Libyan coast and vanished. The war ended and as time passed the plane and her crew were forgotten. Then, out of the blue, in 1959 came news that oilmen working in the Libyan Desert had found the bomber's wreckage four hundred miles south of her take-off point and in the opposite direction from which she had taken off. It was a mother of all mysteries.

The bomber had not been in battle - parachutes were missing so the crew had bailed out, but where, and what had become of them. It was a riddle that perplexed much of America at the time.

The Air Force had come under pressure as to what had happened to the crew, but they were stymied. Responding to events they began a lengthy investigation in the vicinity of the Libyan Desert where the plane had been found.

By 1960 all but one of the crew's remains had been found. Two diaries among their possessions spoke of their struggles to survive in the desert while trying to walk their way to civilisation. The crew of The Lady Be Good was much on Dennis' mind as flight 666 was nearing its crushing altitude.

After the McClendons had taken off Heather rang the von Schneiders to see if they needed shopping, which they did. She and Peter were supermarket bound in Douglas. After a burst of rain the sky cleared, the sun shone, but to the east on the British mainland the weather was bad, there was rain, thunder and lightning.

Following their shopping the Moores spent a nice afternoon sitting in the garden of the von Schneider's bungalow having tea and cakes. Neptune was still unsettled, he was not his usual self even with the elderly sisters whose lives he had saved.

So enjoyable was their visit with the sisters that the Moores stayed longer than intended. By the time they reached home, fed Neptune and received a call from their son in New York it was after eight p.m. It was then that Peter and Heather realized that they had not heard from Dennis. At first they thought little of it but as the evening wore on their concern grew.

When nine p.m. came and went without a call Peter decided that he would ring Dennis in Pateley Bridge after the ten p.m. news; hopefully he would hear from his friend before then. No sooner had he decided this than the telephone rang.

"Peter?"

"Yes?"

"It's Jean."

"Hello, all well?"

"No Peter, have you heard the news?"

"No…what's happened?"

163

"My parent's plane is missing."

"What?"

Jean's voice trembled.

"It's on the news. Helicopters are searching."

All evening Neptune had been unsettled, he didn't seem to know what to do with himself.

Twenty-four hours after take-off there was still so sign of the aircraft. An amateur radio operator in North Wales had reported that he thought he may have heard chatter between a male and female shortly after flight 666 had taken off. It was a mystery that began to echoed the puzzling story of *The Lady Be Good*.

THIRTY-FOUR

By early 1943 reality's walls were closing in on Hitler, his Sixth Army had been beaten in Stalingrad. After a week of fierce fighting Field Marshal Von Paulus had surrendered to a young Lieutenant. Even though German resistance remained north of the city, the greatest battle of the war to date was over. Hitler had an unbridled fit.

Von Paulus had been captured in the basement of a Stalingrad department store. The young Russian officer who negotiated the surrender told him: "Well, that finished it." von Paulus' reply was a miserable look. The loss of life on both sides had been immense, 100,000 German soldiers had been killed or died of starvation in the previous weeks, and twice that number had been lost since Hitler's Army's entrapment in November.

Although hopelessly in check, von Paulus had twice rejected surrender ultimatums. Hitler's promises to fly food, fuel and ammunition to Stalingrad had appeared to be empty promises, that he had been let down was closer to the truth. Goering had assured him that the air force would make the deliveries but he had not been true to his word. German troops had been eating meat from dead horses to survive.

When ready to surrender, Hitler forbade it and promoted von Paulus to Field Marshal. Up to this point no German Marshal had surrendered in the war. Hitler's message to him was unequivocal: *The Sixth Army will hold its position to the last man.* – von Paulus did not obey. The siege of Stalingrad and the Caucuses region had collapsed.

Hitler was being squeezed from all sides. Allied troops had captured Tripoli, the last city held in North Africa by Mussolini. It had fallen three months to the day from the start of the El Alamein offensive by the Eight Army. The pressure from North Africa was only the beginning of worries heaped on Hitler at the end of 1942. The following year Warner Brothers Pictures released the film *Casablanca* about wartime intrigue in North Africa.

In January 1943 Casablanca would again be the setting for a drama; this time real life was in force not a motion picture about wartime intrigue in Morocco. Churchill and Roosevelt called a press conference to say why they had met.

Roosevelt announced that the Allies were pledged to continue the war until Germany, Italy and Japan had surrendered unconditionally. Mention of Italy was a surprise because the story was circulating that Italy might change sides.

There was the usual trouble from General de Gaulle at the press conference; he had yet to forgive Roosevelt and Churchill for invading French North Africa without consulting him. It was clear that Italy would next be in the line of fire after North Africa had been cleansed. By now the Eight Army and General Leclerc's Free French troops had crossed the border into Tunisia in pursuit of the retreating Germans.

Not only had Hitler been beaten in Stalingrad and North Africa, but the Allies were planning to crawl up his backside through Italy and southern France. Is there any wonder that the Fuehrer was sleepless at the Berghof despite its beautiful setting and detachment from the daily flow of German blood.

Something else was irking Hitler, Berlin had been bombed in daylight. The first had taken place as Reich Marshal Goering was set to deliver a radio broadcast marking ten years of Nazi rule; taken by surprise the British planes had met with little resistance. The second had occurred as Goebbels was also broadcasting on the radio. With his options limited, Hitler ordered the mobilisation of the German male population aged sixteen to sixty-five. No longer was he laughing at Britain's Dad's Army, he was now at the bottom of his own human barrel scavenging for help.

Nor was the war going well for his Japanese Allies. They were fleeing Guadalcanal where a US offensive was underway. A sense of desperation was growing in Hitler's mind, his dreams of victory were waning and his anxious state was bubbling over.

Most German Generals knew the future looked grim and prepared a document blaming the SS for the killings of Jew.

They knew the day was coming when war crimes would have to be paid for. But all was not gloom for some German soldiers; the lucky ones were in a loving mood passing life on not ending it. Soldiers like the SS were having a jolly war with French women as well as stuffing their pockets with money made with French collaborators.

From the moment German troops occupied the city, Paris, like London during the Blitz had become a sex-mad environment, but sexual abandonment often led to serious consequences. The tall troops were highly rated by many of Paris' women. Parisian ladies, well known for their chic appearance and allure frequently were drawn to the invaders. Prostitution was also rife. The occupation of Paris had sparked the sexual liberation of women in the Catholic France where only married men played the field or if single had many affairs. Paris was sizzling with sex.

Venereal disease among soldiers was common in all occupied countries especially in France. Some had to be hospitalised for months so steps were taken to ensure that hygiene was practiced in brothels and the rules had to be adhered to in all countries. Hitler had said that if a soldier was willing to fight and die for the fatherland, nothing should stand in the way if love was his desire. Well ahead of the times he had provided blow up dolls but his gesture failed to quell urges, his soldiers were too embarrassed to use them.

At the same time as many Parisians like the singer Edith Piaf were active in the resistance - in her case helping captured French soldiers to escape from prison camps – others, like the fashion world's Coco Chanel, a Nazi sympathiser and collaborator was taking them to her bosom.

Wherever there was darkness or hotels or cinemas, soldiers and French woman were locked in sexual combat. Except for officers who could afford expensive hotels, the most common place for sex was the Parisian Catacombs.

Living with the uncertainty of tomorrow sex was exciting for French women; it helped them survive the war and occupation. With husbands and fiancés prisoners of war life was a struggle. For normally respectable women, sleeping with Germans was a way of acquiring the essentials of life like food, clothing and fuel to keep warm.

German soldiers were not the only ones to take advantage of available sex; women had affairs with anyone who could help. With coal in short supply during winter months, sex was used for warmth. And with the city under curfew, the indoors were an inducement. By 1942 while Hitler was mostly in the Berghof and up to two million Frenchmen were in captivity, the birth rate in France escalated. Germans fathered thousands of children during the occupation of Paris.

Paris' sexual collaborators came mostly from the lower classes of French society like chambermaids and waitresses who, by the nature of their work came into contact with soldiers.

Driven by hunger and need, middle class women often surrendered their bodies, upper class ladies also became romantically involved. One such person was fashion designer Coco Chanel who, for much of the war lived well at the Ritz Hotel. In 1940 she began an affair with Hans Von Dincklagel, a military attaché much her junior. Condemned for her affair, when Paris was liberated she fled to Switzerland.

Sex was not the only thing at play in Paris that sparked one's life. While German soldiers were fighting in Russia, North Africa and at sea, the black market was thriving, profiteers were making fortunes.

Within a few years of Paris' surrender, French construction companies were making fortunes building Hitler's Atlantic wall with French workmen and slave labour. Stretching along the French coast and beyond, the concrete structure consisted of blockhouses, reinforced pillboxes and gun emplacements.

German soldiers were often willing partners in this weird and wonderful world of wartime enterprise. It enabled them to entertain ladies with wine and food while civilians went hungry and their fellow soldiers were dying in far-off conflicts. Meanwhile, in the Berghof, Adolf Hitler, king of the crumbling master race was slowly going mad while many of his troops in Paris were firing droplets of affection into friendly French females.

THIRTY-FIVE

Two days after take-off the McClendon's flight continued missing, it had vanished like The Lady Be Good. It was déjà vu all over again. The coast guard were searching the Irish Sea and helicopters were flying grid patterns over the mainland from the west coast of the midlands to Manchester and beyond. No crash had been reported anywhere in Brittan.

Everyone was worried and Neptune remained unsettled, he knew something bad had happened just as he sensed danger the night Otto Schmitt died.

After take-off in the mist and while flying east, the Saab-Fairchild's pilot had not followed rules and radioed his position to air traffic control at Manchester or Liverpool airport, nor had he replied to any calls. Stranger still was the perplexing fact that the aircraft had not appeared on anyone's radar. This was very odd indeed, yet another mystery. From a few miles east of the Isle of Man to beyond Manchester the British midlands were blanketed with rain-bearing clouds.

The plane's fate and flight numbers were news, newspaper headlines were wildly emotive with the emphasis on the numbers 666: 'Satan's Flight Vanishes', 'Devil in the Cockpit?', 'Lucifer's Flight Lost', the words picking at the bones of misfortune eager to link Satan with tragedy. Television coverage was non-stop.

The story gripped the nation and was the subject of talk radio, the type of yarn the media love, it concentrates the minds, and sells papers. As far as the media are concerned, *If a story bleeds it leads*.

The plane with Satan's numbers would have been news on its own but now there was an added twist. Twenty-four hours after going missing news broke that former US Vice-President Dan Swail had been a passenger on the flight.

He had been on the Isle of Man visiting relatives and was flying to Manchester for a linking flight to New York. Keeping a low profile, no one knew who he was much less the high office he once held in which he was never more than a heartbeat away from the US presidency. But three men on the plane knew who he was, they hijacked the aircraft precisely because he was on board. Swail was the focus of media attention and the hijacker's bargaining chip.

One of the hijackers was a former commercial pilot who had been fired for excessive drinking. The trio were members of the Real IRA, a group that had split from the Provisional Wing of Sin Fein. Their intention was to hijack the plane, fly it to a secret location and hold everyone hostage until political prisoners held by the British without charge in Belfast jails were released.

It didn't matter to them if their comrades were not released. Their motive was to focus world attention on the strife in Northern Ireland and its occupation by British troops since 1968 – their ambition was a united Ireland free of Britain.

The riddle of the missing plane was as riveting as the disappearance of The Lady Be Good. But the Saab Fairchild had not vanished during wartime, it had not been lost in a foreign land. This was Britain, 1991, not North Africa, 1943, a time gone by when allied bombers were blasting Axis targets in southern Italy.

Except for an amateur radio operator from Wales who may have heard talk at very high frequency on the 1082136 meter band, no airport had heard anything from Flight 666. Enter another spooky occurrence, but a man 3,000 miles away did hear something – which was unbelievable – as if preordained and supernatural. He heard it at the intended destination of Hitler's bottle fifty one years earlier: it had been heard briefly by forty year-old James Jones the keeper of the Montauk Point lighthouse at the tip of Long Island in New York. At first he hadn't connected what he heard with the missing plane in Britain. It was not unusual for him to hear talk between amateur radio operators on certain meter bands of the VHF channel.

Jones was turning his radio's dials when at high frequency on the 182136 meter band he heard the crackling sounds of a man's voice asking what the weather was like down there. He took the question to mean how is the weather in your part of the country and assumed the country was America. It never dawn on him that

170

the question was being transmitted from an aircraft over Britain. It was nothing short of a miracle to hear anything at high frequency on that meter band from such a distance and at ground level to boot. This was the kind of weirdness that was hard to believe.

The response Jones heard was from a woman who was probably using a hand-held scanner to receive and send radio messages. She said: *Clear from here to Horse Head. Clear, Clear.*

Ronaldsway Airport on the Isle of Man was tiny with little security, it was easy for the hijackers to spirit pistols on the plane and take over. Dan Swail said nothing and none of the passengers made a fuss. Dennis and Vivian sat tight. After taking over the plane, the only thing said by the hijackers was that the plane was being flown to a safe location and that all would be treated well. Except for a woman with a youngster that began whimpering all the passengers reacted calmly to the polite hijackers who had northern and southern Irish accents.

With one of the hijackers now at the plane's controls, he turned the aircraft to a heading of 310 degrees and flew above the clouds towards the North Channel, which runs between the east coast of Northern Ireland and the west coast of Scotland. The plane was now flying over the Irish Sea at 12,000 feet.

This was when the hijacker made the call to his female accomplice. Where the woman was speaking from is unknown but over the North Channel, a thick layer of mist hung everywhere. Such was not the case thirty miles south as the Moores were shopping at the Douglas supermarket. There it was sunny. Peter was paying for his goods when the life of everyone on board Flight 666 had come to an end. As their plane was screaming down, Dennis and Vivian held hands, most others were also accepting of their fate as their envelope of life was being sealed.

For reasons that will always remain a mystery the aircraft had suddenly lost power, stalled, and then plunged into the North Channel at a point fifteen miles west of Port Logan between Northern Ireland and Scotland. The Saab-Fairchild had sunk quickly leaving no trace of wreckage in the channel. This too was a mystery.

When it was learned that the keeper of the Montauk Point lighthouse may have heard talk between the plane's pilot and a woman on the ground little or no interest was attached to the claim; it was deemed to be far-fetched and impossible.

No one would ever realise the link between Hitler's bottle, the Point Ayer lighthouse on The Isle of Man, the one at Montauk Point and the people who suddenly died because of their contact with the bottle, or because they were privy to its existence. But Neptune could sense a presence that he feared, something foreboding. Even before the Saab-Fairchild had gone missing, he had been hard to live with.

THIRTY-SIX

As 1943 progressed Germany's defeat was certain. Long gone was Adolf's notion of scaring America with his silly bottled letter and notions of setting it ablaze with Operation Pastorius.

Even under the command of Fieldmarsall Ritter von Leeb there was little chance of victory on the Eastern Front; it's siege would end 872 days after it began, one of the most destructive military struggles and costliest in warfare.

In Stalingrad the last pockets of resistance had surrendered, Kursk was back in Russian hands. By the middle of February the Red Army was driving the foe out of their country, city after city was back in the Soviet fold. In a ten-day period four major cities had been liberated from starving Germans.

In step with the Russian push, hundreds of miles away US troops were driving the Afrika Korps out of the Kasserine Pass Mountains of central Tunisia after they, themselves, had been routed. The tables had been turned, the Germans were in retreat with no support to help them fight.

Like Frankenstein re-born the Yanks were back and motivated. Rommel was retreating trying to establish new lines of defence in the southeast but he was nearly surrounded. From the east and west, the Eight Army and US forces were on course to hammer the honourable but sick Field Marshall Rommel.

In the midst of all this, for a man who often said: *I am now and always will remain a Catholic*, whatever humanity Hitler ever pretended to embrace had gone, he had strayed far from the tenets of The Roman Catholic Church. For his catechism with the Benedictines he had committed to memory: *God is the supreme spirit, who alone exists of himself, and is infinite in all perfections.* In the madness of his self-belief he and God were one, he the God of flesh, kin to the supreme spirit sent to save Germany.

With Hitler's blessings a decision was reached to destroy the Warsaw ghetto and send its Jews to the ovens. After all, they were only blacks turned inside out.

Although the German Navy was active, its losses were heavy. Allied bombings of their slips in France was making U-Boats harder and harder to replace.

In the Pacific Japan had failed to regain control of the Solomon islands and were fleeing having had enough of the Marines' flame throwers that were reducing them to smouldering cooked flesh.

In Rome Mussolini had fired his inept son-in-law Count Ciano and assumed the foreign minister's post. Hitler was not impressed.

Allied bombings were smashing German industry. Reports to Parliament in March by Air Minister Sinclair painted a picture of damage done to the Ruhr industrial heartland. Some 2,000 factories had been blown to bits or disabled, tons of steel had been destroyed, coal output had been reduced and more than 400 acres of Dusseldof had been gutted. He reported that in a strike on Essen, thirty-six engineering shops had been hit and that one blast had set off a sheet of yellow-orange flame 1,000 feet into the air.

Berlin too had been hit in March. Tons of high explosives had lit up the capital with fires visible 200 miles away. The myth peddled that German cities would never be hit was now exposed as nonsense. The bombings had left the Nazis with no choice but to admit that the populace needed self-control and grit. Churchill had told the RAF to *light a fire in the belly of the enemy and burn his black heart out.* They and their Yankee cousins were doing just that.

There was more bad news for Hitler in March. Saboteurs had blown up key Frankfurt bridges on the River Oder. But a chink of light pierced the dome of Hitler's sour mood. His worn-out troops had recaptured Kharkhovin in Russia but the victory was meaningless when viewed against the scope of defeats.

Having moved headquarters from Wolf Lair to the Berghof and now Vinnitsa in Ukraine, Hitler was sending angry missives to his generals and ministers. He was in a rage, a whirlwind of mood-swings. On another sleepless night, only a neat pile of letters on his desk brought a measure of relief.

Written to him before the war, he had read their translation into German but had never replied. They travelled with him wherever he went – they were the comfort blanket to which he would turn when he needed to escape reality along with drugs. Next to the letters sat a book of poems sent by the writer of the letters; they had never been translated into German.

Hitler seldom answered personal letters like the ones before him on his desk but these were different and worthy of re-visit, they would divert his mind. They came from Marie Stopes, a British admirer, the pioneer of birth control methods and family planning. Although Stopes meant well, she was nonetheless mired in odd views held by people of merit in Briton, Europe and beyond before World War Two. Her letter's thrusts were a mirror of Hitler's thinking.

Religious conservatives who objected in principal to contraception had always been opposed to Stopes' views. H.G. Sutherland, a Catholic doctor wrote a book condemning her work as *A dangerous and immoral campaign, a sinful practice under the guise of scientific knowledge.*

There were other strings to the bow of Stopes that rang a sour note worldwide and called into question her morality. She was a keen exponent of eugenics, a school of thought that called for the sterilization of the poor, the diseased and the racially impure – this is what her letters to Hitler were mostly about.

After reading what Hitler had written in *Mein Kampf,* and what - referring to Jews – he called 'the lower races', she had written to say she hoped sterilisation would be on his agenda when he came to power. He, of course, agreed that there were mongrel people who should be kept from having children so their inferior bloodlines should cease.

Stopes' admiration of Hitler could not be attributed as coming from a smitten girl like Unity Milford. In 1935 she had attended the International Congress of Population Science in Berlin where Nazi ideology on race was discussed. Her birth control clinics were, for a time, organised under the name: The Society for Constructive Birth Control and Racial Progress.

Stopes' views on eugenics were not unique in Europe; they were also held elsewhere. Well-known individuals in the twenties and thirties shared her belief including H.G. Wells, Winston Churchill and Virginia Wolf; it was being practiced in America. Held up one day on a walk by people with learning difficulties Stopes said, *They should be killed.* Scores of prominent people of the day held the same view.

Leaving sterilisation aside, Stopes did valuable work in the field of birth control. She had opened her first clinic in London in 1921 when she was only thirty-one. Life for some women at the time consisted of endless pregnancies followed by premature deaths. Her books awakened women to the science behind their sexual behaviour.

She was a thirty-six year-old virgin when she wed and thus she would remain during her brief marriage until she wed again. For her first husband sex was a stranger that never came calling despite the invitations. The year before she opened her first clinic she published *Radiant Motherhood* which was full of facts on birth and gave rise to her views on those unfit for parenthood.

She was soon sharing platforms with well-known people of similar views who proposed banning anyone from breeding without a license. After the war that saw the sterilization of unknown numbers, belief in eugenics died. But as Hitler was re-reading Stope's letters, his belief in the practice was a work in progress. And he was feeling better, he knew many non-Germans shared his view and this gave him heart to continue with the war. Thinking along the lines of sterilization he wished that Churchill and Roosevelt's parents had drowned the little shits at birth.

Today, all over the world, the name *Marie Stopes International* is still carried by clinics that deal with family planning. And in Britain, in 2008, Stopes, Hitler's admirer and the advocate of sterilization had a fifty-pence stamp with her image issued by the Royal Mail.

For many people, not least women who recall the liberation that came with the arrival of 'the pill', Stopes will always be a heroine. But for others, the stamp, which pays tribute to her work is causing anger among Catholics and others because of her sympathy with eugenics theories and her admiration of Adolf

Hitler. Whatever about birth control and family planning, the fact remains that she and Hitler and countless others in the 30s were in harmony when it came to the subject of forced sterilization. Today, though silent, others still wish that it be so.

THIRTY-SEVEN

It was hard to believe that a commercial plane on a short flight within Britain could vanish. No aircraft had been reported missing anywhere in the world the day Man Air Flight 666 went missing. It was a riddle with no apparent answer, theories abounded but no one had a clue.

Except for the fellow from Wales, a Mr. Joe Williams, who may have heard chatter at very high frequency on one of the meter bands and James Jones across the Atlantic at Montauk Point who amazingly did hear talk between the plane's pilot and a woman, no one had heard a thing on their radio. And no one had taken the Jones claim seriously.

Not one US or British TV or radio news outlet had contacted Jones. Although it was possible to hear pilot chatter at high frequency, they felt it impossible on the VHF channel from a distance of 3,000 miles and at ground level to boot. What Williams may have heard was hampered by interference - what Jones heard was crackly but clearer.

Only a provincial paper from West Hampton, Long Island carried the Jones story, and they had only spoken to Jones on the phone. To *The West Hampton Echo*, the story was considered to be of mild local interest and used mostly to fill space.

Only the Real IRA knew where the hijacked plane intended to land. But they too were in the dark as to its fate and were keeping quiet. After they had split with the Provisional wing there was bad blood between them. Joyce O'Brady of the Real IRA, the one who spoke with the plane's pilot after Flight 666 was airborne had gone to ground, not even other members of the Real IRA knew where she was. She had slipped out of Ireland and was in America at the home of a US Senator whose grandparents were of Holy Cross extraction, a village in County Tipperary.

With her hand held scanner tuned to the 1082136 meter band from atop Cave Hill – one of the highest points in North Belfast – it was 11.50 a.m. when she heard from her hijacker colleague calling from the Saab-Fairchild. Unlike the rain and mist that covered the North Channel, western and central England and parts of Scotland, the weather was clear in Northern Ireland all the way north to the islands of the Outer Hebrides near the Scottish west coast.

O'Brady had radioed the words, "Clear from here to Horsehead, Clear, Clear." There was no such place as Horsehead. It was 'code' for the secret place where the plane was to land.

The civil aviation authorities were stymied and the media were asking questions of anyone who might shed light on the mystery. The fact that former US Vice-President Swail was on the missing plane and two other Americans made the story juicy for the media.

The American TV networks, the BBC, ITV and newspapers had sent reporters to the Isle of Man to interview relatives of Swail. They were also hunting for relatives or friends of the other passengers and had descended on the Moores as well as the McClendon's relatives in Yorkshire.

High above German targets in World War Two, with bullets and shrapnel hitting his bomber, young Dennis McClendon had survived fifty-eight missions without a scratch. Now, at the ages of sixty-seven, he and his wife were missing on a flight within Britain.

When the TV and the press interviewed the Moores Neptune was not at home. Heather had left him with the von Schneiders. Having been at the centre of attention when he helped save the elderly sisters, Peter and Heather were hoping the press would not recall the event and concentrate on the issue at hand and the two passengers on the plane that had been their guests.

Fortunately the media were so focussed on the story of the missing plane that they forgot Neptune's heroics of the year earlier. Had they made the link life for the Moores would have been unbearable, there was no telling what slant they would put on the story if they realized that two of the passengers on the missing plane had been visiting the home of the celebrated

Neptune. It was not beyond them to embellish a story to boost viewer ratings or sell more papers by adding a layer of intrigue to an already baffling story.

After weeks of investigation and speculations as well as television and newspaper coverage, no one had any idea what had happed to the plane and that a splinter group of the Provisional IRA had been involved in its disappearance. This possibility was an amazing oversight because rebels from southern and northern Ireland were at war with Britain.

Flight 666 was at the bottom of the North Channel and no one had an inkling it was there – no one, except the crew of a Russian nuclear submarine that heard it slam into the water. The vessel was in British waters close to Scotland and should not have been there. Its mission had been to snoop on the movements of an American nuclear submarine base on the west coast of Scotland.

Taking advantage of the mist to surface for a bit of exercise, the crew heard the sound of a plane in its vicinity that was in trouble; its engines were stuttering. No one on the sub saw the plane crash, but they heard it smash into the water not far from where they were, at which point the sub dove and headed north.

Fearful of a diplomatic incident that would expose the presence of one of their subs in British waters where it should not have been, the Kremlin never reported the matter.

THIRTY-EIGHT

1943 was Hitler's Annus Horribilis. All the signs of what lay ahead were there by the end of 1942. Gone was his 'letter-in-a-bottle' fantasy to scare America into neutrality. The Jesuit Ralph Hatton had returned it to the Atlantic and now, in early 1943 it was still drifting between Nova Scotia and Newfoundland,

Hitler's 54th birthday was in April. To celebrate the occasion Bomber Harris organized a party with lots of fireworks by blitzing Berlin and other cities. It did not overjoy the Fuehrer, 1943 was becoming a very nasty nightmare. Hell was raining down on the master race with only the heavily guarded little limping Goebbels out in the streets to reassure the public.

Harris and the US Air Force had not forgotten Churchill's words that they should *light a fire in the belly of the enemy and burn his black heart out*. The RAF 25th anniversary was also in April. To mark the occasion they gave Churchill wings to pin on his chest. In response Winston urged his airmen to *carry on bringing doom to the tyrants*. The RAF obliged by dropping 'blockbuster bombs' on Stuttgart and smashing its factories.

With the situation grave in North Africa, Hitler met with Mussolini to see how their fortunes could be reversed. It was a waste of time. Having pulled troops out of Tunis, the Allies would soon enter the city to the acclaim of its people.

With the threat of invasion now lifted, church bells rang throughout Britain. Churchill told a delighted House of Commons:

Church bells can now be rung on Sundays and other days to summon worshipers to church. Every peel of the bells was a stinging slap across the face of Hitler, Goering and the Luftwaffe.

Black smoke hung over the Warsaw ghetto as the slaughter of Jews continued. General Juergen Stroop, a cold-blooded SS officer had been sent to crush an uprising. He recruited troops from local garrisons and sent them into the enclave as if ready to face an Army.

When the gates of the ghetto were thrown open allowing troops in, the sight was of soldiers standing guard, while beyond the fire-blackened houses, the rattle of machine gun fire was joined by a great explosion. What followed was the crash of dynamite, the rush of dust and smoke and the rubble of a building crumbling. More soldiers appeared in trucks wearing dark goggles, they were mostly Ukrainians from the Soviet Army that had switched sides. Those captured by the Allies and returned to Russia after the war were not greeted warmly by Stalin.

Himmler promised Stroop that if the Jews were dealt with swiftly, honours would be given to those taking part. Stroop said that the matter would soon be settled.

When the Nazis set up the Warsaw ghetto in 1940, the Jewish population was 300,000. After two years most had died of starvation or been sent to death camps. In May 1943, not even the Germans knew how many remained. Jews had been dying every day, dropping in their tracks, their bodies being tossed in heaps onto trucks. Of the original number only 60,000 remained, but these were gritty Jews who had acquired guns and were standing up to the brute strength of Stroop's troopers.

Jittery soldiers were pointing to the high ghetto wall topped with broken glass and barbed wire. They were calling to one another about those that were there fighting back. It was thought that these raggedy few would go quietly as scores had gone before them - but not these Jews. As the troops advanced through the warren of gutted buildings, dynamiting and killing, the Jews retreated into the sewers.

Stroop's task was proving harder that he thought. How could it be that these sub-humans could be so troublesome? His solution was to flood the sewers and drown them like rats. After this incident Goebbels said that it was time for every single Jew to be sent to death camps.

Just as the pot calls the kettle black, the Warsaw killers were accusing the Russians of murder. In April a Germany Army unit had found a mass grave of 4,000 Polish officers in a forest near the Soviet city of Smolensk; they insisted that the Russians had killed them.

The discovery was causing friction between the Russians and the exiled Polish Government in London, as well as between Stalin and the Allies. The murdered Poles had been among 15,000 officers taken prisoner in 1939 by the Reds after they and Hitler had carved up Poland. The exiled Poles had been asking the Russian government questions about the fate of their officers to which no answers were coming. With Nazi war crimes escalating, Hitler's men did not want what happened to the Polish officers added to their own war crimes.

As 1943 progressed, more nails were being driven into the coffin of the Third Right and its Axis partners. In the Pacific the sun was sinking on Japan's killers thanks to relentless US force. In May a Japanese sub had torpedoed a clearly marked hospital ship with the loss of 300 lives - their war crimes were also escalating.

With US bombers now attacking Sicily, Italian airfields and German held Sardinia, in southern Italy a state of emergency was declared amid fears of an Allied invasion. Another state of emergency had been issued in Germany's Ruhr area following the RAF's 'Dambuster' raid. Walls of water had swept down the Ruhr and Eder valleys sweeping everything before it after the planes had attacked and breached two huge dams. Lancaster bombers had used 'bouncing bombs' designed to penetrate the dams.

Flying sixty feet above the water at 240 mph, Lancaster bombers had dropped barrel-shaped bombs that skimmed over the surface of the water before sinking and then exploding at the foot of the dams. The result was a flood of water that swept through Mulheim swamping coalmines and ironworks. People had to flee to high ground or drown. The banks of the river Ruhr had broken, one flood stretching for miles and crashing through the industrial city of Dortmund, filling its air raid shelters and causing huge damage. The bomb had been the brainchild of the British scientist Barns Wallace.

Irritated to the point of near madness, Churchill – again on the move – was causing Hitler more grief. In May he had made another historic speech to the US Congress. Broadcast on radio and speaking with his easy style, Churchill had delivered yet another masterpiece. While he spoke bells pealed in St. Paul's in London as King George VI led the nation in thanks for the Allied victory in Tunisia.

Churchill had been introduced to the Congress by the speaker of the House who said, *He was one of the great figures of our time,* a description that upset Hitler and Japan's warlords greatly. Churchill said to the Congress:

We will wage war at your side against Japan while there is breath in our bodies and while blood flows in our veins. He pledged help to reduce Japanese cities to ashes. The speech brought such cheers that it enraged Hitler. After the speech an angry Roosevelt castigated the media for indulging in dangerous speculation; they were asking how Winston had travelled to Washington.

In 1943 Hitler's Navy was productive up to June. U-Boats were sinking allied vessels in the Atlantic, the North Sea, the Mediterranean as well as in the waters north of eastern Europe. They were also prowling off the east coast of America and the southern states of Florida, Louisiana and Texas, but the war at sea was getting costly, of the 1,150 subs built, U-Boats were now being lost at an alarming rate.

Early in the war the German High Command said that if 800,000 tons of Allied shipping could be sunk monthly, the war against the Axis would fail. In 1942 the U-Boats had kept up a crippling series of attacks on merchant ships, claiming more than 650 tons a month. Up to March they had sunk over 600,000 tons in the Atlantic. It was their last productive month. By late May the tonnage had been reduced greatly, many subs were being lost in battle and by other means. This reversal was due to escort ships and aircraft carriers previously used in North Africa. When sent to the Atlantic it was the first time the Allies had planes capable of hunting U-Boats. Prior to this, the subs had feasted at will.

New devices like a radar system that detected smaller objects were now spotting U-Boats. There were also depth charges that exploded at shallow depths and a mortar system that fired twenty-four bombs around a sub all at once. In a convoy attack in May, eight U-Boats had been lost off the coast of Greenland, an area once deadly for Allied shipping and lethal years later for the fisherman Carl Erickson.

The change in fortunes was affecting U-Boat crews. Much to Hitler's ire, fewer and fewer subs were now venturing into the Atlantic. The tide had turned in the U-Boat war; subs were withdrawing from the Atlantic to prepare for the invasion of Europe.

By June Allied troops had occupied the fortress on the island of Pantelleria using a tactic new to modern warfare. It was the first time a fortress had been conquered from the air without the forceful use of troops. Situated between Tunisia and Sicily, Pantelleria had been bombed for thirteen straight days. Less than an hour after British troops landed on the island the garrison surrendered.

By early July the first Allied troops had landed in Sicily along a wide front and captured Augusta and Ragusa, they had also landed near Catania. With the Allies storming into southern Italy, Hitler travelled to the north of Italy to again meet with Mussolini. In the meantime the RAF was bombing Hamburg savagely.

It was all coming apart for Hitler. The greatest tank battle in history on the flatlands south of Moscow had resulted in a smashing defeat for his army. It started in July when he threw his best divisions into a pincer attack aimed at biting off a bulge in the Russian line at Kursk. Badly in need of a victory after his disaster at Stalingrad, Hitler had predicted great things from this offensive: *It will shine like a beacon around the world.* It failed – the Red Army was waiting.

Fighting had been fierce. The summer sky was stained by columns of smoke rising from hundreds of burning tanks and aircraft, villages had been torn apart by shellfire. Aircraft from both sides had been roaming above the field of battle. Ordered by Stalin to 'bleed the enemy white', the Red Army were doing just that. Hitler had no choice but to call a cease-fire.

In the Pacific at July's end the Americans and Japanese had clashed near the island of Bougainville. By now Palermo had fallen. In a thrust to the north from the south of Sicily US troops had overwhelmed the city trapping Axis soldiers who now had to give up or die; they were on the run all across the island. The assault had been so swift that no time remained to demolish dock and railhead facilities. The victory had deprived the Germans of ' a tactical base for subs on the Mediterranean. It also gave the Allies access to a new airfield from which planes could strike German and Italian points behind enemy lines.

Sick of Mussolini and a war few Italians wanted, El Duce's downfall was inevitable. After twenty-one years of dictatorship he was now in jail with only a nicer looking Rome and trains that ran on time to his credit. The bombastic, sex-crazed poser was all but finished. King Victor Emmanuel had taken command of the military and Marshal Bodoglio – an anti-fascist – was now Prime Minister and Chief of the Government.

The news broadcast by Rome Radio on the 25th of July came when Italian troops in Sicily were giving up in droves; the invasion of the country was poised to begin. The King and Bodoglio had appealed to the populist for loyalty saying that the war would go on. The reality is that Italy's surrender was near. Mussolini had made no public appearances for weeks. News of his downfall had not come as a surprise given the appeals for help he had been making to Hitler.

His fate was sealed when US bombers rained tons of explosives on Rome in a daylight raid that killed 1,000 people; the city shook as bombs blasted rail yards, airfields, factories and government buildings. Under strict orders the Vatican and historical buildings had not been struck.

A journalist who toured the city after the bombing said: *All the well-known streets and squares look as peaceful as ever, but around the US targets fires are still raging, the dead are being dragged from under the ruins.*

After freeing Italy's political prisoners General Eisenhower offered Italy peace with honour if it severed links with Germany.

In August everything continued to unwind for Hitler. Bombers had hit Axis oil fields at Ploesti, the Allies had broken through in Sicily, the Soviets had retaken more towns, a million people had been evacuated from Berlin, Rome and Messina had been bombed again, the Germans had quit Kharkov, the Red Army were advancing into the Ukraine and Winston Spencer

Churchill, Hitler's sixty-nine year-old Rambo nightmare, once more on the move, had arrived in Quebec for talks with Roosevelt and Canadian premier Mackenzie King.

In addition to all this, British and US bombers had virtually obliterated Hamburg. In one week alone seven square miles of Germany's second city had been reduced to rubble including its shipyards and factories - U-Boats had been smashed on their slipways.

Nor had the onslaught on Nazism ended in August. The RAF had blitzed the rocket development site at Peenemunde. Some 800 staff, most of them foreign POW's had been killed. The Baltic Sea raid had been so severe that the entire operation was moved underground.

No let-up in September. The Allies had landed near Messina. A vital point at the toe of Italy had been captured and German troops were now clashing with the Allies near Naples. The heel of Italy had also been taken, German forces were now retreating from Salerno as the Allies joined forces across southern Italy and entered Naples. Italy was crumbling.

Hitler was taken by surprise in September when Italy surrendered. Before the news broke Berlin radio was reporting resistance by Italian and German troops to the invasion of southern Italy. Adding to Hitler's miseries, schizophrenic Italian units were now switching sides in the Balkans and joining Tito's partisans in Yugoslavia.

Hitler's mind was on Europe's Italian underbelly through which Allied forces could strike into Europe and join with the Soviets who now were near Kiev.

With Italy unravelling and Mussolini in jail, in order to save face, Hitler went to his aid and announced: *Parachutists and the SS today carried out an operation for the liberation of Mussolini. He is now at liberty.* This was the first news of El Duce since his resignation. No details had been given as to how his rescue had been carried out - he had been jailed in a mountain stronghold north of Italy. One of the self-appointed glider commando rescue team sent to free Mussolini was the tall, scar-faced SS Colonel Otto Skorzeny, an unashamed egoistic self-publicist.

Hitler's horrible year continued. The Red Army's rapid advance was crowned with the capture of Smolensk, where the Blitzkrieg of 1941 first ran into trouble. The Russians had liberated a large territory since the huge tank battle around Kursk in July. A series of strikes on German lines had led to the recapture of many cities as well as the rail junction on the east bank of the River Dnieper.

In October the same dismal story continued for all the Axis forces. If the Germans or Japanese had a victory it was brief, the Allies responded like wolves.

Early in October U-Boats had returned to base after sinking few ships in the Atlantic. Corsica had fallen to the French Resistance and in Rome German troops were looting the city of art ahead of the advancing Allies. In Russia the Red Army had mounted new attacks on German positions along the River Dnieper.

In the Arctic the British had sunk the battleship Tirpitz in an amazing luck-filled raid in which no Lancaster bombers were lost. In the Atlantic the Allies had used the new midget submarine and also landed on the Portuguese Azores. In Italy they were breaking through more defences and had carried out air strikes from Italian soil. And in a move that concentrated the Nazi leadership's minds, a War Crimes Commission had been created.

By the end of October the Red Army had crossed the River Dnieper and in places broken the German's 1,300-mile defences. Key positions had been captured but the Germans still held Crimea. In November Kiev fell, the Allies had seized a position leading to Rome, 60 U-Boats had been destroyed and Allied bombers were now engaged in precision night bombings.

Events were moving at a rapid pace. The Gilbert Islands had fallen to the Allies and in November a secret and historic conference had been held in Cairo between Churchill, Roosevelt and Chiang Kai-shek. It was the first time the Chinese leader had joined the British and US heads of state. The top items on the agenda were the war against Japan and post-war aims. Her unconditional surrender and the stripping of territories taken by force was resolved.

Three days later, Churchill, Roosevelt and Stalin met in Tehran. Their aim was to agree on plans for the defeat of Germany and a clear declaration of post-war aims that would rid the world of tyrants like Hitler. Stalin, a monster himself, was assured that the invasion of France was set for 1944. Service chiefs and Allied leaders discussed plans with their Russian counterparts in order to co-ordinate efforts that would squeeze German forces from all sides.

From the outset Stalin made it clear that not only would Germany have to be carved up, but that border adjustments must be favourable to Russia. Neither Churchill nor Roosevelt argued the matter; they hoped to soften him with drink at a social event in the next few days. When the gathering took place the Russian leader arrived in a prickly mood surrounded by huge bodyguards with machine guns. Stalin's face was like thunder.

At the end of November Bomber Harris said: *Berlin will be bombed until the heart of Nazi Germany ceases to beat.*

In December Churchill, Roosevelt and Stalin, the first two with Jewish blood, the third a thug who had robbed to help finance the Jewish heartbeats behind the Bolshevik Revelation continued to burn into Hitler's guts.

The invasion of Western Europe would soon begin. Germany and Japan were doomed, what the leaders of these countries hoped to gain by continuing the conflict other than killing more people is a mystery.

Now back in Cairo from Tehran, Churchill and Roosevelt met with the president of Turkey for talks about closer ties. A few days later, Roosevelt, the sixty year-old New York aristocrat in a wheelchair with the heart of a lion and iron on his legs was in Malta.

In London the government gave notice that the list of war criminals and collaborators numbered in the thousands; they warned that crimes would be paid for. Hitler heard this loud and clear. Here and there the retreating Germans were making a stand in Italy but it meant little at this point.

What did have meaning was the choice of General Dwight D. Eisenhower as supreme commander of the Allies' invasion forces of Western Europe. The Texas-born West Point graduate with Jewish blood had never heard a shot fired in anger nor held a field command until he led the invasion of French North Africa the year before.

President Roosevelt, who praised Eisenhower's work in North Africa announced the appointment. The General had shown a gift for getting senior Allied officers to work together and this was a factor in his surprise choice. His field commander would be General Montgomery, the self-assured strategist who some feared might not get on with the Yanks. He and Eisenhower had been recalled to Britain to begin planning the Normandy invasion with Air Chief Marshal Sir Arthur Tedder, Eisenhower's deputy.

Where was Hitler's black bottle now? In six months it had hardly moved more than a few miles; it was still bobbing in the waters of the North Atlantic nearer to Newfoundland.

On a night in early 1943, U-Boat number 666 had skimmed the bottle in the process of surfacing. A week later the sub had vanished off the west coast of Ireland with a crew of fifty-one and without a trace. Its captain was Herbert Engel, the craft had not been involved in battle at the time. Like the also vanished Saab-Fairchild with the flight number 666, its fate would always remain a mystery.

Hitler's Annus Horribilis had ended but it was not the finish of killings by Nazism, his mind was indeed the devil's playground. But not all Germans believed in Hitler. Some despised him and were chivalrous.

THIRTY-NINE

Sophie and Hans Scholl knew of the death-camps and despaired at the killing of Jews and Nazi anti-democratic behaviour. The siblings were beheaded for their beliefs as were others who yearned for freedom. Their courage is unknown to most non-Germans.

There is, however, a tale of chivalry that recently came to light, the story of a German pilot who refused to shoot down a crippled American bomber and helped it to safety. This humane act came from twenty-eight year-old Oberleutnant Franz Stigler. The event took place on the freezing, overcast morning of December 20, 1943 at a time when German pilots were killing and being killed, a period in which Hitler knew the war was nearly lost and was lashing out at his generals and everyone around him.

Second Lieutenant Charles S. Brown was about to embark on his first bombing mission from England as commander of a B-17 which was part of the 379th Bomb Group. The target was a factory in Bremen. At twenty-one Brown was older than most of his crew. What he and his men did not know that morning was that they were soon to take part in a unique adventure that for years would remain shrouded in secrecy and mystery.

Charles guided 'Ye Old Pub', his ship's nickname, behind other B-17s and was soon airborne from his Cambridgeshire airbase. On reaching the target the bombers began their raid at 28,000 feet. As they flew in and out of cloud the flack increased but before dropping its bombs Brown's plane was hit. The blast shattered the Plexiglas nose, knocked out number two engine and damaged the aircraft's controls.

Ye Old Pub was in trouble – rattling and shaking. Unable to keep up with the group it was quickly a straggler vulnerable to attack from enemy planes. Swiftly, seemingly from nowhere, about a dozen Messerschmitt 109s appeared and attacked hitting

191

the number three engine which was now almost powerless. With hydraulic and electrical systems no longer of use, Brown struggled to keep his aircraft in the air, his controls were so badly damaged that they were only partly responsive.

The bomber's eleven guns were reduced by flack damage to top turret guns and one forward-firing nose gun. The tail gunner was dead and all but one of the crew was wounded. Brown had a bullet in his right shoulder.

Faced with these problems and the slim chance of survival, Brown took to the offensive. Each time the attackers approached he would turn his bomber into them, attempting to disrupt their aim with what remained of his guns. At one point he reversed into a steep turn and became inverted – Ye Old Pub was upside down.

Starved of oxygen by the inversion, Brown lost consciousness. When he came to his B-17 was right side up and level at 10,000 feet and though dazed, he started a slow climb using his one good engine. He considered the alternatives. With men seriously injured, he rejected bailing out or a crash landing. The only other option was the slight chance of reaching his Kimbolton base in Cambridgeshire.

As he struggled to guide his crippled bomber towards England, he looked out of his right window and suddenly felt doomed. Flying near his right wing was a Messerschmitt 109, it had Ye Old Pub at its mercy, a burst of fire would have sent him and his crew to their deaths. But this was not to be - a prince among bandits had appeared. The enemy pilot waved at him and smiled; he then flew across the B-17s nose and motioned to Brown to land in Germany, which Brown refused to do.

Charles grew increasingly nervous as the enemy fighter escorted him for several miles out over the North Sea. Then, unexpectedly, the Luftwaffe pilot saluted, rolled his plane over and flew away. Charles could not believe what had happened and it would be years before he knew the answer to the haunting question: why had the German pilot not shot him down – why had he acted so gallantly?

Charles made it across the North Sea and landed near the English coast. He and those in his crew who were able were debriefed about what had happened on the mission. After the affair with the Messerschmitt had been reported, Ye Old Pub's mission was classified 'secret'.

On that day in December 1943 there was good reasons why Stigler should have shot down the bomber. He had already downed two bombers and needed one more to earn a Knight's Cross; he was also taking a risk in letting the B-17 escape, it could have led to his court-martial or execution. Years later Stigler admitted that these thoughts had crossed his mind but he could not shoot down a damaged aircraft that was trying to get home with its wounded crew. He said; *It was the most heavily damaged aircraft I ever saw that was still flying, I could see the injured men aboard and thought to myself I cannot kill these half-dead men.*

Stigler accompanied the bomber some distance over the North Sea towards England. He then saluted Brown and turned away, a merciful act greatly at odds with the evils of Nazism, he was no Bloodthirsty Guttersnipe.

When he landed Stigler reported that the bomber had been shot down over the sea and he kept the secret of what really happened for years. Brown and his crew were ordered never to discuss the incident.

Charles completed his combat tour and retuned to America where, after the war, he finished college. He would later accept a commission in the Air Force where he served with the office of Special Investigations, but the episode of his encounter with the Messerschmitt remained embedded in his memory.

In 1986 he began a search for the anonymous pilot to whom he and the remaining members of his crew owed their lives. Four years later Franz Stigler, who by then was living in Canada, responded to a notice about the famous encounter published in a newsletter aimed at former German fighter pilots. He compared the time, place and aircraft markings and it proved that it was he who had spared Brown and his crew. The two men met when Charles, who lived in Seattle, Washington, tracked Stigler down to the town of Surrey in British Colombia. Stigler was still flying a Messerschmitt 109 at air shows.

When they met Stigler gave Brown a huge hug. Charles replied by calling him 'big brother'. *It was a touching sight and everyone was moved to tears,* said Stigler's wife Helga. It transpired that the two men had been living fewer than 200 miles apart for many years.

Following their reunion they remained friends and met almost yearly until Stigler's death in March 2008 at the age of ninety-three. Charles died later that year aged eighty-four.

Stigler's act of chivalry was belatedly recognized and honoured by many American military organizations. Charles, however, was never decorated for his part in that day's events and his Bomb Group never reported the incident up the chain of command. It would be many years before Ye Old Pub's story would finally be known.

FORTY

Anger swept through Britain and America in January in 1944. They both denounced Japan's brutality and inhumanity. Almost 1,800 men on a ship torpedoed by the Japanese were left to drown and thousands of war prisoners in their clutches had died on forced marches in the Philippines.

Captured at the fall of Bataan and Corregidor, the Americans were tortured, starved and murdered. Escaped prisoners had signed sworn statements citing acts of Japanese brutality, crimes that were hard to believe.

The cancer of Nazism continued to spread. In January 1944 after General Eisenhower had been appointed Supreme Commander of Allied forces in Europe, Hitler's inhumanity continued, the purification of the Aryan race was being stepped up. The idea came from Martin Bormann, Hitler's personal secretary for whom an example of human perfection was an SS officer. He was pouring moral convention into a sewer of depravity by encouraging chosen unmarried women to bear the children of the Nordic elite. Lebensborn – *The Fountain of Life Society* – would look after the pregnant women and rear the children. The plan was to house 10,000 such children in specially selected homes. Thousands of Aryan-looking offspring had already been stolen from the arms of mothers in occupied countries to be raised as Germans.

The invasion of Europe was imminent, in four years Hitler's fortunes had declined greatly. His plans for Britain had been well laid out. In 1940 he could see it all ahead of him: Blackpool would be his holiday paradise, a playground for his troops. Other landmarks would also feature in the 'Occupied England' of his dreams.

Operation Sea Lion, the plan for the invasion was prepared by Spy Chief Walter Schulenburg, its details gleaned from British guidebooks, pamphlets, government publications and spies.

Having conquered France, Operation Sea Lion would begin after the Luftwaffe had bombed Britain's railroad and manufacturing infrastructure and broken the moral of its people and government. Blackpool, Blackpool, Blackpool, in 1940 the town was often in Hitler's thoughts.

The image was delicious, a huge swastika flag flapping from the top of Blackpool Tower and troops marching along the resort's Golden Mile with him at the head in his six-wheeled G-4 Mercedes, his face ruddy from the wind that swept in from the Irish Sea. Along the route more troops and flags would be on view and a large military band would be playing the Nazi anthem, Deutschland, Deutschland Uber Alles. This day would be an immense triumph, he could see it all in his mind's eye.

He had ordered the protection of Blackpool and its Tower and planned to use the town as a recreation area for his troops. His invasion would see columns of soldiers along the coastline after parachuting into Stanley Park; its Italian Gardens and compass sheered pathways would serve nicely for his paratroopers to aim for. He had visited Blackpool in 1913 when staying with his half-brother in Liverpool. Over the years the town had grown in his mind as an ideal place for recreation, the type of town he had always been drawn to and planned to create more of in Germany. He adored the splendid architecture of Blackpool's three 19th century piers.

Whenever Hitler's thought about Blackpool so too did he think of his half-brother Alois Hitler Jr. and his distasteful family. Up to the point that Alois left Britain for Germany and was divorced by his spouse for violence and abandonment, Alois had lived in Liverpool with his Irish wife Bridget. Their son William Patrick claimed to hate his uncle Adolf but he and his mother were not averse to writing about him for money.

At the age of eighteen William Patrick had gone to Germany to sponge off his uncle but things did not worked out for him.

Under pressure from the Nazi Party when he tried to blackmail Adolf with false claims that his uncle had Jewish blood, he had fled Germany. In 1939 he and his mother had left for New York on a lecture tour about his uncle who by then was the chancellor of Germany. All these treacherous acts from Alois's family would surface whenever Hitler though about Blackpool.

Hitler believed in promoting invigorating health programmes in Blackpool where soldiers could rent rooms and homes close to the sea. Blackpool, with its bracing climate had been designed as a holiday centre for the mill workers of Lancashire. This link with the 'working class' attracted Hitler. The town's appeal was its hotels and bed and breakfast facilities. Its pubs and bars would suit his off-duty troops nicely.

The plan to invade Britain was based largely on reports sent by spies before the war. They provided pictures and maps of towns which, like Blackpool would not be bombed. Among other places not to be raided was Oxford which Hitler planned to make the capital of his conquest; he had long admired the beauty of Oxford's colleges and did not want them destroyed. He also greatly admired the academic traditions of its universities.

Northampton too would not be bombed, it would be his northernmost outpost after Britain's invasion. In 1940 the Nazis had devised a plan to land forces on the south coast. They expected to take major towns and cities as far north as Northampton, at which point they were certain Britain would surrender. Another headquarters would be the Shropshire town of Bridgnorth, it would be a strategic site close to the 'geographical centre' of England. All the plans for the conquest of Britain were in a 'Black Book'.

Albert Speer, Hitler's architect, a highly committed conservationist was determined that no one should touch Bridgnorth's High Street. He was captivated by the old shops and considered the Town Hall a jewel of architecture; he said that the Fuehrer had no wish to destroy beauty.

Not only was the 'Black Book' a profile of British institutions, including details of the British way of life and culture, it also held a list of nearly 3,000 'undesirables' to be done away with as soon as German forces had landed. Among them was Winston

Churchill, Virginia Woolf, Noel Coward, H. G Wells, Lord Baden-Powell, Lord Beaverbrook, Sylvia Pankhurst, the list went on and on.

Of special interest to spy chief Schulenburg was education and Britain's elite private schools such as Eaton. To have attended one is the pride of any Englishman, he said. Under the Nazis the school would be turned into a 'Hitler Youth Educational Centre'.

Schulenburg was suspicious of the British Boy Scout Movement considering it a disguised instrument of power under the command of British intelligence. He believed that they, together with the Freemasons, would provide the basis for a movement of resistance to be done away with.

After securing victory, Hitler planned to stand on the balcony of Buckingham Palace and savour the moment as he gazed up along the Mall right up to Admiralty Arch. His aim was to dismantle Nelson's Column and ship it to Berlin where it would be re-erected close to the Brandenburg Gate. He knew it was a symbol of British Naval power and world domination; its capture would be one of his best trophies. This may account why Nelson's Column remained intact despite all the bombing in the vicinity of Trafalgar Square.

Had Hitler fulfilled his dream and taken over Buckingham palace, he would have found it empty. The Royal family would have exiled themselves to Canada, Bermuda or America. Nor would he have been able to grace his head with the crown of England. Along with Britain's gold reserve, the crown jewels were stored in a vault under the Montreal office of the Sun Life Assurance Company.

Churchill, however, had vowed to remain in London at 10 Downing Street, pistol primed and ready, his bodyguard Walter Thompson watching his back. He was determined to go down fighting, he was quite clear on the matter: *At least I can take a few of them with me,* said Churchill.

In early 1940, when Hitler's dream of conquering Britain was about to be realised, the country was not prepared for invasion. It was May when the Chiefs of Staff started taking the threat seriously. The Home Guard was not marshalled until then and most of the needed concrete anti-tank pillboxes had not been built or started.

Many felt that Britain stood no chance if Hitler invaded and isolationist America seemed not to care. Joseph P. Kennedy, JFK's father, then US ambassador to Britain and a hater of the country said that Britain would be defeated and that Hitler should not be trusted. In a letter to President Roosevelt he said – *Britain is appallingly weak and the people haven't a chance. The belief is that Hitler will be in London by the middle of August. All the plans for the defence of Britain will not amount to a tinker's damn.*

It takes little imagination to guess what attracted Hitler to Blackpool, it was its vulgarity. One need only look at the blueprints for his redesigned, gaudy-looking new Berlin. Blackpool was without question the vulgarity capital of Britain, perhaps of all Europe.

Hitler liked the pointless Blackpool Tower, with its theatre organ rising through the ballroom floor. He could imagine it playing *Horst Wessel Lied*. He would have loved the illuminated trams trundling along the seafront as far as Fleetwood and back; he might well have ordered a fleet of similar trams for his own use. No doubt an underling would have told him about the obscure single-track that winds its way through the back streets, a good escape route in case of attack.

His dream of conquering Britain was not realized and as the weeks passed in early 1944 the invasion of Europe drew closer - would it be at Calais or Normandy? And would his Atlantic Wall of concrete and steel help stop the Allies? That was the question. German spies were beavering away trying to discover the location of the thrust while the Allies were using every device to cause them to alter their defences from Normandy to Calais.

While German spies and intelligence were searching for an answer, General Eisenhower was struggling with a problem. How to keep secret the tragedy in Lyme Bay on Slapton Sands, Devon during 'Operation Tiger', a mock military exercise. Due to a series of errors, on April 27th 1944, more than 800 American soldiers practicing a landing in preparation for D-Day had been killed when German torpedo boats attacked tank-carrying vessels filled with soldiers heading for a beach. Ten times more American young men were killed in England that day than would perish on Utah Beach on June 6th. The US Public and kin of the soldiers who perished would know nothing of the tragedy for years.

FORTY-ONE

Neptune had been very disobedient since the disappearance of Flight 666. He was irritable, his posture sagged, his tail was limp and his intake of food had diminished. A visit to the vet proved inconclusive, something was wrong but no one knew what it was.

The impulses coming from Hitler's bottle were upsetting him even though he knew nothing of the man's life, and he had not gone near the living room since the Saab-Fairchild had gone missing. He was out of sorts, not the dog everyone knew and loved. Another visit to the vet gave no real clue to Neptune's disposition. He didn't have a temperature or infection but it was obvious that something was stressing the animal and for this an 'Adaptil' collar was prescribed that gave off a calming scent.

On several occasions he had stayed out all night, something he had never done before. And it wasn't that he was dating, he simply wanted no part of Avoca. He seemed to know that the death of Otto and the disappearance of the plane were linked with the bottle; in truth he was Hitler's chosen telepathic channel, his conduit, his supernatural top frequency meter band. There was something paranormal and unearthly about it akin to the occult driven Medieval Church that was mysterious, weird and not of this world.

Neptune knew how the mood at home had changed since his American friends had gone missing, how distraught his owners had become, how they were always on the phone and attentive to the latest news reports; how nothing was as it was before he found the bottle.

In the cross-fire of events the last thing on the mind of Peter and Heather was what to do with Hitler's bottle, it had gone out of their heads, it was now insignificant in lights of their friend's fate. But Neptune knew - he knew the link between the bottle and the grief unfolding and he tried to convey it.

On more than one occasion he had stood outside Avoca and barked until Peter or Heather or both appeared. Then he would bark again and run off, stop, turn and bark again as if to say *Follow me, get away from that bottle, there is danger there, follow me.* But he had failed, his owners had not made the connection his super senses had made.

Two weeks had passed since the Saab-Fairchild had gone missing and Neptune's strange behaviour persisted. It was worrying his owners and making them jumpy, Neptune was getting aggressive. On one occasion he had shown his teeth. There were other unusual things too, he had not checked on the von Schneiders or others on his daily rounds, nor had anyone seen him near the lighthouse and beach.

Since the plane had vanished and despite searches of the Irish Sea, nothing had been found of the aircraft, no wreckage or personal belongings. No plane crash had taken place on the British mainland nor in any country within range of the aircraft's fuel capacity. It was a riddle of high magnitude, in fact nowhere in the world had an aircraft been reported missing on the day in question.

Neptune had quit Avoca; there was no sign of him and the Moores were worried. They had informed everyone and made up posters with his photo for display around the island. His normal dog collar gave his name and phone number so Peter and Heather were hopeful someone would call with news. His 'Adaptil' collar gave off a scent to help reduce his stress level; Heather had neglected to remove his normal collar and was now glad she had not.

A week went by and still no sign of Neptune, he had vanished like the Saab-Fairchild and The Lady Be Good. No one on the Isle of Man had seen him.

One morning at nine a.m. the Moores' phone rang and Peter answered. The call was from Lieutenant Colonel John Smithwaith, the commanding officer of the Cheshire Regiment posted in Northern Ireland. The night before, two of his soldiers on patrol in the Falls Road in West Belfast had come upon a starving, emaciated Neptune. Only the Labrador knew how he managed to get from the Isle of Man to the scary streets of West Belfast.

On a day of intermittent rain, Neptune had made his way south along the east coast of the island from Port Cranstal to Douglas Bay from which ferries come and go to mainland Britain as well as to Southern and Northern Ireland. He had slipped aboard the Douglas to Belfast night ferry undetected.

FORTY-TWO

Hitler had no wish to conquer the world, but he did delve into spreading Nazism to a land whose resources could sustain life and provide living space for the Third Reich. Encouraged by Heinrich Himmler, in the 1930s this venture was a work in progress in a distant land of promise.

In 1938 the Nazis had been in power for five years and Hitler's eyes were on a far off colony as a potential breeding ground for the Reich he said would last a 1,000 years.

His book *Mein Kampf* spoke of 'Lebensraum', living space for Germans in Poland and Russia but Himmler's thinking reached further. He had already sent a geologist to the jungles of the Amazon to investigate and prepare the ground for a takeover of British and French possessions.

The twenty five-year old geologists with the iron name of Otto Schulz-Kampfhenkel was to send copious reports on the indigenous population of the Amazon. The aim was to enslave them for the German farmers Himmler would send to settle and plant Nazism in the rainforests of Brazil. The geologist had already sent a report with encouraging news saying that the two least populated but resource-rich areas were Siberia and South America, that both offered great, spacious immigration and settlement possibilities for Nordic people. Given that Siberia in the 1930s seemed likely to fall to China, he recommended colonising Amazonia because it offered vast exploration possibilities for the more advanced white races.

The geologist agreed with Nazi race purity. He said that the people of Amazonia could not be thought of in civilized terms, that he viewed the jungles of Brazil as a place where the 'higher white people' could breed to offset the threat of being swamped by 600 million Chinese.

He also said that with a million Germans already settled in Brazil, the seed was there for the expansion of the Third Reich, and that Germany could then stifle American influence in the region. His thesis clearly spoke to the issue of conquest and colonization of the rainforest.

It is no secret that after the war many Nazis fled to regions of South America and were helped by fascist governments, the basis of which were planted by German settlers in the 1930s, many of whom came to Brazil and spread Hitler's gospel. Help to those fleeing also came from within Germany.

Munich based Gudrun Burwitz, Heinrich Himmler's fanatical daughter who adored her father - now in her late eighties if still living - has dedicated her life to helping run a charity called Stille Hilfe (Silent Help) to shelter and finance Nazi war criminals from justice. Among those helped since 1946 are Adolf Eichmann and Josef Mengele who like many Nazis fled to Argentina and Brazil.

In recent years a graveyard of Nazis sent to create an Aryan outpost was discovered in a remote area of Brazil's Amazon Forest near the River Jary. A tall, wooden cross-decorated with swastikas was found carrying the inscription *Joseph Greiner died here on 2.1.1936 from fever in the service of German Research Work.* Other explorers who died for Hitler did so from similar tropical illnesses.

In researching the subject of Nazis in Brazil, the discovery of the grave was made by the author Jens Gluessing. Joseph Greiner was a member of the Schulz- Kampfhenkel team who arrived in 1935 charged with exploring the region bordering French Guiana; of interest also was the near-by British and Dutch colonies now known on Guyana and Suriname.

Ostensibly collecting specimens of fauna and wildlife, the explorers also produced a documentary film which they later played to cinema audiences in Germany. The true purpose of their mission of course was to send plans to Berlin for a future expeditionary corps that would land troops in Brazil.

The explorers had a Heinkel seaplane to test its performance in the humidity of the Amazon basin. In their eighteen months travelling through the steaming jungles they interacted well with the natives and played them German music on gramophones. In fact they despised the low-intellect of the natives that by contrast was so inferior to theirs.

As they made their way through the jungles they wrote their ideas for the colonising of the region. They visualized scores of German farmers travelling to settlements such as where Greiner died, spreading the Aryan race and using the locals as labour.

As the explorers moved closer to the British and French colonies their plans for military conquest began to formulate. From the aerial photographs they had taken, the maps of the rainforests they had drawn, and from their own research into the natives, a plan had developed for the establishment of a German stronghold in South America.

Ways to subdue tribes were thought through and chronicled. Schulz-Kampfhenkel felt that these 'wild men of the forests' would leave Germans free to conquer as long as they were allowed to retain their hunting grounds and given trinkets.

On the borders of Guyana and Suriname he made sketches of landing points where he thought troops could be unloaded secretly from U-Boats and where the river was still enough for seaplanes to land. When he returned to Berlin in 1937 he was a hero. Museums across Germany were eager to display the exotic flora and fauna he had brought back, he was also a rave on the academic lecture circuit talking about a world that in one of the most advanced societies on earth could scarcely be imagined. He wrote a book, which was translated into English in 1938 under the title: *Riddle Of Hell's Jungle.*

The document produced for Himmler was studied by an aid and deemed worthy of action - an immediate takeover of French and British interests in Amazonia and a large part of the northern Amazon basin was recommended to Hitler.

The aid posed a question in his report: *What do the people of Guyana mean to the Fuehrer?* He threw up the possibility of great mineral wealth – gold and diamonds – so abundant in quantity that in a few years all Germany's debts would be erased.

He spoke of German enterprise in taming nature, of harnessing the power of waterfalls, of building factories, roads and highway crossings and the re-birth of land where only jungle now existed. What German colonisation means, he said, *Is the takeover of French and British possessions, something our Fuehrer will be able to speak about and point to with pride.* He added that a marine base in Amazonia would threaten England's interest in South America should war come.

It was not until 1940 after Germany had over run Western Europe that The Project was studied in detail. By then Hitler and Himmler were busy with other matter; the Fuehrer's mind was on the invasion of Britain and Russia and Himmler's was fixed on setting up death camps. The Project was to be considered again later but it never was.

At the end of the war Schulz-Kampfhenkel was arrested and sent to a POW camp in Austria. He dies in 1989 still clutching to his dream of a German colony in the Amazon.

Dr Josef Mengele held the power of life and death in Auschwitz. As trains rolled in with Jews the first person they often saw was him directing streams of other Jews to the left and to the right. Twins were then separated from mothers and delivered to him. Given better food and forbidden to do hard work they were often not parted from their mothers. Mengele once killed fourteen pairs of twins by injecting chloroform into their hearts for the purpose of immediately dissecting their bodies for study. A lift of his finger could determine a person's fate. Now, years after his death, it appears that his Frankenstein work lives on.

With the Russians advancing in Poland, Mengele fled Auschwitz in 1945. Using a false name, after his arrest he slipped through the fingers of the Allies and hid in Bavaria and Italy. With help from Himmler's daughter he arrived in Argentina during 1949.

In central Brazil there is a small town called Candido Godoi. It's different from others towns because a fifth of all pregnancies result in twins with blond hair and blue eyes, not the norm in a country whose people descend from native Indians, Africans and southern Europeans.

The first such twins to be born in this town was in 1963, the year Candido Godoi was founded, the same year that Mengele's presence was first known in the town. Using the name Rudolph

Weiss, he had travelled the Brazilian region working as a medic who treated women.

After the war and during the flow of Nazis on the run to South America, Mengele chose the town as a place for experiments dealing with the study of genetics. Candido Godoi had important prerequisites because people of German and Polish blood had mostly settled there.

Testimony exists that he attended women, followed their pregnancies, treated them with drugs and that he often talked of artificial insemination in human beings. His final years of life were marked with fears of being caught by Jewish Nazi hunters. It is thought that he died in February 1979 while swimming in the sea off the coast of Bertioga in Brazil.

In 1940 Himmler's plan to colonise Amazonia may have been put aside, but not the dream of breeding a master race of blond, blue-eyed Germans. Its implementation before and during the war would take the most grotesque of forms.

Two year-old Folker Heinecke was one of thousands of children whose lives were shattered, but in the long run his bitter-sweet-good fortune was due to Hitler and Himmler's wild desire to breed a master race of people. Folker was one of the Lebensborn Children.

FORTY-THREE

The plan was for Peter to collect Neptune so he took the ferry from Douglas but by the time he reached the army barracks in West Belfast, Neptune had again fled. Peter rang Heather with the news.

Uppermost in their minds was the fact that Ulster was a dangerous place. The IRA had shot and killed Peter's friend Marcus McBride in 1972 near the coastal town of Londonderry; his body with two bullets in the head had been found in a ditch near his Limavady home.

A tall man with an upper class accent, Colonel Smirthwaith was embarrassed. Neptune had slipped through his fingers and was again on the loose. In the two days since he was found, Neptune had been well cared for. A vet had examined him and said that he was sound of health though dehydrated, disoriented and irritable, his 'Adaptil' dog collar said it all.

At this point neither Smirthwaith nor his soldiers knew how the dog had escaped from the compound. Slick Neptune had done it like a well-practiced escape artist reminiscent of the American bank robber 'Slick Willie Sutton' who, on three occasions had broken out of maximum-security jails on the US east coast. Just like Sutton, Neptune had done something fiendishly clever, he had planned, organised and implemented his getaway with skill. Not wanting to coop the dog up, Neptune had been allowed outside the barracks to wander around the inner perimeter of the compound. It was early afternoon and drizzling. Neptune was outside sniffing around, keeping a low profile and sizing the situation up, looking for his escape opportunity.

The soldiers had been good to him but the rhythms of military life were not to his liking, he cared little for the sounds of heavy boots or shouted orders; he didn't like sharp, aggressive voices.

A sergeant and corporal were loading the back of an army truck with bed frames and mattresses they were driving to a barrack on the outskirts of Londonderry forty miles away. When they returned to the storeroom for the last items, Neptune leapt into the back of the truck and into an empty box large enough to employ his body, there he stayed hidden and silent.

With the truck loaded, the back gate was lifted and secured, the canvas lowered from the vehicle's roof and fastened. Driven by the corporal the truck then drove from the compound heading towards north Belfast. The sergeant sat in the passenger seat heavily armed. From north Belfast the truck swung west destined for Londonderry, the scene of much IRA violence.

By now Neptune was out of his box ready for the next step leading to his freedom. The signals coming from Hitler's bottle had put him in a travelling mood with an eye on self-preservation. He had tried to warn the Moores but without success, it was time for him to think of himself. He didn't know what lay ahead, but he knew he had to keep moving, the impulse even as far away in Belfast was hard to resist; there was an urgency about the matter. Rain or no rain something was telling him to quit the vehicle just as the wolf within him had urged him to be brave.

As the truck drove west Neptune's head was out the back right side of the vehicle through a gap in the canvas. But a question remained. Could he force his body through the narrow gap when the time to flee came? He would try the next time the truck stopped; if successful he would wiggle his way out, jump and sprint for cover.

The truck had been on the move for over an hour and had driven through three Ulster towns. Ever on guard, the corporal and sergeant's eyes scanned the roadsides for suspicious signs because the IRA was on the warpath. Roadside bombs triggered remotely were their latest way of killing British soldiers. In the last few months similar devices placed along barren roads had exploded destroying the lives of four young troopers.

It was now raining hard. The green army truck was on a narrow road heading towards Dungiven, tall fir trees lined both sides of the road. A blue Ford Escort was driving some thirty yards in front of the truck. Up ahead an RUC car was parked width-wide across the road; two policemen were flagging the Ford down.

When it stopped so did the truck but well behind the Ford. It was a tricky situation; the sergeant and corporal were on alert. 'Carpe Diem' Neptune seized day, plucked the moment, he forced himself through the canvas, fell heavily on the road but he quickly recovered and was swiftly gone through a cluster of trees.

Forty minutes later, while driving on a quiet road between Dungiven and Londonderry, the truck was blown up by a roadside bomb killing the corporal and sergeant. Neptune had escaped with his life thanks to an irresistible impulse from beyond logic.

Perhaps it was premonition, perhaps it was luck, perhaps there was no connection, but close from where Neptune leapt to safety, there is an islet called Lough Swilley near Londonderry town. The peculiarities of Northern Ireland's partitioning from southern Ireland in 1921 meant that despite the northwest coastal county of Donegal being geographically in the north of Ireland, politically it is part of the south. The county directly east of Donegal is Londonderry, which is part of Northern Ireland.

On the 'Inishowen Peninsular' in county Donegal, east of Lough Swilley – In the war years it was part of neutral South Ireland - sits the hamlet of Buncrana and on a hill is to be found the Swilley Hotel. To the east ten miles away at the mouth of Londonderry's Foyle Lough, the British had a naval base.

Between 1940 and 1942 U-Boats would slip into Lough Swilley where their crews would avail of the Swilley Hotel's hospitality and where they would gather information about British shipping in the convivial atmosphere of Irish Bonomi. They always seemed welcomed by the southern Irish of Lough Swilley, it was an opportune location for pro- German IRA spies to gather information and pass on to U-Boat crews for transmission to Berlin.

In June 1940 Captain Emile P. Schultz and the crew of U-Boat 619 were at the Swilley Hotel. Hitler's bottle had been given to him to release off Montauk Points but plans had changed and the task was given to Captain Schuhart and U-Boat 29 who, at the time, were also at Swilley Lough.

After fifty-one years did Neptune sense his proximity to the bottle's changeover in 1940 before making his escape from the truck? Maybe yes, maybe no, the answer will never be known. But it does make one wonder - the supernatural dances on the head of a pin whose prick is unreality with a purpose.

Ten minutes before the truck was blown up, a passing motorist in a Wolsley stopped and picked up a rain-soaked Neptune who was trotting along a narrow lane that connected with two roads, one of which, in whose direction the Wolsley was heading, led south to Dublin and then county Kildare. After examining the dog's collars, the motorist had no trouble persuading Neptune into the Wolsley, a plumb coloured car with crimson leather seats and wide, comfortable arm rests. The motorist was a Jesuit priest.

In his soft, southern Irish accent he simply said, 'Neptune, get in' and the dog did. The priest was Jack Brennan, the amiable rector of Clongowes Wood College in County Kildare, the most prestigious Catholic boy's school in southern Ireland, a school with grounds of 700 acres and the castle of the once opulent Wogan-Brown family. It was the same college where the young Jesuit in training Ralph Hatton had taught American history before the war. And it was the very same Hatton who had found Hitler's bottle in July 1940 at the shore of the Montauk Point lighthouse.

Father Jack was returning to Clongowes after visiting his sister Dee in Ballymena. The journey would take a number of hours during which the priest spoke quietly to Neptune against a background of soothing songs from a Nana Mouskouri audio tape. Sitting in the passenger seat Neptune would look at Fr. Jack. He liked what he was seeing and hearing, he felt in safe hands. Although the soldiers in Belfast had treated him well, he cared little for the sounds they made.

It had been raining for a number of hours. Light was slipping from the sky and rain was pouring down. It came in waves, slapping at the side of the Wolsley. "Only a little longer Neptune" said Fr. Jack, "Just a little longer and we'll be at the college, then I'll call your family." It was natural for Fr. Jack to wonder about Neptune's Adaptil collar, he has never seen one before.

Heather was home by the phone and Peter was in Belfast among soldiers, two of whose comrades had been killed that afternoon. Unbeknownst to everyone, Neptune was in Southern Ireland poised to arrive at Clongowes Wood College, a long way from where the Jesuit had picked him up and the two soldiers had bombed to death.

Colonel Smirthwaith had come to the conclusion that the dog had slipped out of the compound in the back of the truck that was destined for Londonderry and its date with destiny, and that Neptune too had perished. His remains had not been found in the wreckage of the truck but that meant little as the blast had been terrific. Not much remained of the corporal and sergeant.

There was nothing left for Peter to do but to return to the Isle of Man. Heather was gutted by the news that Neptune had met a tragic end along with those poor, unfortunate soldiers. Within an hour of the bombing the world knew all about it.

Little did the Moores know that Neptune would soon arrive at Clongowes Wood College where the boy James Joyce was deposited by his parents in the late 1800s and about which he would write in: *Portrait Of An Artist As A Young Man*. A college whose heart is its castle, a setting with a long tree-lined driveway and ghosts like John Sullivan, a Jesuit known in Kildare for his miracles; a priest whose clone was the actor Robert Stack. A college dating from 1814 founded by the cunning Jesuit Peter Kenny contrary to the Penal Laws of the times when Britain ruled Ireland - the sister school of Stoneyhurst College in Cheshire where the young Otto Schmitt taught among Jesuits in the 1930s.

Neptune would adore Clongowes Wood College from the outset, so had the Jesuit Ralph Hatton during his time there.

FORTY-FOUR

In early June 1944 the stage was set for the invasion of Western Europe. Hitler's generals were jumpy, it had to be repelled, the Allies must not gain a foothold in France.

The probe into Europe's underbelly through Italy was grinding away, filleting German and Italian strongholds on route. It was hard, but Axis bases in Italy were now exposed, a daily growing German and Italian wound was evident. The brutal battle of Monte Cassino for the high ground and a passage to Rome was over. It had started in January and ended in May. German resistant from the Benedictine Abbey above the Allied forces had been fierce.

It was now the turn of Hitler's western fortress to be invaded - would it be at Normandy or Calais? That was the question Hitler and his generals pondered. If, through deception, the Allies could trick the Germans into believing that Calais was their aim, troops and firepower would be moved from Normandy to Calais thereby saving the lives of many Allied soldiers. And so it came to be; through a cobweb of ploys German intelligence was duped into thinking the invasion point was Calais. The table was set for the eating, chewing and spitting out of Nazism in mainland Europe.

Although the Allies focus was the liberation of Europe, the US was also making headway in the Pacific. In April Japanese troops had left their positions in New Guinea so quickly that when the Yanks landed they found uneaten food on the beach. General Macarthur's troops had bypasses Japanese enclaves and struck 500 miles further along the coast taking the foe by surprise. They had seized the town of Hollandia near an airstrip whose capture had given them air dominance over New Guinea.

Yet again there was grief for Hitler. In May the Red Army was powering its way through the Crimea, sweeping his troops out. Adding to his woes, in Italy the Allies had captured Cassino and begun an offensive from Anzio. Even before the Normandy invasion had started the Allies had taken Rome.

Hitler was being squeezed as a rope for war crimes would squeeze his neck unless he was killed or took his own life, that was the reality of the situation and he knew it. The guttersnipe was checkmated; the blood of his troops in Russia and Italy gushed like from a ruptured fountain.

By early June the blitz on Japan from captured islands was poised to begin by Super-Fortress B-29s. The targets would be centres of industry in Kyushu, the most southerly Japanese island. At this moment however, the focus was on the liberation of Europe and the destruction of Nazism by overwhelming power. Although the stage was set for the Normandy invasion, a problem raged behind the scene from who else but the prickly French. During the war Winston Churchill said that the greatest cross he had to bear in the war was 'The Cross Of Lorraine', the symbol of General de Gaulle, the wartime Free French leader - an unbearable, disagreeable self-centred Anglophobe.

By 1944 officials were almost immune to the tantrums that followed when things were kept from him. In his memoirs de Gaulle wrote how Anthony Eden told him that he had created more problems for Britain than all its allies combined. The egomaniac fool was proud of it.

In London, as D-Day drew near, de Gaulle surpassed even himself by refusing to broadcast on the BBC or to provide Free French liaisons to go with the first wave of allied troops. He did this on the eve of the greatest sea borne invasion in history whose perils were made more acute by bad weather and whose purpose was the liberation of France.

As far as Churchill was concerned this was treason to the cause. He threatened to have the general flown to Algiers in chains. After hours of upheaval, aids managed to calm Churchill and persuade de Gaulle to cooperate, which he did but in a huff giving little credit in his broadcast to the British, Americans and Canadians who would soon be dying on the beaches of Normandy and elsewhere to liberate his France.

The most prolific military invasion in the history of mankind began on D-Day, June 6th 1944. Code-named Operation

Overlord, it involved 300,000 troops. Often stained by criticisms involving Dunkirk, Tobruk, Arnhem and Singapore, these episodes were not as daring and robust as the Normandy invasion. D-Day by contrast shines as a triumph of planning, imagination and human endeavour. This was a task the Allies did beautifully in the defeat of Nazism.

The Allied forces launched the invasion landing on five beaches codenamed Omaha, Utah, Sword, Juno and Gold. The British and Canadians made shore at Juno, Sword and Gold relatively easily, so too did the Americans at Utah. Not so at Omaha beach, savage German fire and explosive power cost the Yanks huge casualties before establishing positions inland.

A tense, low-key broadcast from Eisenhower's headquarters told the world that the long-awaited invasion had begun. He said: *Allied naval forces, supported by strong air forces began landing troops this morning on the northern coast of France.* No place names were given, nothing that could help the enemy.

The Germans were saying landings were made in Normandy at about twelve points along more than a hundred miles of coast from west of Cherbourg to Le Havre, that fighting was raging, and that the town of Caen was under attack.

Operation Overlord began on the evening of the 5th June when airborne troops departed from airfields in southern England. Between midnight and the June 6th dawn they had landed men by parachute or glider at points behind enemy lines.

Throughout the night bombers had struck batteries along the French coast. By daybreak more than a thousand US bombers had already started their attack. Fighter escorts had been at it non-stop since before the dawn bombings, strafing and patrolling while naval forces were sweeping mines from the invasion route.

A huge force of several thousand troop-bearing ships had converged on the Normandy coast soon after 5 a.m. The coast and invasion rout were being readied for the troop landings. Battleships and destroyers were pounding German defences while engineers were demolishing beach obstacles. Troops followed with tanks and artillery. Weather had delayed the invasion, a strong north-westerly was blowing off shore and high seas were causing problems for the landing crafts, many of the troops on board were sea-sick.

The Germans had been outfoxed, they still believed that the Normandy thrust was an attempt to distract attention from Calais. Reconnaissance flights had confirmed that the strongest German defences were still in the Pas de Calais, and that an armoured force had not been moved. The question generals on both sides were asking is whether the Allies could reinforce faster by sea using their artificial harbour 'Mulberry', than the Axis could by land. Land-based forces always had the advantage, but the Allies had been hitting railways, bridges, radar stations and supply columns so the Germans could only re-supply at night.

In the House of Commons on the evening of June 6th, Winston Churchill said that the landing was proceeding in a satisfactory manner, that many of the anticipated dangers were now in the past, that losses had been less than feared, and that the resistance of enemy batteries had been weakened by bombings from warplanes and ships.

By nightfall he revealed that Allied Forces had advanced several miles inland on a broad front, a fact that was giving Hitler as many fits as de Gaulle was giving his allies. His great Atlantic Wall had been breached – the Allies had cracked open his last chance of averting defeat in the west.

A veteran of the Normandy landing described the day as chaotic, terrifying and bloody in ways most people can never imagine. Hitler understood, his soldiers, though brave and gritty, were bleeding and dying in great numbers and losing ground. In the meantime the guttersnipe's letter in a bottle was still bobbing in the Atlantic off the east coast of New Foundland.

Among those storming the beaches of Normandy were Americans, Yanks under fire, scared but there, walking or crawling into the carnage that lay on the beaches before them. Many were already dead or wounded, butchered in seconds by machine gun fire and shelling at Omaha Beach. But they were there on the north coast of France in great numbers, at the heart of the merciless din of gunfire and explosions. This is what Otto Schmitt was recalling while driving to lunch with the Moores and listening to the BBC.

Adolf Hitler may have been an evil genius of a shaven ape who was also nothing but a guttersnipe, but he respected the gravel in the guts of his opponents like those displayed by the Yanks, British and Canadians at Normandy.

FORTY-FIVE

Folker Heinecke's looks brought him to the attention of Heinrick Himmler, the prime mover of the plan to populate Europe and Brazil with people of the Aryan race. But Folker Heinecke was not the boys birth name. Blond haired and blue eyed, the beautiful near two year-old child was the centre of attention in the Crimean village of his childhood.

He was chosen to be one of the elite 'new breed' of genetically superior Germans and ripped from the arms of his parents when Nazi tanks entered Crimea in 1942. Taken to a medical facility and checked for traits of Jewishness he was then deemed suitable for the 'Lebensborn Programme' – The Well of Life - Himmler's breeding plan to ensure the future of the Third Reich by providing 'racially pure' generations to replace those lost in war.

First mentioned in *Mein Kampf,* the 'Lebensborn Programme' had different facets. In addition to stealing suitable children from occupied lands, another strand involved breeding clinics where pure SS officers were told to mate with equally suitable German or other chosen women.

In countries like Norway where blond hair and blue eyes were part of the genetic-make-up, 'officers' were encouraged to father children with local women even if they, and in some cases the women were married. For Himmler these women were like gold dust due to their Viking looks; they were forced or induced to mate with SS officers stationed in Norway.

As the Nazis stormed across Europe, these Aryan babies were born into a life of privilege and power, often baptized in a ceremony involving oaths spoken on their behalf pledging loyalty to Nazi ideology. The reward for these children and their mothers was the best of everything, so that they would grow up use to the spoils of war. In other cases the children were sent to orphanages or assigned to wealthy German families.

The most demonic facet of the scheme involved stealing children who fitted the Nazi racial stereotype who could then be Germanised with suitable families. This was the fate of Folker Heinecke who was stolen from his parents, given to a Nazi couple and raised to adore and obey Hitler.

Now in his 70s, Folker says he recalls the day he was chosen to be part of the Lebensborn Programme. Perhaps the traumatic nature of his young life to that point fixed the event in his memory as he was less than three at the time. He says: *I remember people coming into a room, around 30 of us children were lined up like pets to be picked for a new home; one couple were to be my parents. They returned the next day and picked me to be their son - my new name would be Folker Heineche.*

Folker remembers seeing Himmler at his new family home. He vividly recalls the man who oversaw the 'Final Solution' and was keener than Hitler when it came to killing Jews, and who took his own life when captured by the British at the end of the war.

The boy from Crimea was now part of the 'Master Race', he would be one of many Lebensborn children who, since the war, have been social outcasts and have no memory of their real parents; they never saw them again or know of their fate.

The privileged life of the Lebensborn finished with the capture of occupied countries such as Norway. Thousands of their mothers were labelled 'German Whores' and sent to prison camps as slave labour.

The Norwegian government officially classified Lebensborn children as 'rats' – 'Nazi whore children'. Some of those still living continue to be looked down upon. Attempting to rid themselves of them after the war, the Norwegian government tried sending some to Australia but failed. It was not unusual for former Lebensborn children to commit suicide or drift into drug-use or crime. Depression and low self-esteem was common among them after years of being labelled worthless bastards with no right to life. Some were sent to asylums where drug trials were conducted on mothers and children by the Norwegian military, others were force-fed harmful experimental drugs.

The best-known issue of an SS officer father and Norwegian mother is Anni-Frid Lyngstad, the dark haired singer from ABBA. (She was a natural blond with dyed hair). Her family fled post-war persecution and moved to Sweden where she was unknown. Others such children were not so fortunate, at times being beaten and raped, mothers were often labelled 'people of limited talent and psychopaths'.

In Scandinavian countries the words 'father was a German' was enough to send children to a mental hospital where they were often abused and deemed dangerous due to their 'Nazi genes'; they were thought capable of forming another Nazi state.

Norway born in 1942, Harriet von Nickel suffered years of abuse after her mother agreed to have a child with a German officer. Fostered after the war she was chained with a dog in a yard. When she was six a local man said, *I want to see if the witch drowns or floats*, and threw her in a river. Three years later she had the shape of a Nazi symbol scored into her forehead with bent nails.

By comparison Folker Heinecke's life was sweet. He was so young when the Nazis stole him that he had no memory of another life. The only inkling came after the war when a local kid he was playing with said, *You know you're a bastard, don't you, they're not your real parents.* Folker didn't know what that meant and he never discussed it with his German parents who may have been loyal Nazis, but they gave him a good life and never abused him.

In 1975, the Heineckes died within months of each other. Folker, then thirty-five, was devastated but he inherited the family firm of shipbrokers and went on to make millions. It was then that he found papers among his father's files that shocked him. They showed that Folker Heinecke was born on October 17, 1940 in Oderberg in Upper Silesia, which is now part of Poland, but was then part of Germany.

He criss-crossed Europe in search of the truth about his origins and found that his adoption papers and SS birth certificate were forged. This being the case he was an orphan and he could live with that. Years later, as he dug deeper, it began to appear that he was part of the Lebensborn Programme.

He collected boxes of documents from US authorities, the German and Polish Red Cross, the International Tracing Service, the British Army of Occupation and other agencies and church offices - all pieces of the puzzle of his past. Then, in 2008, at the age of sixty-eight he made a stunning find by way of the biggest Holocaust archives in the world at the Red Cross Tracing Centre in Bad Arolsen, Germany.

He found a document dated November 12, 1948 which stated: 'The childless couple named Heinecke applied to the Hamburg youth office for adoption of a child. They were given permission and went to a Lebensborn home to select one. The child was collected on May 20th, 1943. Other documents were found on which the name, birth date and place of the adopted boy was given as: 'Aleksander Litau, born October 17, 1940 in Alnowa, Crimea, USSR.

The mystery was near an end. Folker Heinecke was Aleksander Litau, a Russian by birth. An SS document referred to a military operation near Alnowa in 1942, in which the blond, blue-eyed Aleksander was taken to Germany for 'Aryanisaton'.

In 2008 Folker journeyed to the Crimea and found a road and house where locals said a family named Litau once lived. He didn't find his parent's grave but elderly locals said they recalled the day soldiers came and took a 'beautiful blond child' away. After the war Stalin sent millions of Russian to the gulags – many for simply being overrun by the Germans. The Litaus may have been among them.

Folker says he has to keep searching to find something that might lead him to who his parents really were and where they are buried; then he will have done his duty as a son, then he will have honoured his real parents. The journey of this Lebensborn child is not at an end.

FORTY-SIX

In Father Brennan and other Clongowes Wood College priests Neptune had found new friends. Their soft, southern Irish voices were good for his soul, one that was troubled by the supernatural ghost of Adolf Hitler, the telepathic-sending spirit that had prompted his escape from home.

Contrary to the beliefs of the Roman Catholic Church Neptune had a soul. Had this been voiced in the Vatican the Pope would have tripped on his ankle-length cassock and had an outburst albeit less vocal than those of Hitler and de Gaulle in their stride. But his Holiness didn't know Neptune, the Labrador who was better of nature, instinct and behaviour than many who claim to be Catholic as Hitler often did. Too much about Neptune spoke to that truth; he was too humane of character for it to be otherwise, too aware, too sensitive of people's needs for God to deprive him of afterlife in whatever kingdom follows death for those deserving.

More than any being that had contact with the bottle only Neptune sensed it past, quite the opposite of the vibes that filled his senses from the smiling, Very Reverend Jack Brennan SJ and his fellow Clongowes Jesuits, many of whom were ageing, wise beyond the subjects that they tough but still teaching; they suited Neptune nicely. Their black attire and white collars were new to him but he felt at home among them.

On arrival at Clongowes Neptune was briefly in the care of Brother John Adams, the school's administrator who approached every task with clarity of thought and pride in his work. Nothing short of perfection was good enough for him.

From head to toe his appearance was like his work, neat and precise. What you saw is what you got from Brother Adams.

A cleric in his forties with closely set eyes, dark haired Adams like most Jesuits was not about humility. The sin of pride was not in the makeup of Jesuits. Educationally superior to other religious orders, Jesuits could be ruthless when, in rapier like fashion, they drew their blade of knowledge in debate. Wisdom was a weapon they eagerly marshalled into action; they relished drawing blood from the educationally inferior.

Adams fed Neptune and took him for a long, easy walk around the school's spacious grounds. He didn't tether him or anything so demeaning; he talked to him, treated him with respect. He didn't ask Neptune why he was wandering alone in the rain on a road in scary Northern Ireland, or where he lived or who his owners were or why he wore two collars. Father Jack would soon have the answer to these questions when he called the number on one of collars.

The rain had stopped. It was, as the Irish say, 'a soft evening'. The days were longer so there was ample daylight for their walk and for Neptune to enjoy the new sights and smells of the surroundings.

Here and there a priest or brother or student would stroll by and the Labrador, whose tail would wag, was introduced. He met Father Breardon and then Father Leonard and then Father Looby and then a student from Cork named Connor Rock whose aim was to be a commercial pilot which in time he did become. They liked Neptune and he liked them.

On these occasions pats to the head would follow along with soft-sounding words that fixed the feeling in the frisky dog that he was welcomed in this world of Gaelic hospitality upon which he had come, perhaps by fate, perhaps by chance, perhaps to widen his vistas and that of those he met.

Their walk was in the vast area at the front of the college with the castle behind them. To the right, where they were heading, were the pleasure grounds, an enclosed area of trees with overhanging branches and monuments of people from yesteryear pre-dating the Jesuits of Clongowes. Neptune sniffed around while Adams walked ahead crunching and snapping damp branches and twigs that lay underfoot.

Next on their walk was a visit to the cemetery, which, with the castle still behind them, stood up the college driveway to the right behind tall, masculine trees planted by a Jesuit of renown years earlier. And there in the cemetery he lay – the man himself – with other priests that were hopefully at peace. Even in life, despite their leaps of faith that promised heaven, not all were sure what lurked beyond the veil. Father Frank Frewen whose golf swing was perfection was always in doubt; he was never certain how his life's-story would end, when the coffin lid lowered and shut on what the Irish would have said was 'himself'.

Except for two rows of black gravestones that faced each other, the cemetery was similar to the pleasure grounds with trees that arched to meet, whose ever-thinning arms with clinging raindrops formed a halo of branches and leaves above the graves below.

If silence is golden the Jesuits who lay here would forever be in credit. The stillness was profound. Except for the occasional visitor, all others were God's gifts like robins, magpies and the Clongowes red squirrels with their long, bushy tails, as well as the occasional bandits of Kildare, the black squirrels, the cunning, swift, Robin Hoods of the college who robbed from birds and other squirrels but kept the booty.

Not so with Neptune, he came in peace with Adams who walked softly just as his voice stepped with care. And stopping at different graves he would say to Neptune, *And this was Gerry O'Bierne, he planted all the trees on the driveway, and this was Frank Frewen, a convert from Tipperary who spoke like Dr. Watson in the Sherlock Holmes movies, and this was Jim Casey, the tall, broad shouldered master of Latin and Gaelic who lived in the same Clongowes bedroom for forty-two years. You could set your clock by him, and this was Brother Glenville and Brother Fitzgerald. They toiled at Clongowes for years, hanging from the castle roof, fixing tiles, banging nails, mending this and that in between which they would talk of the old days and the boxes of fruit that came to Ireland from abroad and one box that ticked their fancy that had written on its side: 'The Good Juice of the American Apple'.*

And when he came to the grave of Cyril Power Adam's voice lowered even more. His old friend had gone to his reward providing one was waiting. *He was brilliant*, Adams whispered to Neptune, never took himself seriously, a whiz at maths, a master of the subject, he had a face like Churchill and a heart that was fair but tough. His passion was Red Rum, the horse with invisible wings that thrice won the Grand National."

Neptune listened to Adams' words. He sniffed around keeping an eye on the hopping magpies and the scrambling squirrels, each of which he was leaving in peace for this was not the place or time for frolic. Then, respectfully like a man of breeding, Neptune would hang back, melt away and find a tree on which to lift a leg.

While Neptune's leg was up so was the phone in Jack Brennan's hand pressed against his ear. He was speaking with Heather saying he had found her dog, that he was well and not to worry, that he was in good hands and ready for collection at any time.

It didn't take long for her to call the barracks in Belfast and leave a message for Peter who was out in the streets of Belfast asking people if they had seen his missing dog.

The following day Peter collected Neptune and they were soon back home on The Isle of Man. Although happy to be back, Neptune continued to avoid the living room.

At last Peter and Heather understood, their dog didn't like Hitler's bottle. Too much badness had befallen their friends since it was found but for the time being a decision was made, Peter would bury the bottle at night in a field near Avoca.

The location did not escape Neptune's notice.

FORTY-SEVEN

The final squeeze on Nazism began on the day of the Normandy invasion. It was the beginning of the end not the end of the beginning. With Rome now in Allied hands, the Red Army was grinding its way to Berlin. American and Free French troops had already landed in southern France and were pushing north.

Despite their dire situation since D-Day, Hitler's troopers fought on. In December they had counter- attacked through the Ardennes and stalled the Allies advance culminating in the Battle Of The Bulge. They even tried infiltrating US positions by posing as American soldiers. But it wasn't enough. By March 1945, as the Soviets were encircling Berlin, other Allies were crossing the Rhine and on the 30th of April, Hitler and Eva Braun committed suicide having married the day before. It was all over in Europe on the 8th of May. Germany surrendered unconditionally.

Hitler's Thousand-Year Reich had lasted twelve years. His loopy idea of keeping America out of the war by way of his letter in a bottle had proved an act of folly.

By July 1944 many of Hitler's general staff were fed up. With defeat inevitable they hatched a plan to kill him and surrender with honour hoping to save themselves from war crimes they had taken part in or knew were in progress.

The attempt to kill Hitler occurred in July 1944 at Wolf's Lair during a meeting he was holding with his generals, a bomb was planted by Colonel Claus von Stauffenberg, a self-styled devout Christian. Hitler survived the explosion. An hour later and partly deafened by the blast and burns to his legs he was lunching with Mussolini who had arrived by train. Hitler had gone to meet him.

Retributions against the plotters were swift. All but one plotter were rounded up and executed including von Stauffenberg who was shot in a Berlin courtyard.

A plotter who recently died at the age of ninety-one and was never suspected was Inga Haag. She escaped detection even though she was deeply involved in German resistance and knew all the plotters. As the assassination attempt was being carried out Inga was lunching with two Gestapo offices, having cleverly invited them for a meal at her home to divert suspicion from herself. It worked; she slipped under the radar of suspicions.

In recent years the impression has been given that the army officers who tried to kill Hitler were staunch Christians and democrats who were shocked by the Nazis' treatment of Jews and wanted peace and justice for Germany's neighbours. This is nonsense. If von Stauffenberg was a Christian it was of the Ala Carte variety, he fully shared the racial views of his class, as did many in Germany at the time.

Far from being a democrat, von Stauffenberg despised the belief that 'all men are equal'. He once had described Poles as 'an unbelievable mix of Jews and mongrels'. Like his fellow conspirators he was brave, he carried out the plot to kill Hitler despite the injuries he had received in North Africa the previous year in a bombing raid. He and his conspirators only become concerned with the welfare of their fellow men when their options for self-preservation were sinking.

During the Nuremberg trials surviving Army officers claimed that as honourable soldiers of the Wehrmacht they knew nothing of the way the SS were killing Jews, gypsies, Russian POWs, the disabled and so on. They said they were too busy fighting the Red Army and knew nothing of the crimes taking place. Their claims were hollow; there was no dividing line between the guilt of the Army and the SS because the Army took part in the rounding up, transpiration and execution of its victims.

Not all Germans were Hitler lovers, some saw through him and what he stood for. They were true democrats who paid with their lives for their beliefs. Two such people were a brother and sister who were guillotined, to this day they remain symbols of the German resistance.

In February 1943, seventeen months before Colonel von Stauffenberg and his group tried to kill Hitler, Sophie and Hans

Scholl, twenty-one and twenty-four, quietly shared a cigarette then embraced. This would be their last day on earth.

'The sun is still shining' cried Sophie as she was led into a courtyard. The Gestapo had brought her to the execution place in Munich's Stadelheim Prison and placed her in a guillotine; a few seconds later the blade dropped. Minutes later Hans suffered the same fate. 'Es lebe die Freiheit – 'Long Live Freedom' he cried before the blade fell.

The Scholl siblings are an example of those in the resistance who today are admired in Germany as much, if not more, than Claus von Stauffenberg - nearly 200 schools are named after them.

Sophie and Hans were Munich University students and members of The White Rose, a protest group who would mail leaflets to people randomly selected from phone books. The leaflets gave details of the Holocaust and spoke to the ideals of freedom, religious tolerance and democracy. Late at night Hans would scribe anti-Nazi graffiti on building walls like 'Down With Hitler' and 'Hitler the Mass Murderer.'

The siblings were caught after leaving leaflets outside the university lecture hall. Four days later they were put to death after a swift trial presided over by Roland Freisler, the fanatical Nazi who later tried Hitler's plotters.

In recent years a poll taken in Germany named Sophie and Hans the 4th most popular Germans ahead of Einstein, Mozart and Bach, von Stauffenberg was hardly mentioned. Evidence exists that at least in part helps explain why the brother and sister defied all sense of caution to denounce Nazism. Hans Scholl was an active homosexual.

Tall, handsome, athletic and full of leadership qualities, Hans reflected the Aryan Master Race in every respect. At the age of fourteen in 1933 he had joined the Hitler Youth and become squad leader quickly; he was allowed to form a special squad to train future leaders. At first he was committed but he listened to his father who believed that the Nazis were leading Germany to destruction. This explains why Hans' squad was based not on Nazi principles but on soon-to-be outlawed ideals. As leader of the squad Hans took them on camping trips often outside Germany.

As the SS bore down on opponents, Hans was ordered to disband his group by the Hitler Youth Commander, but they continued meeting secretly. In 1937, the Gestapo started crushing 'subversive' groups by raiding their homes and Hans, then eighteen, was arrested.

During the long and brutal interrogations that followed, a friend of Hans made an admission; he confessed to a yearlong homosexual affair with Hans. He spoke of the attention Scholl paid him on several camping trips. Kept in confinement for a month, Hans finally admitted that the allegations were true. Totally mortified, he apologised to his family profusely. To be charged with any offence linked to sex between men under twenty-one was a crime in Germany. Being sent to a concentration camp wearing a pink star, then kicked out of the Army and banned from higher education were the prospects Hans was facing.

The trial of Hans and other group members took place in June 1938 in the Special Court in Stuttgart. His CO gave him a glowing reference and his friend helped by saying that their affair had been brief, and that it was only teen-age fumbling. Summing up, the judge described Hans' behaviour as the 'youthful failing' of a normally heterosexual youngster with a bright future. He acquitted Hans on all charges.

Hans was lucky, but despite his good fortune, the humiliating experience points to the trigger that ignited the siblings opposition to Nazism. Hans was traumatized by his interrogation and tormented by the fact that the Nazis knew of his sexual past. But he never lost the support of his family. On her part, Sophie was showing her own rebellious streak and hatred of Hitler and all for which he stood.

At the time her brother was going through his interrogation and trial, Sophie began an affair with Fritz Hartnagel, a captain in the army. By way of dangerous correspondence, she was doing her best to turn him against Hitler. She did not believe that the war was started for the good of Germany. Fritz did not agree, but in time he did consider her views.

In one letter she wrote: *Don't turn into an arrogant officer.* But she expressed her love and said she prayed he would survive the terrible times ahead and urged him to oppose the war, which eventually he did. It was a great reversal for him to now be against the war and admit that Germany was on a path to doom.

Sophie longed for Fritz to share her Christian beliefs of universal brotherhood. She was certain that Hitler aimed to replace Christianity with the ideology of Nazism. A society that embraced all religions was her longing.

In 1942 Sophie began at university and Fritz was sent to fight in the battle for Stalingrad. From this point forward she started living a secret life of contradictions: a university student engaged to an army officer whose leader she was active in opposing.

Hans and other students started the White Rose. Munich based, the group was non-violent, its purpose being to influence people against Hitler and militarism. The first leaflets began with a vengeance in the summer of 1942:

Nothing is less worthy of a civilized people than to allow itself to be governed by a clique of bandits of dark ambitions without resistance.

Mailed in several cities, members of The White Rose took suitcases full of leaflets on trains and began living on their nerves.

They ceased operating in the summer of 1942 when Hans and other White Rose members were sent to the Russian Front, but they were back later in the year more determined than ever to overthrow Hitler. With their own eyes they had seen the treatment of Jews and Russian prisoners by German soldiers; the defeat at Stalingrad was the subject of the last leaflet.

Within days disaster struck. Even though Munich was alive with police and soldiers, for three nights running in February 1943, Hans and two others painted anti-Nazi slogans along the city's main thoroughfare.

Soon after, Hans and Sophie were distributing leaflets in one of the buildings on the campus of Munich University. As they were hurrying away they realised they had left leaflets in the suitcase in which they were carried. Having retrieved them, they climbed to the top of the building and threw what was left to the

231

wind to fall on the students below. Spotted by the building caretaker and caught, they were handcuffed and taken to Gestapo headquarters. They went to trial on February 22nd.

During their interrogation neither cracked. They were both beheaded along with another member of The White Rose. Three others were also arrested and executed. Hans and Sophie were buried in Munich at Periach Cemetery on February 24th. Soon after their burial graffiti appeared on walls in town saying *Their spirit lives on.*

Is there any wonder that Hans and Sophie are more highly thought of than Claus von Stauffenberg and his fellow plotters? These Hitler followers believed in racial purity, many had taken part in the killing of Jews as well as other war crimes.

From the time Hitler's bottle was released in the Atlantic off the US east coast on July 1st 1940, and throughout its slow, wayward Atlantic journey in the years that followed, Hitler's ghost continued weaving it's spell.

Due to their contact with the bottle, among the lives it had probably taken were the crews of two U- Boats, and possibly a third, U-Boat 619, the sub at Swilley Laugh whose orders were changed blew up mysteriously on its slipway on the coast of France.

Four months after the guillotine had whistled down on the necks of Sophie and Hans Scholl, Luftwaffe bullets were piercing the body of a DC-3 aircraft that was flying over the Sea of Biscay on its way to Bristol, England from Lisbon, Portugal. Its flight number was not 666 but it was spookily close-777-A.

Including its Dutch KLM crew of three, there were seventeen on board the BOAC aircraft. Leslie Howard, one of the stars of 'Gone With The Wind' was a passenger. Joseph Goebbels was aware of his propaganda value, he knew that killing Howard, one of Britain's idols of the screen would damage the country's morale.

FORTY-EIGHT

Actors risked their lives as soldiers in World War but not as secret agents. Leslie Howard may have been the exception; he may have played such a role for Britain in 1943. Although no hard proof of this has ever been produced, it may have been the case. The matter is puzzling and complex.

Howard was killed at the age of fifty when BOAC's flight 777-A was shot down by the Luftwaffa over the Bay of Biscay on June 1st, 1943. Three people jumped clear of the burning plane but their parachutes were ablaze. Everyone on the aircraft perished.

The DC-3 had taken off from Portela Airport in Lisbon bound for Whitechurch Airport in Bristol, England. Howard and his accountant were priority passengers so two people had to leave the plane to make room for them. A third person, a priest also left the aircraft after boarding.

During the war Howard was of great help to the British government for his anti-Nazi propaganda work and the films he produced and starred in, which supported the war effort. Prior to his death he had been in Spain and Portugal on what was supposed to be a lecture tour to promote The film *The Lamp Still Burns*. Lisbon was then known as 'The Capitol of Espionage'.

The tour may have been cover for its real purpose as Anthony Eden, the British Foreign Secretary, had vigorously sought his services. On the surface it is doubtful that Howard was a secret agent but it may have been the case; his film-star fame would have opened many doors and provided good cover.

Over the years it has been said that Howard, the well-spoken Englishman may have been involved in keeping Spain from joining the war on Hitler's side at a critical point in the war. At the time and under General Franco, Spain was already neutral.

Assuming that the question of Spain's neutrality was truly at issue, what may have been making Franco rethink his position probably involved neutral neighbouring Portugal with whom Spain had a treaty of friendship.

Although Spain was also neutral, it was an unabashed fascist state, its loyalties being to Adolf Hitler and Benito Mussolini, for it was they who had helped him during Spain's Civil war with aircraft and troops. The Messerschmitt 109s operational début had been in Spain's civil war. Unlike Spain's neutrality however, Portugal's was flexible. Up to the end of 1942 they had been more or less even- handed, they were selling sugar, tobacco and tungsten to both the Axis and Allied powers.

In 1943 however, Antonio de Oliveira Salazar, Portugal's head of state had allowed the Allies basing rights in the Azores thereby enabling British and American aircraft to protect Allied shipping from U-Boat attacks in the Atlantic. This, for Franco may have been going too far, it was an act favouring the Allies, not the behaviour of a truly neutral country.

General Franco, no fool, was aware that the Anglo-Portuguese Treaty of 1373 was the oldest alliance in the world and that Portuguese military units were quietly helping Britain. All this may have been making him anxious about its neighbour Portugal and the Allie's intentions towards Fascist Spain. Churchill knew that Spain in a more active alliance with Hitler would change the complexion of the war and prolong it.

The claim, therefore, is that Howard, armed with a message from Churchill met with Franco to assure him that the Allies had no intention of involving Spain in the war and that Spain should remain neutral for its own good because the Axis Powers were well on the way to being defeated. Whether the meeting between Howard and Franco ever took place is unknown but one thing is certain, Spain remained neutral throughout the war.

To this day some believe that the Germans were certain that Churchill was on Flight 777-A and that it was the real reason for its attack. In his autobiography Churchill certainly acknowledges the possibility by expressing sorrow that a mistake about his own whereabouts may have led to Howard's death.

If, indeed, Howard met with Franco on behalf of Churchill he would almost certainly have also met with Salazar, a brilliant academic and master politician adept at playing one side against the other while keeping his country neutral.

If Howard's meeting with Franco actually took place, perhaps, to some extent it is the reason that Spain remained neutral. This would have angered Hitler given that he and Mussolini had helped Franco in his rise to power.

Some of this information stems from an interview given to a Spanish author by one of Howard's former lovers, Conchita Montenegro who, in the 1930s was known as the 'Spanish Greta Garbo'.

She and Howard had an affair in 1931 while filming *Never The Twain Shall Meet*. Later in the 30s she had married a man in charge of foreign relations for the Falangist Party which backed Franco's uprising against Spain's Republican government. It was her claim that she arranged a meeting between Howard and Franco through her husband. She revealed this to the author Jose Rey-Ximena shortly before her death at the age of ninety-five.

Although Howard has not been viewed as a secret agent in any account of World War Two, new details suggest that propaganda chief Josef Goebbels was aware of Howard's importance as a symbol of what Britons were fighting for. As far as the Nazis leadership were concerned he was no ordinary actor. One of Howard's films had ridiculed him no end.

In his book *In Search Of My Father* Ronald Howard describes the circumstances that may have led to his father's death, including the belief that the Germans were bent on shooting his plane down. His book claims that his father was involved with Franco on Winston Churchill's behalf but it has never been revealed to what extent if any, Howard was connected with Churchill and Franco or what the nature of their links may have been.

Howard was a highly prominent figure in wartime Britain and his death must have lifted the spirits of the Nazis. There can be no doubt that his trip to Portugal and Spain at the height of the war prior to D-Day was for reasons other than the promotion of a film - its purpose had to have been relevant to the times.

Ronald Howard's book goes into detail about German orders to intercept Flight 777-A, as well as dispatches from the British that seem to confirm reports of a deliberate attack on the actor's aircraft. The German orders say they were aware of Churchill's movements at the time; they were not so foolish to believe that he was flying on a commercial aircraft in wartime. Given these revelations, Churchill's feeling of sorrow at Howard's death take on new meaning: he would have felt guilty for sending the actor on a mission that cost him his life.

The Germans have always insisted that the shooting down of the DC-3 was an accident; it was one the fighter pilots who attacked the plane that reported seeing three people jumping from the aircraft with their parachutes on fire.

Leslie Howard was a British born Jew of Hungarian decent, the eldest son of Frank Stainer, an immigrant who changed his name from Steiner after adopting British nationality. Before marriage, Leslie's mother had changed her name from Blumberg to Howard.

In 1893, shortly after Leslie's birth, the Stainers moved to Vienna, the result being that Leslie only spoke German when his family returned to Britain. After completing college and a brief career in banking, Leslie had joined the cavalry in the First World War and become a lieutenant with the 20th Hussars. Marriage followed to Ruth Martin from which Ronald and Leslie Ruth resulted.

Shell-shocked in WWI and invalided out of the Army, Howard did not follow his father's wishes and return to banking; he took his mother's maiden name and with her blessings began a stage and film career. Brains, good looks and charm won him fans and rolls on the stage, some of which he produced and directed like Berkeley Square, a play that brought him to the notice of Hollywood. Nominated for Oscars several times, he was a lifelong friend of Humphrey Bogart who insisted that Howard be cast opposite him in *The Petrified Forest*.

With a stunning career ahead of him after his success *in Gone With The Wind*, Howard left Hollywood and returned to England with the sole purpose of helping Britain in the war.

Fully aware of propaganda value and his status in the film world, as actor and director, he made movies to maintain spirits at home. Many of his finest roles like the Scarlet Pimpernel portrayed the illusion that inside every foppish man hides a hero poised to strike. In Howard's case it may not have been an illusion.

It is likely that Josef Goebbels knew that killing Howard would damage morale in Britain; doing so was therefore desirable. Eight JU-88s attacked the DC-3 in which Howard was a passenger, yet Luftwaffe patrols in the Bay of Biscay usually entailed only one aircraft. Sending so many fighters to down one unarmed plane suggests that Goebbels knew how dangerous Howard was to the Third Reich. Or maybe he genuinely thought that Churchill was on the plane. No one really knows.

Another figures from the world of entertainment who perished in wartime in mysterious circumstances was the forty year-old American bandleader Glenn Miller. The single engine plane on which he was a passenger vanished on December 15th 1944 while on a flight across the English Channel. It had taken off from Croydon Airport near London heading to France. A book published in 2010 claims that Miller did not die in a plane crash but was tortured and then killed after he tried to help Nazi scientists escape from Germany. Other theories, some unflattering have also been put forward about him over the years.

Four months elapsed between the guillotine killings of Sophie and Hans Scholls and the shooting down of Leslie Howard's plane on June 1st, 1943. In between the two and well after, Hitler would kill many more. In the meantime Hitler's bottle continued bobbing in the Atlantic near Newfoundland.

FORTY-NINE

A lady who was close to Hitler wrote in her book: *Suddenly, after one of his mood-swings, a sensitive side to his nature would appear*. She recalled an incident in the autumn of 1944 when allied forces were heading for Berlin and squeezing him from all sides.

In *He Was My Chief, The Memoirs of Hitler's Secretary* she writes: *He was behaving oddly, the frown that often spread across his face was gone, he was smiling strangely and without warning his arms flung open and he said: 'How lovely when two people are in love!'*

The people around him were stunned - this was not the Fuehrer they knew, this person was different, this was a sparkling person. His mood was sunny. A jittery aide asked doctor Morell if the Fuehrer was ill. With the hint of a smile the doctor replied: *You've noticed? I'm giving him hormone injections from bulls' testicles – that peps him up.* What probably prompted Hitler's remark was that sex with Eva Braun the night before had gone well, he had risen to the occasion.

The author of the memoirs may not have known it at the time but a crude form of Viagra – testosterone extract – was among the eighty-two drugs Hitler had come to rely on daily by the end of the war.

These revelations come from Christa Schroeder, Hitler's secretary from 1933 to 1945. She had been hired for her shorthand skills after answering a newspaper advertisement. Her work was in the Munich office of the Nazi Party. When Hitler became Chancellor in 1933 she was appointed to be his main secretary. She was twenty-five years old at the time.

On becoming Chancellor Hitler installed himself in Berlin's Radziwill Palace where he lived and worked among aides who often quaked around him. Schroeder and the other secretaries worked in what was called the 'Ladies Saloon'.

In passing one morning Hitler happened to see the girls on a break and politely asked if he might join them, it was the first time Christa had spoken to him informally. He would soon visit the girls regularly for conversation, which he called 'an hour of easy chatter and tea'.

He was so relaxed in Christa's company that he would talk about his life as a child: *The Ladies Saloon was a place where he felt unburdened and I always had the impression that what he said there came from a secret memory box which he mostly kept shut,* Christa wrote in her book.

Often he would speak affectionately of his mother with whom he was close and at times of his father. I never loved my father but I feared him, Hitler told Christa. *Father was prone to rages and would resort to violence. My mother feared for me. I had read that hiding pain was a sign of bravery so I decided that the next time he beat me I would not cry out. When the beating came I knew mother was anxiously waiting at the other side of the door in the next room. I counted each stroke out loud. Mother thought I was mad when I reported with a smile – father gave me thirty-two strokes. He never beat me again.*

Working alongside Hitler could be unpredictable but his eyes spoke. Christa found them expressive, even friendly and warm-hearted. But in the last months of the war they became bulging and watery. She could also judge his mood from his voice, it would start calm and clear but suddenly it would increase in volume and become loud and aggressive.

The word he used mostly was 'ruthless'. She often heard him use it regarding particular orders. *Force it through ruthlessly whatever the cost* he would bark punching the air with his fist. He was also a health fanatic and placed high value on personal hygiene taking as many as nine baths a day, especially after meetings and speeches from which he would return sweating. In social occasions he mostly only drank mineral water and prided himself on reserves of energy about which he would boast to aides who could not keep up with him. But as Christa Schroeder says in her book, from 1944 Hitler was no longer master of his body. His trembling left hand became an embarrassment; he would cover it with the other. She was also aware of his reaction to bad news, which was a slight movement of the jaw.

He enjoyed displaying his knowledge of different subjects and was obsessive in looking up facts in encyclopaedias. He often convinced people that he was a deep thinker with a sharp analytical brain. He was also fanatically against smoking and wanted a skull and crossbones printed on every packet of cigarettes made in Germany. Chocolates are what he thought his soldiers should be given. He would eat them a lot, sometimes two pounds a day.

One day after tea with the girls Miss Schroeder spoke up. *Ah Mein Fuehrer, let the poor boys have this pleasure, they don't get many.* Hitler looked serious and explained how nicotine and alcohol ruined people's health and muddles the mind, and without another word he walked out giving her a cold look. In her book Schroeder says: *I no longer existed for him, it was months before he forgave me for challenging his views with my opinion.*

Among his obsessions was his liking for vegetables which he would eat in large quantities; this had the effect of giving him bouts of flatulence which could be amusing but also deadly for those near him. He insisted on huge vases of flowers on tables and as much apple pie as his chef could make and he would spend hours listening to classical music, Aryan composed only and mostly Wagner.

In addition to his loathing of smoking and alcohol he deeply disliked meat and surprisingly cats, they made him nervous. He had a fear of cancer and suffered from high blood pressure, stomach cramps and bad headaches, he had polyps removed from his vocal cords several times. And he had terrible, terrible breath and very poor table manners.

A sure way to annoy him was to make a fuss of his dogs, especially Blondi. He was very selfish in their unflinching affection, if they responded to stroking from anyone but him he became irritated.

Christa was arrested at the end of the war and convicted as a war criminal. Reclassified later as a collaborator, she was released from prison in 1948. She died in 1984 at the age of seventy-six knowing many of Hitler's secrets and quirks. It would be more than twenty years after her death that her book was published.

Had Schroeder been alive today and was up to date on Hitler's past she would have recalled that he seldom spoke or went into detail about his sister Paula, his half-sister Angela, his half-brother Alois Hitler Jnr, or his distasteful nephew William Patrick Hitler, Alois' son, who, since 1939, had been living in America with his Irish born mother.

Nor had he probably ever mention another nephew by way of his half-brother Alois Jnr's second marriage, Heinrich 'Heinz' Hitler who had fought as a Nazi and died valiantly in a Soviet prison camp at the age of twenty-one after much torture.

FIFTY

Franklin D. Roosevelt died suddenly at 3.35 p.m., April 12th, 1945. He was sixty-three, seven years younger than Churchill, and seven years older than Hitler.

Life drained from his courageous body when victory in Europe was near and the outcome of war in the Pacific was certain but not yet achieved. Japan would surrender in August after atomic bombs were dropped on Hiroshima and Nagasaki.

By April 1945 German resistance was totally collapsing, the Soviet army would soon be in Berlin. In the Pacific the Japanese were fighting to the last man on islands like Guadalcanal, surrender was not in their nature even though bombers were blitzing their cities in Japan at will.

Roosevelt died in Warm Springs Georgia where he regularly went for treatments on the polio that had crippled him for years since the age of thirty nine. Unbeknownst to Eleanor, his wife, Lucy Mercer Rutherfur, his lover of years earlier was him when he died. With the help of his daughter Anna Roosevelt Boetinger, FDR and Lucy had been in close contact over the years without the knowledge of Eleanor.

The brave but often devious aristocrat from upstate New York who ran the war from a wheelchair had fainted after complaining of a headache while having his portrait painted. A cerebral haemorrhage brought his life to an end two hours later. Vice-President Harry S. Truman was sworn in at the White House a few hours later as the 32nd President of the United States at 7.09 p.m. He was the no-nonsense sixty-one year old former Senator from Missouri who would coin the phrase: *The buck stops here* – meaning at his desk.

How different from Roosevelt's death was that of Hitler's eighteen days later and Mussolini's end two days before Hitler's. Mussolini and his mistress had been shot in Milan by Italian partisans and strung up by the heels. Such an indignity would not happen to him so Hitler and his new wife committed suicide. The German Army surrendered in Italy the following day.

As Berlin burned around him, Hitler cowered in his bunker beneath the Chancery. The Red Army were near, he would soon be in their clutches. Gone was his bravado, he was a sick man in a terrified fury. Just as victory has many fathers, in defeat Hitler found himself almost an orphan. Before he and Eva Braun killed themselves he raged to the few people around him who loyally stayed at his side:

It was not my fault, he cried. *It was the English and Americans serving the Jewish-Bolshevik plot. They are to blame! My generals are incompetent! My comrades have deserted me!*

Hitler had spent his last days below ground ranting about the betrayals, cowardice and lies all around him.

Two of the people with him were Hanna Reitsch, a fearless test pilot and the wounded General Robert Ritter von Greim. With the Russian Army poised to engulf Berlin, Hanna and the general had flown into the heart of Berlin in a light plane on the 26th of April. In doing so von Greim had been hit by Russian ground fire. Loyal to the end the pair pledged to stay with the Fuehrer but Hitler would not hear of it. He ordered them to leave, which they did on the 28th with the brave Hanna at the plan's controls. Several days earlier she had landed on a city street and from there she had taken off. In 1937 she had been the first person with the guts to fly over the Alps in a glider.

According to those who fled when the Russians were virtually hammering on the Chancery door above ground, Hitler slipped away to his quarters. Minutes later a shot rang out. Members of his staff found him slumps on a sofa, dead from a bullet in the head. A revolver lay on the floor. Slumped beside him was the body of Eva Braun who had taken poison. Blondi had also been poisoned. Ten days earlier had been Hitler's 56th birthday. Just as Roosevelt was seven years younger than Churchill when he died, Hitler was seven years younger than Roosevelt when he fired a bullet into his own head.

No one knows what Hitler's last words were before he shot himself but it was well within his character to believe he would return. He shot himself with a 7.65 revolver.

Much can be learned about the last days of the man who hypnotized millions of ordinary Germans and others such as the industrialists, army generals and landowners who put him in power. At the end of his life the gap between the real and unreal did not exist in Hitler's mind. Long after Goering, Himmler and others had seen the war was lost and had fled Berlin, Hitler retreated into a world of fantasy and continued issuing orders for counter-attacks by Army divisions that no longer existed.

The delusions of his last days were as deranged as his conviction-filled words and deeds of triumphant years earlier when he murdered his party comrades and set out to gas Jews and kill others deemed unfit to live among Aryans.

If the homeless Austrian who earned a pittance from his sketches in Vienna and went on to cause the death of millions calls for an epitaph, Churchill knew what Hitler's should be long before he was dead: *Hitler*, he said in 1940, *is a bloodthirsty guttersnipe*, a description well justified and deserved by 1945.

In June 1940, Hitler felt on top of the world. Virtually all of Western Europe and parts of the East were in his hands or under his control. His worry was the entry of America in the war. He had urged Japan not to drag them into the fight hence his child-like bottle and letter. But the bottle had a mind of its own, powered by the demon within that waxed and waned and may have ended the lives of many who crossed its path.

Who knows what evil lurks or lurked in the hearts of men, when it came to Hitler's spirit in the bottle, Neptune seemed to know.

FIFTY-ONE

In 1406 'The Isle of Man' was known as the 'Kingdom of Man'. It was granted in that year to Sir John Stanley with all its rights on condition that in order to pay homage to the Crown, he and his heirs should render future monarchs two Peregrine Falcons on the day of their coronation. The Duke of Athol was the last to comply on the coronation of George IV in 1821.

The Peregrine Falcon therefore – the fastest moving animal in the world - at one time held a lofty position in the Crown's eyes enjoying a mystical reputation of great value. The need to possess a replica was depicted in the film *The Maltese Falcon*.

Neptune was home from his Irish adventure, he was more his traditional self but no fool was Neptune. Hitler's bottle was not in Avoca so he was mostly at ease. His owners were now aware of what irked him, but they remained vigilant to see his reactions when he was in or near home. The bottle was now buried in a nearby field and Neptune didn't know it - that's what Peter and Heather thought.

Unlike his tranquil mood among Jesuits in Clongowes Wood College, his persona around the house was one of caution. With his ears folded back and his tail still, Neptune was semi on-guard; he was eating and back among friends who spoke softly but he missed the southern Irish voices. He missed the Clongowes grounds and the red and black squirrels that dashed and darted up trees and sat alert on branches looking down, wondering who he was. And he missed the chirping robins and croaking crows that watched him with equally questioning looks.

The increasing awareness of Hitler's bottle and its messaging spirit had dampened his urges. Mounting a bitch on heat, decanting her discomfort and passing life on were not on his agenda, other tasks beckoned. He made a tour of Port Cranstal, did a bit of shopping for the von Schneiders and was greeted by friends who were glad to see him and would ask what had prompted his trip to Ireland. *How did you manage to board the ferry undetected?* they would ask. Neptune's response was to relax his ears and wag his tail a little. For him danger still hung in the air just as baby Adolf long ago hanged suspended at birth between the birth signs of Aries and Taurus in the zodiac.

Since Neptune's return a Peregrine Falcon with a slate-grey back and a brown chest and belly had swept three feet above him and come to rest on the highest branch of an ancient oak. Its eyes were on him but Neptune's reaction was indifference. The Falcon had then flown away.

The Peregrine had sensed disquiet from Neptune that he, himself, had sensed on the island; a sensation to which his occult nature now responded as in days past when his mystical reputation was high on the Crown's agenda. Maybe the disquiet he was sensing was the one between Neptune and Hitler's telepathic signals pulsing on a meter band for the occult tuned such as Neptune and he were. Who knows, but the Falcon was sensing something that rattled him.

In the Moore's garden is a picnic table. It was a beautiful day, the sun was shining and the birds were chirping as in Clongowes Wood College but with sharper voices. Peter and Heather were seated at the table sipping tea, their mood was one of sadness. They knew no more about the disappearance of their friend's plane than they did weeks earlier, they were perplexed, they had yet to decided what to do about the bottle which was now buried in the nearby field.

What to do? That was the question. Except for Otto, Dennis and Vivian, no one else knew about the bottle. The Moores hadn't even told their children, no mention of it had been made to their eldest son when he called from New York.

Neptune suddenly appeared and sat on the garden lawn looking at Peter and Heather, he had made his rounds, his tail was active and now he was home with a mild sense of satisfaction.

"All right Neptune?" Heather asked. The Labrador stretched on his side on the warm grass. His ears limp; he was aloof in a world of his own as dogs often are but something was lurking within him.

Heather asked Peter: "What are we to do about the bottle?" Peter responded in the negative by moving his head from side to side - he didn't know. Neptune lifted his head, then he looked sharply at Heather, his ears jumped to attention as if an impulse ruled.

Suddenly he scrambled to his feet and quickly made for the beach and the spot near the lighthouse where he came upon the bottle. "Maybe he's heading for the ferry" said Peter with a smile. No sooner had Neptune reached the beach when he started mooching along the water's edge, sniffing, looking for something; an inner impulses was in command. The beach was barren except for a teenage couple waking his way holding hands. They said hello but Neptune ignored their greeting, his focus was elsewhere, he was alone with his thoughts. He sat primed, his gaze looking east across the Irish Sea towards the west coast of Britain.

Then, if you turned reality inside out and hung suspended in the outer reaches of the solar system followed by a gulp of Johnny Walker it all started to make sense.

From the lighthouse behind him Neptune heard the kek, kek, kek sounds of a Falcon coming from the same big bird that had eyed him earlier. The kek sounds were not new to him, Falcons were not a threat, he was not on their menu; their dish were rodents, birds and small ducks – fish too, like the ones that often washed ashore near the lighthouse, the way Hitler's bottle washed ashore after its journey through time and liquidity space.

The Falcon was perched at the highest point of the lighthouse. He and Neptune stare at each other, their eyes locked through a narrow vacuum of distance.

The Falcon, a male, has long pointed wings and a tail that is also pointed. Its wings extend, he then takes flight towards Neptune who stands his ground. The bird lands a few feet from Neptune who's still sitting but alert - ears up, tail rigid. The bird folds his wings but is unsettled, uncertain of Neptune's reaction. The Falcon and Neptune are face to face, their eyes fixed on each other as if combat is eminent. We see them from a distance, still, staring, poised. Then they settle as if thoughts are being processed and exchanged in a language only they know and understand.

Time passes and all is calm between them. They've been locked not in battle but in a plan of action. Hitler might have been au fait with the occult nature of their meeting. A job needed to be done. The Falcon flies off and Neptune races home just as women and girls raced to hear Hitler speak at rallies. They adored him, some fainted when they saw him in the flesh. At home they gazed in the mirror and felt blessed and proud at their Aryan reflections. Many such females rushed to join the League of German Girls, a slick, brainwashed Nazi unit.

FIFTY-TWO

In Hitler's glory day's women were often his most avid followers jostling for position at rallies to be near him and if lucky even to touch him or shake his hand. They were mostly ordinary girls with typing and shorthand skills in the bloom of youth like secretaries in banks or offices the world over.

They did what girls do, they laughed, gossiped and talked about boyfriends and films they had seen and movie stars like Leslie Howard, the Briton who spoke English better than most Britons and German as well if not better than most Germans. But some of these girls were anything but ordinary - they were part of the Secret Police, the dreaded SS.

What they tapped out on their machines were the records of Jews and others slaughtered in Auschwitz, Belsen, Treblinka and other camps whose purpose, among other things, was for killing.

Until recently the role played by females in Nazi Germany has been given only mild attention. Women like Irma Grese at Belsen and Ilse Koch, wife of the commander of Buchenwald became guards and were known for their cruelty. They hitched their wagon to the Nazi killing-machine and showed that they could be as fanatical supporters of Hitler and his methods as any man. Many women viewed the Fuehrer as a living God - almost as the second coming. His appearances in public were often marked by thousands of excited, swooning women screaming his name in what was close to sexual frenzy. In America from the late 1920s other men were making girls swoon, causing them to melt from the sound of their voices, men like Bing Crosby, Rudy Vallee, Nelson Eddie and in the late 1930s Frank Sinatra. But there the similarity between Hitler, the singers and female fans ended.

With shining blue eyes mirroring promise, pretty blond girls would wave frantically as Hitler passed. Extreme enthusiasm was not uncommon among some ladies. Often faster than men, they would betray Jewish neighbours they had known for years or anyone with communist sympathies. At times they would denounce other women over trivialities or jealousies.

During The Nazis' rise to power Germans had been hypnotized into believing in racial purity and superiority. Boys joined the Hitler Youth and girls joined the League of German Girls, which was similar to the Girl Scouts, in which principles of health, cleanliness and discipline were instilled. But the League's aims were devious and far-reaching: when war broke out they would be a generation of females totally dedicated to Nazism.

For women who had reached their most fertile time of life, the Nazis introduced Lebensborn – The Well of Life – a programme aimed at producing the soldiers needed by the Third Reich, the programme into which the two year-old Aleksander Litau had been sucked when stolen by the SS from his Russian parents and given the name of Folker Heinecke after adoption.

Clinics were scattered throughout Germany and neighbouring countries to which mostly single, pregnant women were sent to give birth secretly. Before admission doctors and nurses would check their racial purity.

To be accepted into the Lebensborn Programme the pregnant woman mostly had to have blond hair and blue eyes and proof of no genetic faults. They also needed proof of their father's identity and their father had to match these requirements.

Many of the men who fathered Lebensborn children had wives, they were chosen SS officers who often had children of their own. By 1945 the programme had produced some 12,000 births and due to its secrecy the father's identities could not be revealed on certificates of birth. Heinrich Himmler had put the programme into practice.

When war broke out the concept that women should stay at home caring for children while their men fought for the fatherland changed to a land of opportunity. With their personal horizons lifted, so too were woman's chances of a career. Some worked in the pre-war sterilization project aimed at removing imperfect people from society as well as programmes of euthanasia that caused the deaths of handicapped children.

On the home front women helped the regime in other ways, such as queuing to buy the often stolen furniture of Jewish neighbours at government sales. They knew where the goods came from but that did not stop them shopping with the zeal of bargain-hunters.

Before the war German women stayed at home, they were no different than females from other countries. Now they were advancing in the civil service, in schools and in hospitals. By 1939 the number employed in German industry had risen sharply, they worked on buses and post offices. Near the end of the war they manned flak guns directed at enemy bombers.

Before the war Hitler spoke of a nation of perfect marriages. Not so in Nazi Germany. Some wives would denounce their husbands as traitors and draft dodgers in the hope that their execution would spare them the trouble and cost of divorce. As the war progressed some women became Gestapo informants, catchers of Jews in hiding whose reward would add to their family purse.

Some women joined the Gestapo, at one point twenty-five per cent of the Berlin Gestapo headquarters were female run. In death-camps female guards were sometimes the most sadistic. Irma Grese, who worked at two camps and became warden of the woman's section in Belsen was but one; she would laughingly send Jews to the gas chambers. After the war she was tried and hanged. Irma Koch was known as the Bitch of Buchenwald. She would rip skin off dead prisoner bodies who bore distinctive tattoos. She hanged herself while in jail after the war. Most women in Nazi German never committed sadistic acts but by default the majority were willing partners in Hitler's evil.

Magazines had more in mind than entertainment while men were at war. Each issue of 'Frauen Warte', 'Women Wait' was propaganda aimed at brainwashing females into accepting Hitler's regime. The cover photo of the February 1940 issue depicted Hermann Goering cuddling his baby daughter, giving the impression that he was a kind-hearted family man. Added to articles that were otherwise proper, pages were often devoted to claims that Britain was responsible for the war because it yearned to dominate the world. Other magazines had their sights on propaganda dealing with every aspect of society. In Nazi Germany women were not backward when it came to helping the Fatherland and its bloodthirsty guttersnipe.

FIFTY-THREE

After their meeting on the beach the Falcon flew off and Neptune raced home, he had a task to perform.

Hitler's bottled ghost had to be returned to a life of limbo, to drift and sleep, as the Mafia would say, with the fishes. Destroying it posed a danger in the occult world of thought inhabited by the Falcon and Neptune. It had to be banished, exiled.

Hitler's life on earth was beyond the dog and bird to comprehend, but they sensed a presence not of the world they knew. They absorbed and processed data differently from humans.

Almost from the start Neptune sensed the history but not the detail that clung to Hitler's bottle and the spirit within. Now the Falcon sensed it too - a presence akin to Satanism, something that had to be banished because Satanism was evil for its own sake, it struck at the essence of the animals - but that was not the end of it. There was more. Then there were the sounds and smells that after years still hung in the air that only they could hear and smell: the bellowing sounds that cried from ovens, and the smells of cooking flesh belching from chimneys in wartime Poland. To rid themselves of all this messing with their senses was the mission of Neptune and the Falcon, the big, rat catching bird called The Zenitram by the Isle of Man's mysterious occult-tuned Masons.

When Neptune raced from home Peter and Heather had no clue what had caused his hasty exit, he had only just returned from his rounds; his normal routine was to head for his bowl in the kitchen. Not so today, he had gone straight to his owners and spread out on the grass.

When Heather asked Peter what should be done about the bottle Neptune had come to life and was off like a shot. They had not linked the question with his departure, perhaps he whiffed a bitch in heat was their guess but they really didn't know.

One minute thinking to themselves about their lost friends and the next wondering what to do with the bottle Peter and Heather continued relaxing with their eyes closed and the warm sun on their faces. They were not to know of past deaths caused to people due to their link with the bottle. Amazed, fearful, apprehensive, perhaps chosen for such insights might have been their mind-set had they known.

They would never know the fate of Father Hatton, the Jesuit who found the bottle at Montauk Point fifty one years earlier, or how he returned it to the Atlantic or of his death after confessing to the Pope, or of the Pontiff's demise hours later. They would never know the tale of U-Boat 29 and Captain Shulhart who flung the bottle in the Atlantic near Montauk Point. Nor of U-Boat 666 or of U-Boat 619's strange and mysterious explosion. Nor would they know of the fisherman who, having found the bottle was then hit by lightning, or of the Irishman who tumbled from his sailboat and died trying to retrieve it from the waters of Ireland's west coast.

Neptune was almost home, his tongue out, his ears back, his tale up. He was on a mission that involved the currents of the Irish Seas. Yes, that's right, currents of the Irish Sea. He and the Falcon had a plan, and each had his part to play. Peter and Heather were still in the garden with no view of Avoca's front, to the right of which, obscured by leafy hedges was an open field in which Hitler's bottle had been buried.

Neptune had not announce his arrival by running into the garden as he normally would, he made for the field where the bottle was buried. There was no fear in him now, he had work to do that would cut the bottle and its spirit adrift. He started digging, his paws like pistons scooping out earth which flew in every direction. The bottle was not deep, it lay on its side. Peter and Heather were still unaware that Neptune was back even though they and the dog were only sixty yards apart. But they were not concerned.

Neptune's fur was speckled with the earth he had dislodged in his haste to reach the bottle. He held the neck of the bottle in his mouth and shook himself to evict the earth. In doing so the bottle fell from his mouth but it was soon back in his grip.

Neptune raced to the beach. Most Port Cranstal folks were at work or sunning themselves in their gardens, children were in school. Only Leo and Bette McShane were out and on their way to see the Moores about a party they were throwing to celebrate the von Scheinder's 93rd birthday. Neptune raced towards them with the bottle in his mouth but he didn't stop, he continues at pace towards the beach. The amused McShanes wondered what he was up to now.

From the lighthouse looking east towards the Irish Sea the Falcon was flying in a wide circles over the water one hundred yards away. Below him running through the Irish Sea were many currents, one of which was the object of his focus. How from on high he could detect and judge their direction of travel is known only to Falcons. High tide was near its end. All the bird's attention was fixed searching for a current that ran from southern Ireland along the Isle of Man's east coast and then continued through the North Channel towards Iceland and the Denmark Straits. That's the one he wanted, the vehicle of choice. The dance of a sea's underworld ballet was familiar to this Falcon. With him on the wing fish had to think deep but they need not have worried today.

There were crosscurrents that might derail the one desired, southern currents from the Solway Firth to the east, as well as those flowing south from the Firth of Clyde off the coast of Strathclyde. The Falcon had to be vigilant, the window of opportunity for the current he was seeking was limited due to many factors. Once he has found the desired one he would fly above it in a tight circle, this would signal Neptune what point to swim towards.

Planning, organization and implementation were everything if the aims of their partnership were to succeed. Neptune's strength of purpose and stamina was a vital final element.

When Neptune reached the beach, there in the distance was the Falcon flying in a tight circle. This was the bird's signal, so with the bottle in his mouth, Neptune plunged into the water and started swimming towards the circling Peregrine.

Paddling hard, it did not take long for Neptune to reach the spot over which the Falcon was circling. He could hear the bird's keck, keck sounds confirming that this was the place so Neptune released the bottle and let it drift. It had been returned from where it came, never to be seen again. Maybe! But a question loomed: would Neptune make it back to shore swimming against the ebb tide which was now starting in a muscular fashion.

The Falcon kecked encouraging sounds and flew towards the beach, he had to rest, catch his breath, rest his eyes, life on the wing was not easy, there were laws of nature to contend with.

Neptune was finding the going hard, on several occasions he had slipped under the water only to reappear. With the grit of an Olympian on and on he paddled, stroke after stroke with legs that felt like led. He had covered fifty yards, another fifty to go. The water was cold, a mixture of currents were working against him. Could he make it, or would Hitler's bottle claim him too? Neptune disappeared under the water but then popped into view.

From the top of the lighthouse the Falcon could see Neptune was in trouble so again he took to wing. On reaching his objective he flew in a circle above the labouring Neptune below. Kek, kek, and kek the Peregrine cried out in a frenzied tone. *Swim, swim* was his message. And Neptune did, until soaked, trembling, and breathing deeply, he reached the beach and collapsed.

Wet and droopy Neptune returned home an hour later. The McShanes were still with Peter and Heather. It was only when they saw him that they told their hosts about seeing him earlier running towards the beach with a bottle in his mouth. They had forgotten all about it. The Moores made light of the matter but all was clear to them now, now they fully understood.

With a north current pushing it, in due course the bottle would clear the North Channel and carry on like a meandering buccaneer of doom of the Hollywood variety to the future misfortune of others.

FIFTY-FOUR

Errol Flynn is remembered for his Film roles but according to CIA files, in the late 1930s some believed he might have been happier as a Nazi officer wearing a swastika arm band. Although this probably is not true, Flynn was an enigma with a dark reputation worthy of suspicion.

David Niven, Flynn's Hollywood roommate in the 1930s summed him up nicely: *Errol*, he said, *will never disappoint you, he will always let you down.*

Only British and American classified files will ever reveal if Flynn was a Nazi spy as some have staunchly maintained. To this day some believe that he met with Hitler in Berchtesgaden in 1938 when the Spanish Civil War was raging.

Flynn's biography by Charles Higham claims that the actor's spying led to hundreds of German deaths. The allegations have angered people in Tasmania where Flynn was born and where his 100th birthday was celebrated in 2009.

Mr. Higham said: *I think it's sad that Tasmanians would want to celebrate this; there is no doubt that Flynn had Nazi sympathies. Prior to the war he worked as a Nazi operative if not an actual agent. He was first noticed for his vocal anti-British pro-Nazi views in 1934. There is little doubt that his work for the Nazis resulted in people being killed.*

According to Higham, Flynn grew up in an anti-Semitic, Irish Catholic family where racism was rife in his youth. The biographer claims that in the early 1930s Flynn was influenced by Hermann Erben, an Austrian doctor and Nazi Party member. They had met by chance while Flynn was on his way to Britain by boat from his native Australia.

Higham says that in declassified US files he found a letter from 1934 written by Flynn to Erben in which he complained about a 'slimy Jew' who was trying to cheat him. *I do wish we could bring Hitler over here to teach these Isaacs a thing or two*, is what Flynn is alleged to have written.

In 1937 during the Spanish Civil War Erben, who would later head German Intelligence in Mexico is said to have travelled with Flynn to Spain to investigate German socialists who were fighting in the Civil War in the 'Thaelmann Battalion' named after the communist leader Ernst Thaelmann. It is claimed that Flynn's celebrity was used as cover for the trip. Hitler, who supported Spain's fascist leader General Franco was enraged that Germans had joined Spain's Republican forces against Franco.

Higham says that information from Erben and Flynn about the German socialists was sent to the Gestapo and used to round up relatives of Battalion Volunteer members, many of whom later died in concentration camps. He also claims that Flynn met with Hitler in 1938.

Although Flynn most probably did not work for the Nazis prior to the outbreak of war, it does appear that he admired Hitler in the early 1930s when he was in his twenties and not yet a film star. Flynn was by no means the only none-German to admire Hitler at the time or to have anti-Semitic leanings, Henry Ford and Charles Lindberg were but two among many. To what extent if any Flynn was involved in Nazism before or during the war has never been proved.

Tasmanian born in 1909, Flynn became a US citizen at the age of thirty-three, he was already a film star but for medical reasons he did not qualify for military service, which, according to him, he regretted. That's one side of the Flynn story, then there is the other.

Errol Flynn *spied for Allies, not the Nazis* according to the English newspaper The Daily Telegraph on 31 December 2000. The reporters were David Bamber and Chris Hastings. The story goes on to say: *According to classified Government documents, Flynn offered to help the Allies in 'unconventional ways'.* The Telegraph reports that the British Home Office has MI5 papers dispelling claims that Flynn was a Nazi sympathiser.

Classified for more than fifty years, the documents detail how Flynn offered to help Britain's security services. They allegedly show that he was willing to use family links in the then neutral Irish Republic to help the Allied cause.

Relatives and friends have been calling for the release of the documents which they believe will restore Flynn's reputation following biographies which have claimed that he supported Hitler. The Home Office documents allege he was a patriot who was willing to do all he could to help the Allied cause. His rejection by the US Armed Forces because of a heart murmur made him determined to help in 'unconventional' ways.

Flynn attended a meeting with officials of the Office of Strategic Services, the fore-runners of the CIA after writing to them about a possible role in the war effort. He also wrote to President Roosevelt. Until the British Home Office, the CIA and FBI release all that they know about Flynn's role in the war, his involvement with Nazism , if any, will remain a mystery.

Flynn was a womanizing, alcoholic who lived a less than wholesome existence but he most probably was not a traitor There can be no doubt however, that in his twenties Flynn, like many others, admired Hitler

Sean, his eldest son and the opposite of his dad in character despised Hollywood and his father's playboy way of life. The two had little contact; he disappeared in 1970 at the age of twenty-eight while covering the Vietnam war in Cambodia as a combat photographer. Reports claim he was captured by Viet Cong guerrillas and held captive before being killed by the Khmer Rogue.

Errol Flynn died suddenly in Canada of an embolism at the age of fifty in 1959. Leslie Howard was also fifty when he died but his character was quite different from that of Flynn's.

Errol Flynn played swashbuckling roles in films, his son lost his life while dealing with real dangers not those in the make believe world of motion pictures.

FIFTY-FIVE

As the years pass those who lived through WWII dwindle in number. The Moores died within one year of each other in 2005 and 2006 never having known what had happened to the bottle after Neptune dug up from the field. They never mentioned its existence to anyone other than Otto and the McClendons. Neptune preceded them in 2004 at the age of fifteen having served his purpose in life by passing it on and helping others. He fathered offspring of various talents among them the apply named Venus, Saturn and Picasso. His happy spirit dwells somewhere.

Hitler's passive ghost also lives on, he's as spoken of today as Elvis Presley but unlike Elvis, Adolf has never left the building.

He must be smiling. When the war ended the world was shocked by Nazi atrocities. Today, however, some seventy years after the fall of Nazism, and despite attempts to atone for its ugly past, there is a lucrative tourist trade in Germany built around interest in Nazi wartime landmarks. But Hitlerism and tourism is far from new.

After becoming chancellor and opening Dachau, after forming the Gestapo, burning books and passing the Nuremberg laws, Hitler passed a new law that promoted leisure travel in Germany. It paid off nicely in the 1936 winter and summer Olympics Games. Contrary to Churchill's belief, Hitler did not always think along predictable straight lines.

Germany uses the wines of the Neckar Valley, the beer of Bavaria and the beauty of its Alps, rivers and forests to attract tourists. Today Nazism's dark past is a new attraction from which income is derived from Germans themselves - it's a money spinner as new generations less tainted by guilt learn of their nation's sinister history through the lure of tourism.

As Hitler's crimes fade in public minds - or maybe because they loom - visitors flock to the V-1 and V-2 rocket site at Peenemunde, the picturesque grounds of his retreat at Berchtesgaden and they go on tours of Nazi sites in Munich and Berlin.

A popular attraction is the 1936 Olympic Games Village. Amid the decayed buildings, the wrecked swimming pool and old running tracks are now to be found German day-trippers and history buffs drinking in the past that once shamed them. The Village is an eerie spectacle. After the Games had ended the Wehrmacht Legions were trained there, and when the Russians had crushed them the Red Army occupied the Village. Their victims once littered the Village fields. Old Nazi bunkers are now one of Berlin's biggest attractions along with the Brandenburg Gate.

After the war the authorities kept silent about the places built to protect Nazi leaders. No longer is this the case. The Berlin Underworld Association arranges tours of the remaining bunkers, the most popular being Hitler's compound under the chancery building. Tourists can't get enough of them. Hitler's ghost surly must revel in this twist of fate thanks to the passage of time, the opportunity for monetary gain and the endurance of his attraction.

It was once feared that the 'Fuhrerbunker' where Hitler killed himself might become a shrine for neo-Nazis. When it was opened to the public it did not become the magnet once feared – but Neo-Nazis do exist and are growing in numbers due to the inflow of people into Europe from other cultures. They see the face of Europe changing and within them the ghost of Hitler resonates and trumpets like an alarm.

A centre has been built in Nuremberg next to the field were Hitler's rallies were held. Tourists now stand where Hitler stood, not thugs, but ordinary people fascinated by the man once called The Fuehrer. The ghost of Hitler likes this too, he may be a star in Satan's gallery of horrors but he's also helping the German economy and though dead he can live with that.

Places have been opened to the public in Munich like Hitler's private apartment at Prinzregentplatz, and the beer hall where he tried to seize power in 1923. Daily in Berlin thousands visit the former Gestapo headquarters at No.8 Prinz Albrecht, once the most feared address in Europe, or they travel south to the lake at Wannsee where the Final Solution was decided. The demand for this tour is so great that walking tours are now held in English. This too brings a smile to the face of Hitler's passive ghost.

There is also a Holocaust industry in Poland. Established for educational purposes, the tours go to former grizzly camp-sites like Auschwitz, Birkenau and Treblinka. Such tours also exist in Israel.

No longer is it shameful to be curious about Nazism. Germans stand on line for a glimpse of a time that for years has been buried under layers of national guilt and shame. But a painting showing Jesus next to Hitler recently had to be removed from the alter of a Bavarian church where it had been since 1939 when Hitler was considered a messiah.

There is no escaping the fact that Hitler is a commercial icon. In addition to films about WWII, German TV airs documentaries ranging from 'the wolf pack' submarines that sank enemy ships, to epics about the army's defeat in Stalingrad. There is also a publishing frenzy dealing with Hitler and Nazism that includes CDs and magazines. In 2012, 680 books were published world-wide on the subjects - the money generated is immense.

Recently Hitler's Mein Kampf was published in Germany for the first time since the Second World War. Entitled "Hitler, Mein Kampf, A Critical Edition" it was published by the Munich-based Institute of Contemporary History. It's a best seller.

Germans and non-Germans are also discovering the Nazi's past through the Internet. A company recently sold out selling blueprints of Germania, the super-capital envisioned by Hitler to replace old Berlin. People have rushed to buy plans for a city that never existed beyond models drawn from Hitler's imagination.

Discovered in a trunk in Austria a Nazi propaganda painting by Hitler is to be auctioned in England which shows a figure of Hitler being handed tools by Arminius, a German hero who defeated the Romans. Painted, signed, dated and with a Nazi stamp, it's a rare work by Hitler as he mostly painted landscapes. It points to the value he placed on propaganda as early as 1929, the year the Graf Zeppelin circled the earth thanks to William Randolph Hurst who financed the flight because Germany was then broke. In 2014 a Hitler watercolour was auctioned in Nuremberg and sold for $161,000. In 2015 seven of his watercolours and pencil drawing were sold at auction in Shropshire, England to a French collector for more than £10,000.

A CD is now available of a virtual *Reich Chancellery* that tours Hitler's office, his dining room as well as his bodyguard's quarters.

In addition to all this there exists a global network of private individuals who collect Nazi memorabilia, one of which is the amazing Kevin Wheatcroft, a British tycoon who, over the years, has accumulated an array of Nazi items worth at least one hundred fifty million dollars. It includes Hitler's bed in which the millionaire himself sleeps.

Among his countless items is the world's largest collection of Nazi military vehicles and sculptures of Hitler's head. Uniforms, machine guns and Hitler's favourite full length portrait of himself are also part of Wheatcrof's collection It even includes the cell door in Landsberg Prison where Hitler wrote Mein Kampf, the Mercedes G-4 he rode in when he entered the Sudetenland, love letters to Eva Braun and an ink blotter with Hitler's signature in reverse. The collection goes on and on and is mostly stored in various warehouses.

Wheatcroft's collection is not the madness of anti-Semite, it reflects the passion of a man who is preserving symbols of evil that he says should never be forgotten. It would appear that for Wheatcroft and other collectors the memorabilia's very darkness is their attraction.

Another Nazi item is worthy of mention: The bullet-riddled tailfin of a Messerschmitt 109 is to be sold at auction. Wolfgang Lohmann discovered the tailfin patching a roof in the village of Hillegossen, Germany. He bought it in 1970 and displayed it at home until 2015 when he decided to sell it. The tailfin is adorned with stencil paintings of the 121 planes shot down by Heinz - Wolfgang Schnaufer, one of the Luftwaffe's deadliest pilot. The 'kill' icons showing British bombers and the dates each was shot down take up the top of the aluminium fin, the bottom half consists of swastikas.

Hitler's red telephone, which travelled with him everywhere, was recently found. It is expected to fetch £400,000.00 at auction.

There is, of course, a down-side to knowledge about Nazism. Neo-Nazis revel in stories of the war in books like *Hitler's Women* and *Death In The Bunker*. People of this persuasion can be found in many east and west European countries including Germany and Austria. And they are growing in number. Further evidence of Hitler's pull is the recent mass killing of left-wing students by their fellow Norwegian citizen Anders Breivik, a Hitler disciple who hates the large intake of Muslims into Europe and Norway in particular.

In Hitler's utopian world his aim in Germany was racial purity and flawlessness: no Jews, communists, gypsies, Slaves and homosexuals wanted or anyone short of Aryan perfection. In essence Nazism was not only nationalism running wild, it was a black hole with the gravitational pull of the devil into which many were sucked.

FIFTY-SIX

Adolf Hitler, Benito Mussolini and Joseph Stalin wrote poetry. Even though they killed millions their words could be sentimental and even tender – they revealed insights into the contradictory world of their minds.

When Hitler's mother died of breast cancer in 1907 - the same year that twenty-nine year-old Joseph Stalin was robbing a train of millions belonging to the Georgia State Bank to finance the Bolshevik Revolution - Adolf Hitler was seventeen. Year later, Hitler's mother's Jewish physician, Dr Eduard Bloch, whom Hitler admired described the scene of her death: *While he was not a 'mothers boy' in the usual sense, I have never seen a closer attachment. In the practice of my profession it is natural that I should have witnessed many scenes such as this one, yet none left me with the same impression. In all my career I have never seen anyone so prostrate with grief as Adolf Hitler.*

Hitler began a five year sentence in Bavaria's Landsberg Jail on April 1st 1924 after being tried for attempting to overthrow the government in his Beer Hall Putsch the year earlier. He was released after nine month. At some point during the year of the attempted Putsch he wrote the following poem:

THE MOTHER

When your mother has grown older,
When her dear, faithful eyes no longer
see life as they once did
When her feet, grown tired,
no longer want to carry her
as she walks

Then lend her your arm in support,
Escort her with happy pleasure,
The hour will come when weeping
you must accompany her on her final walk.

And if she asks you something,
Then give her an answer.
And if she asks again, then speak!
And if she asks yet again, respond to her,
Not impatiently, but with gentle calm.

And if she cannot understand you properly
Explain all to her happily.
The hour will come, the bitter hour,
When her mouth asks for nothing more.

– Adolf Hitler, 1923

On July 4th, 1994, Hitler's bottle was again bobbing in ocean waters; this time after three years in the Outer Hebrides near the Isle of Lewis. As before, the bottle, its letter and the spirit of Adolf Hitler were much like the Holy Trinity, all separate, yet one.

In years to come the bottle will wash ashore on a Norway beach on a supernatural night of brilliant displays by the Aurora Borealis: beams of coloured lights quivering in the sky - but that's another story.

The Zenitram remains unexplained.